The Spring Collection

Paul John Hausleben

Cover photograph, "Cherry Blossoms at Deep Run" and
other photographs by Paul John Hausleben
Cover Design by Mike Z.
Published by God Bless the Keg Publishing
Somewhere, U.S.A.

ISBN: 978-0-9906979-4-7

Dedications

I dedicate this entire collection to, the smell of the air on the first day of trout season, turning over the first shovel full of dirt in the garden after a long winter, frozen packages of Italian-style meatballs, Easter flowers on the altar and most of all, to the look in her eyes on a warm spring day. Individually, "The Rock" is for Kyra Lovell, wherever the hell she is now.

The Lucky Leprechaun

Featuring the brave and fearless Sergeant Walter P. Thrump

Homage to Pussface the cat

Featuring Pussface the cat, dear Mum, the old man, and other characters from the Adventures of Harry and Paul

The Show

A humorous novelette and another story from the Adventures of Harry and Paul

Frankie the Garden Gnome

Featuring characters from the Adventures of Harry and Paul

For You

Some words

The Rock

Featuring Gramps, Paul John Henson and other characters from the Adventures of Harry and Paul

The Look in your Eyes

Some words

Contents

Acknowledgements

Thank you, as always, to Mr. Harry M. Rogers Junior and to my friends and family. Thank you, to Ms. Lydia A. LaGalla for her support and her help with the character's names, her expert consultation and invaluable advice on authentic Italian behaviors, homemade meatballs and family gatherings for "The Show." Special thanks and a hearty shout out to George "The Big Spike" Spina for hiring me for that fashion show so long ago.

"Sometimes, we need to whisper, and sometimes, we need to howl."

Paul John Hausleben

March 2016

Preface from the Author

Finally, with the publishing of this book, I do not have to listen to people asking me, "Hey, Hausleben! When the hell are ya gonna come out with a spring collection of stories?"

It is just not that easy!

I wish it were so easy, but the stories of spring were rather elusive ones. Besides, spring is not my favorite time of year. I rather enjoy winter and I am always sorry to see it leave. It only means the dreaded summer and heat, humidity, and bugs creep closer!

Other than Easter and the opening day of the trout fishing season, perhaps digging in the garden a bit, I honestly found little inspiration for a collection of spring stories.

Deep within the story vaults of the PJH writing command center, I had an Easter novelette in draft, which I had wanted to noodle around with for a very long time. It was a Harry and Paul Adventure and it was a good one, but that was all I had to ride in the spring vehicle.

The spring well ran dry, dry, dry.

Hand wringing ensued. Endless pacing of floors, I consumed beer after beer and a touch or two of a fine single malt Scotch in a desperate search for inspiration.

Drama, drama, drama.

Seldom, if ever, do I suffer from a writer's block, however, when I have to shoehorn stories into frameworks, then it is a bit of a struggle. Inspiration finally arrived, in a form of which I best leave for a story way down the road another time, but when it came, it arrived in a fury.

I wrote and wrote and wrote.

Some favorite old characters wandered in for another visit. Some new characters emerged, Harry and Paul managed another wild scene or two, Gramps shared more of his endless wisdom and a favorite character of readers everywhere returned. Yes, indeed, the brave and fearless Sergeant Walter P. Thrump returned. Once again, the brave little man appeared to hunt down evil perpetrators lurking in dark corners, while he seeks out action, adventure, and justice. Within a few short weeks, the book suddenly became quite a satisfying project.

With the elusive spring book now finished, I feel at ease. Finally, it is complete and no longer, will one season linger outside of the realm of the Hausleben seasonal collections.

All joking aside, actually, the truth is that the springtime does have a number of wonderful memories for me. Memories, such as, trout fishing with Harry and Jeff along icy streams in Sussex County, New Jersey and warm thoughts of joyous Easter celebrations, family gatherings, and yes, even the happiness in turning over the dirt in the garden on that first warm spring day. Spring means many things to many people. It means a rebirth, the world is alive, allergies blossom along with flowers and love is in the air.

Whatever.

For me, spring now takes on a new meaning and no longer will anyone ever ask me, "Say, Paul, when ya gonna come out with a spring book?"

Hell, yeah. The world is now my oyster! Here I am. I plan to put my feet up now for a few months and relax. The storylines will arrive because they always do. At least no one is bugging me with a request to write anything special.

That is no one was bugging me, until, just two days after I completed this manuscript, when the telephone rang in the writing command center. It was the world-famous Harry M. Rogers Junior on the telephone line. The conversation went something like this:

"Hey, twenty-seven! How are ya doing?"

"Oh hey, thirty-five. I am well. How are you?"

"Good, twenty-seven, good. Say, I have been meaning to ask ya. Are ya evah gonna write that story about when you and I went fishin' in the Haledon reservoir and those gigantic turtles ate the whole stringer of fish ya caught? And then after we went fishin,' we went out and met those gorgeous gals at Ice World. Ya 'member what happened that night, don't ya?"

Oh geez! These bloody adventures will never end! I just gave that oyster back. These stories are endless! I never considered *that* subject. Well, I guess that it is back to the writing post. Time to pour some of that single malt Scotch and get back to work.

Here we go again.

It is my fervent hope you enjoy reading this collection of stories as much as I enjoyed writing them.

Thank you for reading them.

Paul John Hausleben

March 2016

Prologue

The springtime is a blessed time of the year. In some places of God's good Earth, the world emerges from a frozen state of dull animation. The world around us slowly recovers, while plants, animals, and people emerge from hiding places and seek warmth after the long months of winter finally leave. The air warms and the tone of the landscape changes from brown to green and colorful birds return. The same birds that retreated rather than face the cold. They join their brethren who were a bit more fortified than they were.

It is all quite profound.

In other areas of the world, it is always green; the springtime brings around changes in attitude, changes in spirit, and changes in energy and enhances everyone's tone.

Spring means many things to many people. For some religions, it represents the holiest time of the year. For others, it means time to go outside and repair all the damage that old man winter invoked.

For me, it means simply a rebirth of sorts. A restart of the seasons. I hear the church bells peal on Easter morning; I see the birds constructing their nests and I see the first flower bulbs mustering enough courage to emerge from a haven within the ground.

Another passage of time, another page in a book that continues to turn and evolve. Young women's hearts are a flutter. Their beauty resonates, and they wear their best spring dresses, and change their hairstyles. Young men chase those young women about with stars in their eyes and dreams upon their hearts. Spring encounters can, nine months or so down the road, lead to interesting arrivals.

The birds sing happily in the early morning light, flowers bloom, trout jump in streams and in placid lakes, and those blasted allergies make us sneeze.

I for one, just go along for the ride, I observe, record it all, sometimes oblivious to all the actual meanings. Oblivious, until later on, when I capture those thoughts and the pictures of the season, from my mind's eye and combine them with memories. It is then that spring takes on a new meaning for me. In my mind, spring is no longer just another change of the yearly seasons.

No, no, no, for me, spring then becomes another season that provides me with another canvas to paint words upon.

The Lucky Leprechaun

1

The Mug Revealed

Walter P. Thrump looked up at the calendar on the wall of his tiny kitchen in his house located at 164 Maple Lane in Jersey City, New Jersey. It was March 1992 and Walter made a careful note of the date.

It was a nice home, a quaint Cape Cod style, and it was a typical New Jersey Cape Cod home, with old style aluminum siding, that was originally gray, but had now faded to being whiter than gray. If you were unlucky enough to rub up against it, then you came away with a grayish-white dust upon your clothing. Somewhat as if the house had a coating of chalk upon it. The house had a small fenced-in backyard, and it sat upon a typical city lot, with a small gate in front to lead you to the front porch of the home. There was no driveway or garage on the property. In fact, none of the homes on Maple Lane had a driveway. Residents of Maple Lane parked on the city street in front of their homes, or as close to the front as a resident could find an open slot to slip their car into along the street. It was an honor system with your neighbors in a city environment such as this one. You did not steal your neighbor's spot, and they did not steal yours!

When it snowed, and it came time to dig out the cars buried up and down the street, you placed "markers" in the road to claim your spot. Virtually anything became a marker, perhaps, a garbage can with your house number painted on the side, or a chair, or a box, you name it and you would see the marker sitting inside the walls of snow, as if the object was a silent sentry of sorts.

Walter loved his old home, and his only dream for the house was to have a driveway on his property. Someday. He knew exactly where he would cut it into the side yard. One day, he even laid it out with a tape measure and some small stakes. He drove the wooden stakes in the ground and then spray-painted them red. The stakes were still in the ground, faded from a deep red to now virtually being pink.

Markers of a simple dream.

All he wished for was a driveway next to his house to bring his prized Whizzer station wagon in off the street. Walter had neither the extra money, nor a sound enough reason (Mrs. Thrump argued that his car was a piece of junk that he should have long since retired) to construct the driveway. When Walter really faced the facts, it was very hard to argue with Mrs. Thrump's logic. The old station wagon was now over twenty-five years old. Its fenders were held on with layers of grey duct tape, the radio worked if you bashed hard on the top of the dashboard to spring it to life, the tires were mostly bald and worn smooth, and the driver's side door inside latch had not worked for many years. You had to reach out the window to use the outside latch in order to open the door. Certainly, a scratch or two from a passing car or city snowplow was something no one would notice!

Yet, despite the present low status of his prized automobile, the driveway dream lingered. . ..

The Thrumps had lived in the house for over thirty years. The same house, the same routine, not too much actually changed in the world of Mr. and Mrs. Walter P. Thrump, and that was just the way that Walter liked it.

"Oh my, only a week or so until Saint Patrick's Day! I have to find my special beer mug and get ready, or I will suffer bad luck the entire year, Gertrude!" Walter proclaimed to his lovely wife, Gertrude W. Thrump.

Mrs. Thrump whirled around from where she was standing in front of the kitchen sink, placed her hands upon her hips, and stared at her husband.

"Oh, so that explains why we are in the situation we are in, Walter! Let's see, because for the last forty-five years or so of our marriage, you have consumed green beer on Saint Patrick's Day from your special lucky mug, as well as spent a fortune on postage to enter every stupid contest on Earth, spun endless prize wheels, flipped lucky shamrocks, and let's see now, we are still penniless and poor!"

Mrs. Thrump was a bit on the rough side, and sometimes, she was a sourpuss who beat poor Walter as if he was a drum. Ever since the two of them shared a wonderful Christmas together last December, Mrs. Thrump had softened her rather staunch previous stance with her husband, but every once in a while, she resurrected her old self to spread joy and happiness.

"Oh well, Gertrude, I know that I have not quite hit the big payoff yet, but I did win that twenty-seventh-place prize in the Big Bob's food contest a year or so ago."

Walter smiled widely at his wife, as he recalled the case of black pens, a special certificate, and seven-foot, inflatable, blow up, balloon version of Big Bob himself that the food empire awarded him. Mrs. Thrump threw her dish towel in the sink, shook her head, and did not comment.

Nothing deterred the forever positive, Walter P. Thrump . . . nothing. Not twenty-seventh place prizes, not old Whizzer station wagons with duct tape holding the fenders on, not a crabapple wife, or not having a driveway.

Nothing.

You see, Walter P. Thrump was a survivor. A New Jersey tough guy.

He was a bulletproof man!

Pollution, foul weather, the stink from the nearby trash dumps when the wind changed around and blew across the neighborhood, the obnoxious neighbor who tossed empty beer bottles on Walter's lawn, all generated no sour reaction from Walter P. Thrump.

He considered each day a gift, therefore, he always projected positive thoughts, positive produced positive in Walter P. Thrump's mind.

He survived walking point next to a first lieutenant, while the bullets flew over their heads, when he served as a radio operator in combat in Vietnam. He faced, and survived, countless other encounters with thugs, potential muggings in dark alleys in shady Jersey City neighborhoods, car wrecks and other tragedies. Walter had only one lung left, due to an adventure with lung cancer, which he contracted from working in a glass factory for most of his life. A fight in which Walter proudly won.

Walter was still alive and vertical, and that was all he needed to know.

Walter was about sixty-five years of age, and he was small, no in fact, he was tiny. If Walter was five feet five in height, then that was a very tall estimate, as five foot four was more accurate. He weighed in at about one hundred and twenty pounds if he was wet, wore a heavy winter coat, and had a collection of spare change in his pockets.

There he sat, smiling widely at his wife with dreams of winning contests, new driveways, and lucky mugs dancing in his head, with his craggily face, with a long, pointed nose, deep-set eyes, and a thick chock of brown hair, which he swirled over to the side. Framing his face on each side were 1970s style long sideburns.

Not a single gray or white hair sat upon Walter P. Thrump's head. He would; defy anyone to find one!

He had virtually no teeth left in his head, and Walter just gummed his endless bologna sandwiches as he chomped them down (no one ever saw Walter eat anything other than the sandwiches and some Big Bob's cheese snacks) He did not intend ever to replace his choppers. He did not care; in the world of Walter P. Thrump, teeth were overrated.

Although he was small in stature, Walter P. Thrump was one tough, little, New Jersey guy. He worked as a sergeant on the security force entrusted with guarding the huge corporate complex of Substantial Industries Worldwide LLC. Walter was the lead officer on the staff, and he loved the job and took it all very seriously. After all, Substantial Industries was one of the, if not *the* biggest company in the entire world. Walter was proud of his job and would never avoid or neglect his duties.

Walter P. Thrump was a serious little man!

"Gertrude, I have to find the lucky mug. Do you know where I stored it after last year?"

Walter jumped up from his chair and frantically started to open kitchen cupboards as his wife stared at her husband's strange behavior.

"Walter, if you are looking for the special mug, then just ask me," Mrs. Thrump complained while shaking her head and pointing towards a specific cupboard. "I put it deep inside the cupboard on the right side there. I did not want to look at that dopey grin on the leprechaun on the side of the mug any longer. You will need the step stool to reach it."

Walter eagerly rushed off to the back porch to obtain the step stool, while he smiled and told his wife, "Thank you, honey. I will get it down now and be ready for the big day." Walter was now obviously very excited to find his special mug. When you are a simple man, with humble expectations from life, then the smallest of items can be very special. Walter P. Thrump required very little in his life in order to be happy.

Perhaps, we all could learn quite a bit from Walter P. Thrump. . ..

Both of the Thrumps were quite short, with Mrs. Thrump being just a bit shorter than her husband was, but not by much. The Thrumps often required the use of a step stool in their house. Walter returned, set the step stool up in front of the cupboard, climbed up, and peered inside. Half of his small body disappeared inside the cupboard while he looked inside.

After a little rustling, around and moving of some objects, Walter suddenly yelled out, "Here it is, Gertrude! My Lucky Leprechaun beer mug!"

Walter's head reemerged from within the cupboard, his face beaming in a wide smile as he held the prized mug up in the air, as if he found a hidden bag of money inside the cupboard. The mug was a pint-size beer mug, designed to hold and to relish lagers in. The mug was a clear glass with a thick glass handle molded on the side. From a distance, and at first glance, the mug appeared to be an ordinary beer mug, and it was only upon a careful study, did you notice the colorful cartoon character printed on the side. Walter held the mug carefully while he climbed down the ladder, being aware of his every step to avoid any catastrophes that an errant misstep could cause in the future fate of the prized heirloom. Walter took a kitchen towel from the counter and carefully rubbed the side of the mug, smiled, and studied the condition of the glass.

"The Lucky Leprechaun looks as if he is still brand new. Well, maybe not brand new, but for how old he is, he sure looks good to me."

Printed on the side of the glass was a slightly faded, cartoon-like imprint of an Irish leprechaun. The leprechaun depiction included the bearded figure dressed in a red jacket with silver buttons, a green vest, and a red jockey cap perched upon his head. In his hand was a sword with what appeared to be somewhat faded bolts of electricity emitting from the sword that may have indicated that the sword did double duty as a magic wand of some sort. At his feet were six small, golden coins scattered around on the ground next to where he stood. He wore a silly, impish smile upon his face, and a person studying the image would have to admit that it was unique and cute, but upon a general examination, there seemed to be nothing particularly special about the beer mug.

Walter stood there studying the mug, still smiling, and Mrs. Thrump shook her head and went back to her dishwashing duties.

"Yeah, honey. One more year. I will set my alarm on my watch for eleven-thirty. I will put a few drops of green food coloring into my Big Boulder beer because those Dingleberry beers are a little too sweet for me, ya know. My luck has already started early, Gertrude. I looked at the schedule and I have off this year from work for Saint Patrick's Day. I can celebrate without worrying about drinking too much beer!"

Walter stood in the kitchen; he wildly explained the traditions surrounding his favorite holiday, and Gertrude seemed to listen half-heartedly. One could easily perceive that Mrs. Thrump might have heard this same speech and witnessed this identical scene acted out a few times before this particular time.

"In keeping with tradition and just as generations of Thrumps have done, all the way back to my great-great-grandfather in Ireland, I will drink a full pint of green-colored beer at exactly one-minute after midnight on Saint Patrick's Day morning! As you know, my darling Gertrude, I am never late, or my name is not Walter P. Thrump. Last year, I had to go to work for the early shift to cover for Officer Davis, and I could only take a little sip of the beer. That may explain why the full, Lucky Leprechaun influence did not quite kick in." Walter emphatically explained his family's yearly tradition once again to his faithful wife, and provided in his opinion, a very sound explanation as to why their luck remained unchanged. A little sip did not quite kick in the full good luck trick. It seemed logical to Walter. This year, he had the remedy!

"And let me guess the rest of the story, my dear Walter. At least one of us has to enter logic and sound reasoning into your pipe dreams and superstitions. Okay, let me see, we do this, so that we have good luck, fame and fortune, for an entire year. So far, your plan stinks. A lot of good it has done us, Walter P. Thrump. No extra money, we live day-to-day even with your pension and security job, you have only one lung, we still drive a twenty-five-year-old car, and the house is going to need a roof this year. I have grown tired of emptying the buckets in the attic."

The ever-positive Walter set his mug upon the kitchen table, turned to his wife and answered her by stating a little twist of hope on her statement, "But Gertrude, last year, I only took a little sip, besides, think of how bad things could have been, or would be, if I did not do this every year. There is no way to measure it!"

There was little doubt that despite her outward gruffness and negative attitude that Gertrude W. Thrump loved her husband. She did not always show it, but this past Christmas made her realize it, as she never had for many years. She turned towards her husband and was about to blast him when she smiled a very rare smile.

He made a good point.

There *was* no actual measuring stick to determine just how bad it would be without Walter and his ever-positive approach and his stupid Lucky Leprechaun mug.

"Walter, I do love you. Nothing ever stops your dreams. That is admirable and in retrospect, I guess you are correct. Since I am not willing to venture a guess or take a chance on how badly it could have or could be, then please by all means set your alarm and enjoy your tradition."

Walter smiled back, scurried over, and gave Mrs. Thrump a big kiss.

"Oh yeah! I will! This is the year, honey! I can just feel

it!" Walter sat at the kitchen table, slid his lucky mug to the side, and then opened a small envelope that he had in his pocket.

"Say, Gertrude, please hand me that black pen from the drawer there. I have to fill out my entry form for the Big Bob's Special Spring O' the Year' Food Contest for this year. He is having two big contests this year instead of the one big one in the autumn. I saved up the required seventy-two flaps of the Big Bob's extra, thick, bologna packs, and now I just have to complete this form to enter. Last time, I won the box of special black pens and a blow-up balloon for Big Bob himself, but this year, it will be the big winner! Oh, boy this year they are giving away a car, a Substantial Industries Rhino 400. A pint of green-colored Big Boulder beer right on time on Saint Patrick's Day and our luck will change. I will mail the entry form on Saint Patrick's Day. Fame and fortune will be right around the corner. I can just feel it, honey."

2

In Pursuit of Evil, Shadowy, Figures

Sergeant Walter P. Thrump did not take frivolous days off from work. He may take a rare vacation day or two here and there every few years, and since his wife and he had grown closer over this past Christmas, he actually spent New Year's Day with her. However, to call in sick, unless he was incapable of functioning, or take a personal day, or even a holiday—that was not going to happen. He was an exemplary employee. Walter was the lead officer on regular shifts for the corporate security force for Substantial Industries Worldwide LLC. Walter knew his job was serious business, and he took his duties seriously and responsibly. He was never one-minute late for a shift, in fact, Walter was never late for anything or his name was not Walter P. Thrump!

After losing a lung to cancer from inhaling glass particles from the glass factory he worked at for over thirty years, Walter found his true love in security work. He was a radio operator in the United States Navy, he still operated daily as an amateur (ham) radio operator in his hobby, and to Walter, the mix of security and the occasional radio chatter they utilized on the job, combined with his tough guy personality and intuitive approach, to create the perfect job for Sergeant Walter P. Thrump.

Now mind you, criminals or persons, who may entertain thoughts of performing something less than law-abiding, or partake in outright and flagrant rule breaking, while on the property of Substantial Industries Worldwide LLC, would face the wrath of Sergeant Walter P. Thrump. His small stature and appearance should not fool anyone into complacency. Walter and his New Jersey street tough guy approach proved himself to be brave and fearless, and a criminal would be gummed into submission, at least until help arrived, to no doubt, save the criminal that is! Walter P. Thrump did not back down from anyone, or anything. Dressed in his security uniform, (the fit was less than optimum, due to Walter's small size) with his sergeant stripes proudly displayed upon the shoulders of his uniform shirt, his polished brass whistle, and a brass badge with his name and rank on his front pocket, Walter was a security officer not to be tested.

On his wrist, he proudly wore his most prized possession. It was the latest custom, Substantial Industries, Super Deluxe, Whiz Bang, model 2-4X12 wristwatch that he had mysteriously obtained as a Christmas present this past Christmas. Walter never determined where, or from whom, the watch and his wife's matching watch came from, but he did not spend a lot of time investigating. The watch and Mrs. Thrump's watch both were the top of the line, with an alarm clock feature, stopwatch, the hour and minute timers, 24 or 12-hour option, digital glow in the dark numbers, a compass, a grid square identifier, a solid titanium wristband that could deflect bullets, and a top of the hour voice announcement feature. It was waterproof, nuclear radiation proof, and explosion proof. Walter loved it, and he cleaned and polished it daily.

Walter generally worked every Thursday night, and he worked right through the weekend, until the following Monday, while doubling up the shifts, in order to work his forty hours. There was nothing in the world that he enjoyed more than work, and sniffing around the building and property for clues, and law or rule breakers.

It was the following day, after his discussion with his wife and preparing his Lucky Leprechaun beer mug for the big event. With dreams of the big holiday and his pending good luck dancing in his head, Sergeant Walter P. Thrump reported for his usual four thirty in the afternoon shift on a late Thursday in the middle of March.

Walter had just a little spring in his step, knowing that next Tuesday was Saint Patrick's Day. Sergeant Walter P. Thrump would be off from work, and he would be home to enjoy some full sips of the heavenly brew from his Lucky Leprechaun mug at the precise time. Walter's faith was strong that his luck would instantly change.

Walter was sitting at his security desk in the lobby of the main corporate headquarters building, preparing for his shift when his boss, Mr. Arnold Plank walked up to check in with Walter.

Mr. Plank was the Executive Vice President of Corporate Operations for Substantial Industries and he had been with the company for many, many years. He was a very tall, thin man who was a nervous wreck. He was a chain-smoker of cigarettes, had beady little eyes, a baldhead, and a thin moustache that he trimmed into a neat line about his mouth. Although he was very soft spoken, he was always on edge, and nervous about everything. Judging by his mannerisms this afternoon, then this conversation was not going to be any different in the nervous levels than other previous conversations with Mr. Plank had been.

"Walter . . . ah, ah, good afternoon. I will need your help with a situation," Mr. Plank haltingly spoke while nervously adjusting his necktie, fingering the end of his little moustache and going through numerous other little nervous twitches. Mr. Plank could not help himself and restrain the nervous habits. The nerves were an unmentioned part of the high-level executive position and they came along with the big salary.

Upon hearing the request from his superior, Sergeant Walter P. Thrump moved into immediate action.

Standing at attention, the brave and fearless, Sergeant

Thrump puffed out his little chest. His polished brass whistle swung from a buttonhole in his uniform breast pocket while he proudly answered, "Of course, Mr. Plank. Please tell me how I might be of assistance. You can count on Walter P. Thrump!

There was nothing that stirred Walter up more than a mission, and he sensed from the body language and extra nervous actions of his superior that his upcoming shift was going to include a special assignment.

"Ah yes, yes, ah . . . yes, Walter." Even though Mr. Plank was quite used to Walter's overzealous approach to his work, sometimes, his eagerness overwhelmed even Mr. Plank.

"Ahem" Mr. Plank nervously cleared his throat as he spoke, "Walter, ah, ah, ah, we had some reports today from some employees, who spotted a suspicious group of trespassers in the north parking lot. I dispatched some maintenance crew out there and our warehouse security officer, to investigate, but they reported to me that they did not see anything or anyone out of the ordinary. I would ask you to investigate during your shift and keep a close eye on this area."

"Sure thing! Absolutely, Mr. Plank. Do you have a description of the evil perpetrators?" Walter pulled his notepad out of his uniform pocket and stood with his pencil in hand to take notes from Mr. Plank.

"Evil perpetrators, Walter? No, I only mentioned some potential trespassers. I did not actually mention any evil perpetrators."

"Oh yes, sorry. Do you have a description of the evil, shadowy, figures, lurking in the dark corners of the parking lot, sir?" Walter asked while looking up at Mr. Plank, while he waited impatiently with his pencil and pad to jot down the facts.

"Walter, I can see that you have been reading your 'Dark Secrets' magazine again. Yes Walter, there were four, very well-dressed men in dark suits, and dark hats and they seemed to be hanging around the corners of the north parking lot and checking out Bruno Crookarelli's car."

Walter looked up, and he seemed surprised and commented, "Hmm, Mr. Crookarelli, huh? If I correctly remember, he is the manager of the print shop operations here.

"That is correct, Walter. When one of our employees asked them if they required assistance, they said no, and quickly drove away in a black, Galaxy four door 5000 sedan."

Walter feverishly took notes and nodded his head as he accurately recorded the information.

When Mr. Plank mentioned the type and model of the vehicle, Walter looked up and whistled while he commented, "Expensive car, huh? That does not sound good. That is a typical, gangster car. I grew up, and I have lived all my life in Jersey City, New Jersey, sir. I know a little something about gangster cars."

Mr. Plank nodded his head and continued, "Well, let's not jump to conclusions, Walter. However, please do remain diligent. I imagine you will step up your patrols and rounds at this location. Please keep me informed of anything you observe or record. Please, do be very careful, Walter. Do not hesitate to call the authorities if you spot something out of the ordinary."

Once more Walter stood at attention, and puffed out his little chest as he proudly spouted, "You can count on Sergeant Walter P. Thrump, Mr. Plank."

"Yes, indeed, I know I can. I always can. Is Russell Hall working in the one hundred building tonight?" Mr. Plank asked while referring to Walter's usual security partner, Officer Russell T. Hall.

Officer Hall usually worked the identical shift in the building directly opposite the main corporate facility within the enormous complex for Substantial Industries.

Officer Hall had been with the Substantial Industries security force for almost as long as Walter had been, and Mr. Plank knew that Russell was a retired civilian and a military police officer.

Russell gave the extra nervous and uptight Mr. Plank an added element of comfort when he worked the same shift as Walter did. It was not that Mr. Plank did not have confidence in the little security officer; it was just that Officer Hall provided a calming influence on the zeal of Sergeant Walter P. Thrump.

"Oh yes, Mr. Plank. I will brief Officer Hall when he reports for his shift and provide him with the description of the evil, shadowy figures and the entire incident." Mr. Plank could not help but smile just a little at the continued zealousness of Sergeant Walter P. Thrump.

"Thank you, Walter. Please have a good night."

"Good night, sir!" Walter shouted as Mr. Plank turned and walked back towards his office in the lower executive wing.

Once Mr. Plank had left, Walter immediately jumped into action as he feverishly transcribed the notes from his pad to his security logbook. Walter was the perfect security officer, and he followed every rule and regulation to the letter while never drifting, or straying, from a single order that may be contained within his official security manual.

Since Walter was the lead security officer on the security force, he anxiously awaited the arrival of the two security officers to begin their shifts. First, Officer Russell T. Hall would arrive and then Officer Juan Mendez. Officer Mendez usually worked in the large warehouse down the road from the two other facilities.

Both security officers were the most trusted and experienced employees on his crew, and Russell T. Hall was, in fact, Walter's only real friend. To say that the two men were friends would be a very loose and broad description of their relationship. In reality, Walter had very few "actual" friends. He did have ham radio buddies with whom he chatted with on the airwaves, but real-life friends were difficult to come by.

If anyone in the world fit the description of Walter's friend, then it would be Russell T. Hall.

Walter glanced at his wristwatch and noted that it was a minute or two before four-thirty in the afternoon. He knew any minute now, his hand-held, two-way security radio would crackle with the security check-ins.

"This is Officer Hall calling Sergeant Walter P. Thrump. I am reporting for duty and onboard here at the one hundred building," the radio crackled with Officer Hall's voice. Officer Hall was on time. Walter smiled, keyed the transmit button on the hand-held, and acknowledged the check-in. Walter ran a finely tuned security machine.

"Roger, Officer Hall. This is Sergeant Walter P. Thrump. Welcome onboard. I need to call you on the landline and give you some special post orders, but I will wait for Officer Mendez to report in." As soon as Walter un-keyed the radio, the security channel filled with the voice of Officer Mendez.

"Officer Mendez checking in for duty at the one hundred and the one-thirty-three warehouse."

"Roger, Officer Mendez. Please standby for a landline call. I need to explain a security situation to you too. This is, Sergeant Walter P. Thrump out."

Walter puffed out his little chest, checked his brass whistle on his pocket, and straightened his badge on his uniform, and then he dialed the telephone extension for the security desk at the one hundred building. Officer Hall answered on the first ring and Walter explained the situation that Mr. Plank had told him about and provided him with the details.

"I will call Officer Mendez next, but on my first building tour, I plan on walking out and checking that parking lot!"

"Well, you be sure to bring your radio Walter, give me a

call when you head out there. Don't be getting into things without help, Walter," Russell warned Sergeant Thrump.

"I will keep you posted on what I find out there, Russell. I will follow the procedures to the letter. Please check the lot over there too. Report to me right away any suspicious activity!"

Officer Hall assured him that he would, hung up the telephone and chuckled at the enthusiasm of the brave and fearless Sergeant Walter P. Thrump. He knew that right now he was on the horn, with Officer Mendez giving him the same report and speech. He knew there was nothing the little man enjoyed more than action or a perceived threat upon his beloved buildings and properties. His smile faded, as his long career in law enforcement had given him a peculiar sense, of when something may be a false alarm and when it may not be. Somehow, from that special sense of a lifetime in police work, he knew that he had to keep an eye out on his little friend.

Superior to him or not, he knew that he needed to watch Sergeant Walter P. Thrump carefully on this mission. He reached down and felt the handgun he always hung over his shoulder. Officer Hall had a license to carry the weapon, and he was the only security officer in the nighttime corporate force who did so. The daytime officers who patrolled the warehouses were armed officers, but those shifts had ended. They had closed the warehouses for the night, and the alarms turned on in order to protect the millions of dollars in inventory stored there. After spending a lifetime in law enforcement, his handgun was something he kept close by him at all times, just in case. This one time, just this once, there was a chance that this threat might be real.

Walter kept his eyes peeled on the security cameras lining the front desk of his lobby posts, watching and scanning the pictures of the parking lots and grounds. He carefully recorded and noted all activities. He anxiously watched the time on his watch for seven o'clock, which was the time to break away from the front desk, and perform his first building tour. He knew that he would head straight to that corner of the north parking lot first. At the stroke of seven, Walter grabbed his watchman's tour clock, his trusty flashlight, put his security jacket on (equipped with his rank patches on the shoulders, nameplate, and a duplicate badge pinned to the breast) and picked up his two-way radio.

He keyed the microphone and called, "This is, Sergeant Thrump beginning my seven o'clock tour now. I am going to check the north parking lot first and then continue on my rounds."

Officer Hall immediately answered, "Roger the info. Please keep us posted."

A few seconds later, the radio crackled with the voice of Officer Mendez, "Roger the report, Sergeant Thrump. This is Officer Mendez standing-by."

"This is, Sergeant Thrump out."

Now, an innocent observer would casually suggest that the odds were very high, that there would be no suspicious cars, or evil, shadowy figures lurking in the north parking lot of Substantial Industries Worldwide LLC corporate headquarters. Perhaps, deep down, Sergeant Walter P. Thrump would agree with that theory, but that did not deter him in the least. He was going to investigate and check out the situation, just in case.

Walter strode out into the cold, early evening air, his flashlight aimed ahead of him, waving it back and forth, despite the fact that the parking lot had bright illumination from the pole lights that dotted the lot. Walter walked out into the parking area, checking all around him while missing nothing. The eagle-eyed Sergeant Thrump made a note of every detail; while his beady little eyes peered into the nighttime. He recognized, and waved to employees leaving for the day, employees who were heading towards their individual cars, and Walter made careful mental notes of anyone he did not specifically recognize.

Very few employees did not know Sergeant Walter P. Thrump, nor were there many employees who Walter did not know. He was a living legend.

Walter stopped in his tracks as he peered into the dark corner of the north parking lot and flashed his light ahead of him.

"Hmm, this is very interesting," Walter spoke his thoughts aloud, while his eyes spotted something in the far reaches of the parking lot. Walter chugged forward until he ran out of the parking lot real estate to patrol. There were no parking lot pole lights nearby this far corner, and some overhanging trees blocked the natural and artificial light from penetrating this dark corner.

There in the corner, he recognized the four-wheel-drive vehicle usually driven by Bruno Crookarelli, and even in the relative darkness, Walter could see it parked alone with no other automobiles next to it. Walter thought how it was a bit strange to see the parked vehicle this late in the day, parked in the farthest reaches of the lot. The little security officer walked up to the car, took his flashlight, and scanned the area.

Nothing. Everything was dark and quiet. Not a person stirred or was around. Walter was disappointed.

Walter then took his flashlight and peered inside of the vehicle. He spotted that the rear of the vehicle had stacks and stacks of boxed cartons packed inside of the interior.

"Hmm, okay, how strange. It looks as if they are the same types of boxes that I see inside the print shop," Walter said aloud as he walked around to the rear of the vehicle and flashed his light inside. He could make out the writing on the side of the boxes and he took out his pad and pencil, and he made careful notes of the numbers and imprints on the side of the cartons.

"Model X4-76 explosion-proof, stainless steel coffee

mugs. Hmm, that's a new one. I never knew we made those," Walter spoke as he wrote down the information on his pad.

The two-way radio on Walter's belt suddenly crackled with the voice of Officer Hall, "Come in, Sergeant Thrump."

Walter's heart jumped in his chest when the radio came to life and he looked around furiously. He had opened the volume control too much on his radio, and if, in fact, there were evil, shadowy figures lurking around, the radio then just gave away his presence. Walter made a mental note to next time be more careful during his investigations. He quickly grabbed the radio and ducked down behind the four-wheel-drive vehicle and Walter looked around in order to double check that the radio did not blow his cover!

Walter keyed the transmit button, and he quietly answered the call, "This is, Sergeant Thrump. Go ahead."

"Just checking on your status. Officer Mendez and I have been standing by to make sure you did not require any assistance."

Walter could not help but smile at the thought that his security staff was always on the stick and looking out for him.

He keyed the microphone again and transmitted, "All clear here, men. Nothing to report. Everything is normal. I will advise you when I am back in the lobby and have completed the tour."

"Roger, the information, Sergeant Thrump."

"This is, Sergeant Walter P. Thrump. Out."

Walter spun the radio confidently in his hands and dropped it back into the holster on his belt with one motion. He placed the notepad back in the breast pocket of his uniform and made his way back towards the building. While he made his way along the parking lot's outermost edges, he suddenly noticed a man moving quickly across the lot in the direction of where Walter just left. The eagle-eyed Sergeant Thrump peered into the darkness, and he quickly ducked down behind a parked car and watched from a distance.

It was Bruno Crookarelli! He had obviously not noticed Walter in the darkness, as Bruno looked all around him and behind him as he hustled along the surface of the parking lot. Bruno was pulling a two-wheeled hand truck loaded with boxes, which were the same type of boxes that Walter had seen loaded in the back of Bruno's vehicle. Walter watched from only a few feet away, as Bruno stopped next to the rear hatch of the vehicle, fished around for the keys, unlocked the door, and while carefully looking around to make sure no one was observing him, he loaded the boxes into the back of his vehicle.

As Walter watched the scene unfold, suddenly to his horror, his wristwatch sounded the top of the hour!

Oh no!

Done in by his pride and joy! The top of the line, Substantial Industries LLC, super-deluxe, whiz-bang, wristwatch he received as a Christmas present.

Yes, that watch! The custom model 2-4X12 with an alarm clock feature, stopwatch, the hour and minute timers, 24 or 12-hour option, digital glow in the dark numbers, a compass, a grid square identifier, a solid titanium wristband that could deflect bullets, and a top of the hour voice announcement feature. It was waterproof, nuclear radiation proof, and explosion proof, but not sound proof! Walter had forgotten to silence the hourly announcement before he had started his tour seeking evil, shadowy figures lurking in the parking lot. It was too late now, but Walter lamented on how he had made two missteps in a row on his investigative tour.

The brave and fearless Sergeant Walter P. Thrump frantically pushed the button on the side of his watch to stop the noise, but it was too late. Bruno Crookarelli had already heard the noise and his head spun around and around as he scanned the darkness for the source of the strange noise. Bruno quickly slammed the door to his vehicle shut and pushed the hand truck off to the side of the lot to ditch it in the woods alongside the parking lot. He moved quickly towards the noise to seek who may have seen his covert activities and maybe to silence the witness.

Walter reached down and turned the volume knob down on his radio, not willing to risk another breach of his cover, and he stared in horror as Bruno made his way towards Walter's hiding spot.

Being a small man in stature, no, perhaps that description is an understatement in describing Walter P. Thrump. Being tiny in stature caused Walter a bit of pain along the way as far as his ego went, but it did have some advantages. Walter looked around, and he spotted a utility vehicle not unlike Bruno's own vehicle, a car away from where he was hiding. Since making a run for it, with his reduced capacity for air intake due to having only one lung, and staying out here and potentially blowing his cover, were not viable options, Walter ducked down and slipped underneath the utility vehicle. His small size, combined with the higher ground clearance of the vehicle, allowed him to fit underneath and hide. There, Walter waited in silence while as he heard the boots of Bruno hitting the asphalt pavement in the cold, March night air.

Walter did not even want to breathe as he spotted the legs and boots of Bruno standing right next to where Walter was hiding! The tenseness of the situation was now overwhelming. Bruno must have been satisfied that whatever noise he heard was not related to a person who had spotted his seemingly covert actions, because after some searching, spinning around, and observation, he finally, slowly walked away.

Walter breathed a sigh of relief as the sound of the boots striking upon the asphalt moved farther away, and he soon afterwards heard the sound of a vehicle door slam, an engine start and the vehicle drive away. Once Walter was sure that Bruno had driven off, he climbed out of his hiding spot, dusted himself off, gathered his thoughts, and made his way back to the building.

That was a close one. He vowed to do a better job on his next tour.

Walter's senses now were on full alert because he was sure that something sinister was going on here and Walter was now determined to get to the bottom of it. He turned his radio back on and called into Officer Hall, and explained he had to conduct a quick side "investigation." Walter was not going to give away any details until he gathered more intelligence.

After returning to the building, carefully checking his alarm panels, he completed his security logbook and logged the details of his tour. He broadly covered the fact in the security log that he observed from a distance, Bruno Crookarelli hauling boxes to his vehicle, and then loading them in the same, but Walter left out the other details, such as hiding under the parked vehicle and the fact that Bruno's vehicle already had stacks of cartons inside. Walter felt as though there was no reason to jump to conclusions just yet.

It was now later into his shift. He would not be due for another building tour for a few hours, but once he signed in and began the nighttime housekeeping staff on their shift, Walter intended to follow-up on his ideas. He knew the location in the building, of where the sales and marketing department of Substantial Industries stored some sales brochures that would reveal the entire lineup of the latest coffee mugs, in which the company currently had for sale. It deeply bothered Walter and his keen mind that the boxes in Bruno's car had labels for a product which did not seem at all familiar to him. He prided himself on his keen attention on detail and that particular model number was a number and product that he did not recognize.

Sure enough, when he could break away, a check of the sales brochures listed all kinds of models of the X line of coffee mugs in stainless steel. But just as Walter thought, the numbers stopped at X4-45. There was no model number X4-76. From walking around this building for years, and observing everything and missing nothing, the keen minded and eagle-eyed Walter P. Thrump knew his product lines.

The plot had thickened considerably, and Walter licked his lips, straightened his belt, and checked his brass whistle, while the little man pondered his next move.

"I know who to ask, just to make sure," Walter spoke aloud enthusiastically, while he snapped his fingers together at his own thought. "Mr. Lathrop will know for sure. He usually always works late. I bet he is in his office tonight." Walter hustled off in the direction of the sales executive wing of Substantial to see if Mr. Robert Lathrop was still working in his office.

Mr. Lathrop was a senior executive in one of the many sales departments, and Walter knew that he was a very important man in the pecking order of the Substantial Industries hierarchy. Walter also was well acquainted with Mr. Lathrop from his many years of building tours and Mr. Lathrop's habit of working late into the night. To tell the truth, Mr. Lathrop was very fond of the little, serious security officer and he enjoyed chatting here and there, with Sergeant Walter P. Thrump. He got a big kick out of him.

Walter reached the corner office of Mr. Lathrop and almost jumped with joy when he spotted the lights still on in his office and the door wide open. Walter was in luck; Mr. Lathrop was still working tonight. Walter peered into the office to see Mr. Lathrop working at his desk, and he smiled as he gently tapped on the office door.

Mr. Lathrop looked up and smiled as he said, "Good evening, Walter. Checking in on me as usual, I see. All is well. I am just finishing here and the later that I stay, no doubt getting in deeper and deeper trouble with my wife. How are you doing, Walter?"

Walter smiled and stepped into his office. Yes, he wanted to check on the executive, but Walter had another motive for this visit, but he had to hide it. He did not want to drag an important man such as Mr. Lathrop into the "investigation" that he was now fully enveloped in tonight.

"Yes sir, Mr. Lathrop. Thank you for asking. I am fine, sir. I hope you are well. You really should be going home, sir. It is growing later and later now."

"I will, I promise. You sound as if my wife has recruited you on her side, Walter. I appreciate your concern. Please, I am fine."

"All right, Mr. Lathrop. I am just checking on you. I am glad all is well. I will be on my way back to the lobby. Mr. Lathrop, can I ask you a product question, sir?"

"A product question, Walter? Sure, sure, sure. Now, you would not be growing more interested in finally buying that new Substantial Industries Rhino 400 automobile you have been talking about as of late, and getting rid of your old station wagon. Please, just say the word. I will make sure we give you the deal of a lifetime, Walter."

"Well, maybe someday soon, sir, but not right now. No, this is a lot less expensive for sure. Do we manufacture a model X4-76 explosion-proof, steel coffee mug?"

Mr. Lathrop leaned back in his chair and rubbed his chin a little as he thought about it.

He piped up and said, "A coffee mug, okay, well, okay, Walter. You are thinking about a gift for someone, huh? I do not think we are that high in numbers yet, Walter. I could be wrong. R and D never tell me about new releases these days. Please, let me check. I have some product indexes that I keep handy right here. . .."

Mr. Lathrop stood up from his desk and walked over to a stack of papers piled on his bookshelf. He pulled one binder book out of the stack, and he thumbed through pictures of the coffee mugs. Walter felt the need to acknowledge the statement Mr. Lathrop made. Since he had surmised the mug was a potential gift, Walter did not mind utilizing that statement to cover his true motives.

After all, it was not a lie to the honest and trustworthy security officer. Walter fiddled with the wording to make sure he was not being deceptive, and he repeated to himself that it was all part of the investigation.

"Yes sir . . . sorta thinking of it as a potential gift of some kind, but I think the person has the number wrong."

"Yes, indeed, they are wrong, Walter. The numbers stop in the forties, we are years away from any seventy's series. Double check the number and let me know."

"Oh, thank you so much, Mr. Lathrop. I thought something was wrong when I could not find that number anywhere. I am sorry to disturb you, sir. Please, I will let you go, so you may finish your work."

"Oh, no trouble, anything for you, Walter," Mr. Lathrop said while he put the binder away and returned to his desk.

After some small talk, the two men bid goodnight.

Walter stepped out into the hallway, puffed his little chest out, and he smiled. The brave and fearless Sergeant Walter P. Thrump was on the case, and his senses were now on full alert. There was nothing that he enjoyed more than pursuing evil, shadowy figures and protecting his beloved corporate headquarters of the empire, known as Substantial Industries Worldwide LLC.

3

Saint Patrick's Day Arrives

"What exactly do you feel is going on here, Walter? I hope your keen eagerness has not caused you to jump to hasty conclusions on this matter," Mr. Arnold Plank asked and commented, as the two men sat in his private office.

Sergeant Walter P. Thrump had just finished explaining to Mr. Plank the details of his previous evening's shift and his observations. Walter had requested an appointment to meet with Mr. Plank, to explain not only his thoughts but also to relay the facts of the incident in the parking lot. Walter knew that his schedule called for him to be off for a few days, until he picked up his shift at the end of the week, and he wanted to speak with Mr. Plank while the details were still fresh in his mind.

Besides, it was almost Saint Patrick's Day, and time for his luck to change with a pint or two of green beer from the Lucky Leprechaun mug.

Walter thought about the inquiry for a few seconds, then leaned in over Mr. Plank's desk and answered, "I truly dislike speaking poorly about a person, but I think that Mr. Crookarelli has become mixed up with the wrong crowd. There is no actual model number that Substantial currently produces that matches up with the brochures that he had in the back of his vehicle. Aside from that fact, Mr. Plank, it was a telltale sign of his evil intentions, when he heard my watch go off. I carefully observed his reaction. I assure you that it was the reaction of a person who is up to something he should not be up to! I know that your next question will be. Why would he be doing this? I think that he might be printing brochures, instruction manuals, and other material, for products that do not exist, with an outside company or within the print shop. He then somehow, bills Substantial Industries for bogus product manuals. I do not like to stereotype, but hey, as I said to you before, Mr. Plank. I grew up there, and I have lived my entire life in Jersey City, New Jersey. I can smell organized crime type relations."

Mr. Plank leaned back in his chair and shook his head gently back and forth. His nervous habits now reached a peak. He tugged at his small moustache, he fiddled with his wristwatch, and his eyes darted back and forth in his head. This was a very uncomfortable situation for the executive.

He sat for a few minutes, thinking about the chain of events. To say the least, it was an impressive testimony to hear of what Walter had found out so far. Although Mr. Plank was hoping that this appointment would be nothing more than a meeting to listen to, and then calm down, the overzealous Sergeant Walter P. Thrump, Mr. Plank had to admit that all of this seemed as if it did have some sinister elements to it.

After some moments to sit and think, Mr. Plank decided to err on the side of caution.

He finally spoke, "Ah, yes, Walter. I am not too sure. It does seem suspicious. However, I think the best course of action here is that we do not need to jump to any conclusions and get ourselves into some kind of trouble with rash thoughts and hasty decisions. I respect your efforts, and opinion, but Bruno Crookarelli has been with Substantial for many years. I do admit that I do not have an explanation for his behavior, as well as the boxes marked with model numbers that we do not manufacture, but I need more evidence."

Walter shook his head because his military background

and his street senses knew that something was going astray here. He just knew it, but he was not going to dispute his superior's feelings or argue with Mr. Plank. The little security officer knew that his role was to observe, deter, and to report situations. He knew his security standard operating procedure manual backwards and forwards; he read it almost every day.

"Walter, I do appreciate your keen observations. I did not realize until now that your investigative persistence was, ah, ah, ah, so . . . eager. Please be careful, but keep an eye on the situation, and keep this in confidence amongst us. Carefully log the details so the other security officers are aware of the situation, and they too, keep an eye out for trespassers, but do not give away too many details. I do wish you to clue in Officer Hall and Officer Mendez with a little more info, since they work the same shifts that you do and may be able to, you know, assist you in observations. Over the next days or so, I think that I may call a meeting with Mr. Crookarelli's executive management, the corporate attorney's office, and a manager from the human resource's department too, but I will think about it for a bit of time. I will call you if something comes up."

Mr. Plank stood up from his desk and extended his hand out to Walter. Sergeant Thrump stood up, and the two men shook hands.

"Good work. Thank you, Walter. Please, enjoy your few days off, and we will see you at the end of the week. I know you always enjoy Saint Patrick's Day, so please have a nice holiday. I need to go outside and have a cigarette now and think about this situation. It is all quite disturbing."

Walter turned to leave and said, "Thank you, sir. Please call me if those evil, shadowy figures show up, you can count on Walter P. Thrump. Saint Patrick's Day or not. I am always on the job, Mr. Plank."

Mr. Plank smiled at Walter's continual insistence on the

fact that the situation included "evil, shadowy, figures" but he appreciated the little security officer's zeal.

"Thank you, Walter. I know I can always count on you."

Sergeant Walter P. Thrump nodded, and he walked out of Mr. Plank's office and into the main hallway of the executive wing. There, he looked up and down the hallway. He straightened his security cap, checked his sergeant stripes for proper alignment, tugged at his radio belt, checked his brass whistle and badge, puffed out his little chest and walked down the hallway. As he strode along, he nodded to fellow employees, while also scanning the entire area for any potential rule or regulation violations. Walter checked for fire hazards, employees breaking storage rules, sneaking pencils or notepads into their pockets, and so on, and so forth.

Sergeant Walter P. Thrump was always on the job, and he was a very serious man.

Soon, it will be Saint Patrick's Day and Walter had a careful pre-holiday ritual; he could not risk anything going wrong. He just had this nagging feeling that this was his year. He returned home from work a little later than usual, since he had waited to speak with Mr. Plank after his night and an early morning shift had ended.

It was now Monday morning, and he had to grab some sleep and then be ready for the big event. Walter crept into the front door of his house, slowly opening the door, while making sure that he did not make too much noise and wake up Gertrude. His wife was still sleeping, and Walter knew that she had been up the entire night watching reruns of her favorite show *El Paso* on the television. She loved the main character, whose name was "RJ" and was a wealthy, evil, oil baron who manipulated and connived his way through life.

Walter was an avid ham radio operator, and he would usually go down into his basement radio shack to tune in the world on his radio and see whom he could contact. He stood in his kitchen, thinking how he always made a point of finding a station in Ireland that he could talk with on his radio set on Saint Patrick's Day, because it was a yearly tradition. He then would exchange "QSL cards" with the Irish station, which were small postcards printed with the individual station call sign as well as contact information, location, country, and the main operator's name. Walter loved to collect them and the walls of his radio shack had cards mounted on them from all corners of the world, which he had contacted and obtained cards from on his radio. Walter lined up the QSL cards confirming the contacts that he made on Saint Patrick's Day with the Irish stations in a long vertical row on the wall, having stapled them in succession for many years. It was an impressive display.

Today, Walter would skip the radio, because the events of his past shift at work had exhausted the little man, not only emotionally, but physically too.

He changed out of his uniform, carefully placing today's shirt and pants on a hook for the laundry, and moving his badge, his brass whistle with the chain and his custom radio belt to a fresh set of uniforms for his next shift in a few days. He took off his prized wristwatch and carefully and lovingly placed it inside of the custom, explosion proof stainless steel, carrying container that he kept next to his uniform rack. Walter shaved, washed up and decided to forego the radio, for now because he needed to relax and then sleep. He thought about how he would sit in the chair in the living room and read the latest issue of *Dark Secrets* magazine for a little while until he went up to his bedroom.

Walter glanced at the cover of his beloved magazine and smiled as he spoke aloud to himself, "This should be a good one. Look at this headline. How evil, shadowy, figures steal your personal information. Oh boy, what is this world coming to these days?" Walter eagerly opened the magazine and thumbed through it.

The next thing that Walter knew was that he was waking up in his living room around two in the afternoon. Walter opened his eyes slowly and gazed around the room. He realized that he never did go up to his bedroom and that he indeed must have been very tired. Pursuing evil, shadowy figures was hard work and exhausting too! His copy of *Dark Secrets,* was still sitting in his lap untouched and it was open to a page. He had not even moved a muscle. The little man stumbled out of his easy chair, hustled off to the bathroom and washed up. He changed into a casual pair of dungarees and put on his Luck O' the Irish sweatshirt and made his way to find Mrs. Thrump. He found her in the kitchen nursing a cup of coffee, glancing at the daily newspaper.

She looked up and frowned at Walter as she said, "Well, finally. It is unusual for you to be sleeping in the living room, all the while, messing up my day. I planned on cleaning and running the vacuum, and now I can't because you decided to sack out in your chair." Mrs. Thrump was angry with her husband for his change in routine.

"I am sorry, Gertrude, but it was a long shift, and I started to read my 'Dark Secrets' and just faded away." He leaned over, kissed her forehead, while she scowled at her husband.

Gertrude W. Thrump was a bit of an extra crabapple today.

"I suppose you want a cup of coffee now?"

"I will get it, honey. I have it. Please, do not get up."

"No, no, no, after all the inconvenience you have already put me through, a cup of coffee is nothing. Sit down there in your chair and I will get it for you." Mrs. Thrump waved at Walter to sit at the table. "I mean, my goodness, falling asleep all day in the living room. I even missed my afternoon show, 'Nights of Our Lives' because you decided to ruin my day."

"I am sorry, Gertrude, but. . .."

"Oh, forget it! So, what was the big deal about this double shift that wore you out so much? Checking for stolen pencils and unlocked doors should not have exhausted you to such an extent."

The ever-positive Walter jumped at the opportunity to explain the intrigue to his loyal and sometimes loving wife, "Oh no, Gertrude, I am on a serious investigation. I am working on a case."

Mrs. Thrump stopped next to the stove and placed the coffee cup that she held on the counter. She placed her hands on her hips, frowned, and then chuckled a little.

"An investigation? I am sure that you are kidding with me now. Ha! What are you checking for, Walter? People sneaking notepads in their pockets to take home. Or are you searching for blocked fire doors? Please, Walter. You are many things, but a great detective you are not."

Walter's testimony of his work activities did not make an impression on his wife, and she remained quite cynical at the thought of her husband performing an investigation.

Walter leaned back in his chair, somewhat taken back by his wife's reaction, but still undaunted.

"No, honey. Mr. Plank asked me to check out some evil, shadowy, figures prowling around in the parking lot and I do think that I may have stumbled upon something. I wish I could tell you more details, but it is a confidential investigation at this point! You know how it is in the early stages of a case. There are a lot of details we have to gather up yet."

"HA! HA! HA! You are kidding, aren't you? Evil, shadowy figures, Walter P. Thrump. Now, you have really flipped your lid. You are such a dreamer. You have been reading that stupid magazine too much. Here is your coffee. I suppose that next on your wacky agenda, is for you to prepare your yearly shrine to the lucky ritual, and your beer mug that never brings us anything. Please make sure you do not move too much on the dining room table and mess up my centerpiece display. There is some bologna on the second shelf in the refrigerator. I am going to dust a little in the living room, and run the vacuum around. I do need you to go to the Foodworld, the butcher, and pick up the dry cleaning for me today, before you become involved in silly, lucky charms and wild Irish rituals. Your shopping list is on the refrigerator. It is under the magnet."

Mrs. Thrump left the room, shaking her head back and forth at what she perceived to be Walter's outlandish behavior.

Walter sat back in his chair and sighed, but at the last minute, he recalled the joy of his favorite holiday and he shouted out to Gertrude, "Oh, by the way. Happy Saint Patrick's Day Eve!"

At first, his wife did not answer the well wishes for her to enjoy a grand pre-holiday. Then, Walter heard some rustling around in the other room, which he perceived to be his wife readying the vacuum cleaner, and Gertrude suddenly shouted back, "I am not Irish!"

The little man carefully whispered, when he heard the vacuum turn on and he was sure that his wife could not hear him, "That explains a lot. Oh well, not everyone can be lucky and great too. . .."

After a chuckle at his sly dig into his wife's heritage or lack thereof, he perked up quickly when he realized how hungry he was. He did not allow his wife's doubts to deter his usual positive behavior. After all, Walter knew that it was almost Lucky Leprechaun time.

He ate his lunch, ran the requested errands for his wife, stocked the kitchen with the supplies from the Foodworld supermarket, changed the oil on his beloved station wagon (after all, Walter still considered three hundred thousand miles on an odometer to be just past the breaking in point of the engine) and soon it was time. It was time to set up the shrine in the dining room for his Lucky Leprechaun ritual. Walter carefully moved his wife's centerpiece from the table, being extra aware not to allow a single flower to roll out of place because he did not want to face the wrath of Gertrude W. Thrump. After carefully laying out the special green tablecloth, Walter pinned his "HAPPY SAINT PATRICK'S DAY" banner up over the table, stretching it from wall-to-wall in the dining room. Soon, the cardboard cutout shamrocks were standing up on the table, as well as the special green candles.

There could be no missteps in this yearly ritual. A year is a long time to wait for another chance at good luck.

Walter found his shiny, green, leprechaun hat with the big buckle on the front of it, buried in the back of an upstairs closet, and he set it on the table next to the shrine. He dug around in the record cabinet for his copy of "Harvey Crooner Sings Your Favorite Saint Patrick's Day Tunes" record album, and set it right next to the record player to be able to play it at the correct moment. There was no way to avoid weeping your eyes out when Harvey broke into those wonderful, heartfelt renditions of "Harry Boy" and "The Roads of Old Dublin Town."

Then, in the place of honor in the center of the table, he carefully placed the Lucky Leprechaun beer mug. Walter bowed in honor as the leprechaun smiled back at Walter from his printed and faded, worn-out image.

All that Walter had left to do now was to find the green food coloring, chill down a few Big Boulder beers, and wait for the stroke of midnight.

The anticipation and excitement were a bit much for Walter P. Thrump. The rest of the night, he woofed down a few bologna sandwiches, listened to his wife preach and complain to him, paced the floor, double-checked, and then triple-checked his custom, Substantial Industries, Super Deluxe, Whiz Bang, model 2-4X12 wristwatch with the alarm clock feature. Walter made sure he had set the alarm to eleven-thirty, just in case he dozed off. The other features such as the stopwatch, the hour and minute timers, 24 or 12-hour option, digital glow in the dark numbers, a compass, a grid square identifier, the solid titanium wristband that could deflect bullets, and the top of the hour voice announcement feature, could also come in handy someday.

You never know in this world!

Walter sat and watched some evening's television shows with his wife, talked to some friends on his ham radio set, and before he knew it, the time had finally drifted away. He had nodded off in his chair, and his alarm sounded loudly and clearly on his wristwatch, shaking him from his nap and springing Walter into action. Mrs. Thrump heard the alarm, and she frowned at him. She was watching the latest reruns of *El Paso* on the late-night station, and Walter's alarm sounding on his watch had interrupted her concentration on the television show.

"Are you going to come and watch, while I bring us a full year of good luck, honey?" Walter asked his wife with a wide, toothless smile.

Gertrude W. Thrump stared at her husband for a few seconds, scowled, then kicked her feet into the easy chair, clicked off the television remote control and said with a loud sigh, "I guess . . . we have nothing to lose except time, I guess."

Walter eagerly charged ahead. He was a nervous wreck as he looked at his watch and made careful note of the time.

"Eleven thirty-five. There is still plenty of time," Walter said as he made his way into the kitchen.

He picked up a book of matches, hustled back to the candles and carefully lit each of the green candles, and watched as they flickered to life, casting a warm glow upon the setting. Walter picked out two Big Boulder beers and unscrewed the beer caps from the bottle. He took the small tube of green food coloring and squeezed the contents into the bottle and carried the two bottles into the dining room, and set them next to the beer mug.

Oh, the drama.

Careful now, one slight misstep and an entire year of bad luck were the result!

"Would you like me to start the record player with the dopey, Harvey Crooner record on it for you, Walter?"

"Oh yes, Gertrude, key up 'Harry Boy' for me, please."

A few minutes before the hour, Walter carefully poured the green-colored beer into the Lucky Leprechaun mug and watched as it foamed up and the head of the beer overflowed the glass. The tension built as Mrs. Thrump dropped the needle on the record at the stroke of midnight. Walter carefully watched his wristwatch. While in the background of the room, the needle wobbled upon the record. Walter's eyes welled with tears as Harvey Crooner belted out the sad ballad telling the story of, "Harry Boy."

Walter watched the second hand as it spun around on his watch and exactly at one-minute past midnight on Saint Patrick's Day, Walter shouted out, "Here is to the help of the Lucky Leprechaun and to ask him for one year of nothing but good luck!" Down the hatch the pint of green beer went, in one, big gulp.

He was, of course, right on time, or his name was not Walter P. Thrump.

Mrs. Thrump was not impressed with the entire situation. She had been a witness to the same ritual for a good many past celebrations. Unimpressed, she wandered off, shaking her head. Given the choice, Mrs. Thrump would rather to continue watching her *El Paso* reruns on the television, then rely upon a silly family superstition to change their luck. At least, by being lost in the world of television drama allowed her an escape of some sort.

Another year had passed and Walter smiled as he placed the now empty mug on the dining room table, sat down and cried at the touching music and words of the Harvey

Crooner song in the background. He poured another green beer and swigged it down too while he stared at the image of the Lucky Leprechaun. One could only hope and it was certainly something to cling to, that was for sure.

"Happy Saint Patrick's Day," was all Walter managed to say as he finished the final beer.

Indeed. After all, one could always wish, dream, and believe in the Lucky Leprechaun.

As well as all the magic and luck that comes along with it too.

4

A Bit O' the Luck of the Leprechaun

Saint Patrick's Day was a wonderful holiday for Walter P. Thrump. He had a few extra green-colored beers, an extra thick, bologna sandwich or two, some cheese puff snacks and he even convinced a very reluctant Mrs. Thrump to dance around the living room to a Harvey Crooner song or two. He ran out to the mailbox and made sure that under the fresh influence of the Lucky Leprechaun; he mailed his entry form in the Big Bob's Special, Spring O' the Year Food Contest.

"This is the year," Walter proclaimed as he dropped the envelope into the mailbox, and he listened as it landed with a loud "thud" in the bottom of the box.

He attended mass with Gertrude at Saint Patrick's Church; afterwards, Walter managed to contact one or two ham radio stations in Ireland on his ham radio set, and continued the holiday tradition of making contacts with Ireland and exchanging QSL cards with them for their mutual collections.

Overall, it was a grand celebration. Walter felt as if it was one of his best!

Walter might have consumed a few more Big Boulder beers and shed a few more tears than he had in the past years, but, nonetheless, he had a grand time of it.

All too soon, the special holiday had passed. Walter carefully took down his shrine for the Lucky Leprechaun mug, cleaned it, and packed the mug and the decorations away for another year. The days after the holiday passed along rather quickly and before Walter knew it, the holiday was a vague memory, and it was now time to return to work. Now, work was Walter P. Thrump's favorite place to be, so it was not that he was apprehensive or sad about reporting for his shift, it was just that after a few days of merrymaking, it is always hard to shift gears into a work mode. Off to work the reliable Walter P. Thrump went, and he, of course, was not one-minute late or his name was not Walter P. Thrump.

Right at four seventeen in the afternoon, on the Thursday after Saint Patrick's Day, he was on duty. His old station wagon with the duct tape on the fenders, the blue and black smoke spitting out of the tailpipe, the driver's door handle that did not work on the inside, (you just rolled the window down, stuck your arm out and pulled it from the outside) and the radio that required a hard bash on the top of the dashboard to turn on, pulled into the special parking spot in the front circle marked, "Security Officer."

The door popped open, and out jumped Sergeant Walter P. Thrump. He rolled the window back up, grabbed his lunch pail, his bag of cheese puff snacks, adjusted his brass whistle, checked his badge and puffed out his little chest. He proudly strode up the majestic steps of Substantial Industries Worldwide LLC Corporate Headquarters building to begin his shift.

After greeting Judy Hicks, who was the long-time receptionist in the front lobby, he checked the huge glass display case of major products, company information, history and memorabilia mounted on the wall of the grand lobby of the corporate building. Walter always checked to make sure the glass cases were intact, and the doors were secure. After all, there were valuables inside the display case! Walter loved to scan the case and study some of the products that Substantial Industries made. Everything the company manufactured, produced, or sold was the best and without question, the top of the line, and was always over the top. There is no room for halfway or the middle of the road for Substantial; it was not acceptable.

Walter looked up at the company logo and motto that was made of solid stainless steel and mounted on the wall, high above the display case, and he read the company motto aloud, "When the wimpy stuff just will not do the job, then go Substantial!"

Walter loved it. He was a Substantial man.

He settled in at the security desk in the front lobby, and he scanned the security logbook entries of the past few days for any suspicious or unusual activity. Walter checked in with Officer Mendez, and then Officer Hall on the radio, and he was reviewing his paperwork, when Mr. Plank came by and tapped Walter on the shoulder. One look at him told Walter that Mr. Plank was a step up from his usual nervousness. Walter could tell that his boss was a nervous wreck.

"Hello, Mr. Plank, sir. Good afternoon."

"Ah, ah, ah, yes, good afternoon, Walter. I hope you enjoyed your days off and Saint Patrick's Day."

"I did, sir, very much so, thank you."

"Good, good, look, I am off to an important meeting and pressed for time, but with regard to that matter and situation we had discussed before your days off . . . well," Mr. Plank's voice trailed off, he looked nervously over his shoulders a few times, and all around the desk to make sure evil, shadowy, figures were not listening.

It seemed as though Mr. Plank might be a believer now too!

Walter leaned in to listen intently and eagerly as he whispered, "Yes, yes, yes, Mr. Plank."

"Well, it seems as though there may be some substance to your discovery, but I must strongly stress that we are still investigating. Please do keep up your observations and patrols of the lot for evil, shadowy . . . ah, I mean, for any trespassers. Please do keep Officer Mendez and Officer Hall diligent at the other properties too, Walter. Call the police right away if you spot anything. It may take us a bit more time to determine the situation here behind the scenes." Walter stood up at attention while saluting Mr. Plank.

"Aye, aye, Mr. Plank. Yes, sir! You can count on my crew and me. We are on duty and at your service."

Mr. Plank smiled at Walter's actions; he gave a half-hearted salute back and said, "Yes, indeed. I can always count on you, Walter." He then gathered some papers under his arms, waved back, and continued his way towards the main lobby elevators.

Walter mumbled softly and smiled when Mr. Plank had left and he fist pumped in the air a little after making sure no one was watching him.

"I knew it. I just knew that bum Crookarelli was up to no good." He puffed out his little chest, checked his whistle and chain, checked his badge for proper alignment, and then sat back down to review his paperwork. He focused his cameras, and panned, tilted, and zoomed in on the north parking lot area, but the spot where Bruno Crookarelli parked his vehicle was just out of reach of the camera's range. Walter knew that was on purpose, and Bruno parked in that specific location to stay out of the view of any prying eyes. No trouble, Walter thought. Bruno might be able to hide from cameras, but not from him. Once the housekeeping crew arrived on site, and Walter met with the executive housekeeper and started them on their shift, he can hustle out there and perform a building tour and parking lot tour too.

It was the part of the job that Walter loved the best!

Over in the Substantial Industries 100 building lobby, directly across from the magnificent corporate headquarters, Officer Russell T. Hall had just hung up the security hotline telephone after having a conversation with

Sergeant Walter P. Thrump. He had received the latest news from Walter on the evil, shadowy figures, as Walter called them. Initially, while it was very easy to dismiss the enthusiasm of Walter, as a bit of overblown huff and puff due to his energy and zeal, somehow, Russell still was not too sure. Just as it was during their previous duty shifts when he first heard about the unusual situation, Officer Hall still had a nagging feeling. A feeling that this incident was trouble of some kind.

He stood up and walked around the lobby a bit, rubbing his chin and pondering the situation. Officer Hall, after his lifetime in law enforcement and despite the fact that he was technically retired, still had the edge earned from the experiences of a long career. He was tall, still strikingly handsome and from playing quite a bit of golf, and walking all the time, for a man in his early seventies, he was in prime physical condition. He was a big, tough man when he was in civilian and military law enforcement, and not much, other than the color and amount of hair on his head, had changed, as the years had passed.

Russell returned to the security desk, picked up the hotline telephone, and dialed the telephone extension for Officer Juan Mendez, while he reached down and felt for the special handgun strapped in his shoulder holster.

Yes, it was still there.

Meanwhile, at the one hundred and one building, Walter briefed the housekeepers on their work, sent them on their way, looked at his watch and confirmed the time. He picked his radio out of the holster belt and called on the security two-way radio into both Officer Hall and Mendez that he was starting his tour. He also reported that he was going to include the ominous north parking lot in his round. The little security officer grabbed his security cap, his jacket (the jacket had an identical brass badge mounted on the front lapel) his watchman's tour clock and his trusty long flashlight. He puffed his little chest out and headed out into the cold March air. It was an unusually cold evening for mid-March in northern New Jersey, but it was clear, starry, and crisp. Walter strode along confidently, with his flashlight in front of him, checking every nook and corner for the presence of evil, shadowy figures. This was his beloved Substantial Industries property, and no one was going to inflict any damage on it, or harm any employees while the brave and fearless, Sergeant Walter P. Thrump, was on duty! Walter made his way up the pedestrian pathways; he crossed some steps and walked across the center parking lot. He passed a handful of employees who greeted him and bid Walter a good evening, but for the most part, there were not many employees remaining at this time of the early evening.

When Walter reached the outer reaches of the north parking lot, he leaned in, because he thought he heard some loud male voices and perhaps some type of argument.

The eagle-eyed, Walter squinted his eyes, and he peered into the darkness while carefully scanning the parking lot. The parking lot pole lights were of some assistance, but it was still a dark area. He listened and still heard what he thought were voices, so he stepped up the pace and he knew right where to head . . . toward where Bruno Crookarelli parked his vehicle!

The north parking lot was immense and sprawling. It was an overflow lot for the parking of the employees who worked in the Substantial Industries warehouse operations building adjacent to the corporate headquarters. Therefore, it took Walter and his little legs a bit of time to propel himself towards the farthest corner of the lot.

As he approached the corner, he could now clearly see Bruno's vehicle parked in the usual location and sure enough, Walter could see a large, dark-colored, Galaxy 5000 four-door sedan parked next to Bruno's vehicle.

He had found the evil, shadowy figures!

Walter's heart jumped in his chest. He tapped his flashlight in his hands, overhung his lower lip in an effort to show his determination, he stuck out his craggy nose; he tugged at his radio belt and holster, slung the tour clock lanyard over his shoulder and puffed out his little chest.

The brave and fearless Sergeant Walter P. Thrump dug into the ground, picked up the pace, and then he stopped dead in his tracks when he spotted three men dressed in suits and jackets standing between the two cars. They were even wearing the typical "gangster" type fedora hats on their heads. Bruno Crookarelli was leaning precariously on his own vehicle while being surrounded by the group of well-dressed men. They were shouting and yelling a bit, and Walter could not make out what they were saying, but he could tell it was not an exchange of casual pleasantries.

As Walter approached the scene, he saw one of the men pick Bruno off the car, then push Bruno forcibly into his car. Walter watched in horror as Bruno bounced off the vehicle and rolled onto the ground. The men were hulking brutes of a huge size, and poor Bruno bounced off the vehicle with considerable force and landed hard upon the ground. One of the men in the rear of the pack took out a stick of some sort and started to beat Bruno Crookarelli with the stick, while Bruno was helpless and prone upon the ground.

Bruno started to scream out, "STOP! STOP! OKAY, I WILL COME UP WITH THE REST OF THE MONEY! I AM CLOSE TO HAVING IT NOW."

One of the gangsters yelled back, "We need the rest of the money now! This printing idea of yours is not bringing in the money quickly enough!"

Upon seeing the horrific attack, Walter jumped into action—all five-foot two, three, or four of him. Hulking, evil, shadowy figures meant little to the brave and fearless Sergeant Walter P. Thrump! He rushed into the fray, while reciting the rules from his security rule book, which he of course, knew from cover-to-cover. This time, he knew the rules of enforcement for private property, and Walter was going to use them too!

The little security officer ran ahead, while shouting loudly, "Hey! Private property here, men. You are trespassing on private property and assaulting an employee. I am in charge of Substantial Industries Corporate Security! I am Sergeant Walter P. Thrump! Take your beef elsewhere, vacate the premises immediately and leave the employee alone!"

The surprised men turned and faced Walter. It was easy to see that until now, they did not see the little security officer arrive on the scene.

"It is all right, Walter! Please, please, please, go back into the building. It is going to be all right," Bruno Crookarelli said as he looked up from the ground and stared at Walter, while desperately waving his hand. Even in the darkness and the dim light of the parking lot poles, Walter could see blood dripping from Bruno's head.

One of the gangsters called out, "Get rid of the little chump. He saw all of our faces and he needs to go."

Another hoodlum chuckled, and then shouted out, "You got it! I will take care of him!"

The man quickly advanced towards Walter, and the brave and fearless security officer froze in his steps. Without a single hesitation, the mobster reached inside his jacket and pulled out a handgun. He pointed the weapon in Walter's direction and squeezed the trigger, before Walter even had any time to run or react!

A loud "CLICK" and a gunshot echoed across the parking lot.

Oh no!

Walter now ducked, closed his eyes, and thought to himself that his luck had finally run out this time. He started to pray, and his mind raced with what Walter thought would be his last thoughts on this good Earth.

Walter instinctively threw his hands up across his body. He felt a sharp pain on his left wrist and he heard a loud noise. In the darkness, Walter spotted a large spark emit from the wristband of his watch at the same time that the noise occurred. The force of the blow to his wrist caused the little man to tumble down upon the asphalt and roll around on the parking lot surface. His security cap went flying, his flashlight fell, the tour clock crashed upon the asphalt pavement, and his brass badge, whistle, and chain flashed in the night. After surviving many firefights in Vietnam and walking point with many first lieutenants, while a hail of bullets flew over their heads, it appeared as if this time, Walter P. Thrump's luck had run out!

A second after firing the shot, the gangster who fired the weapon, grabbed his side in pain, dropped his weapon, and he doubled over and mysteriously fell to the ground.

Suddenly, out of the wooded area in the rear of the parked cars came a voice, and a loud "click" of a gun trigger being cocked.

Officer Russell T. Hall charged out from the woods as he screamed, "On the ground now! On the ground! There are three of us now, the police are already on the way, and I extended one last-minute invite from one other, whose name is, the Substantial Industries handgun division. I hate to tell you bums, but this model X12-2Y cannon-blaster with the single-barrel, advanced propulsion, is the most powerful small-caliber handgun in the entire world! It will most surely leave very little left of your body to plant in the ground."

Officer Mendez then charged into the scene from the other direction, swinging his nightstick and flashlight ahead of him.

"C'MON NOW! You guys! Easy! Down on the ground, face first, arms straight out. I can pull off four or five rounds very quickly here and I do not miss! Toss any weapons to the side. DOWN NOW—OR DAMMIT, I WILL

SHOOT!"

The men all complied and lowered themselves to the ground, while following Officer Hall's instructions.

Officer Mendez held one of the crooks down with his nightstick held to the thug's throat, and the gangster who had the beating stick tossed it away, when Officer Hall waved his gun in his face to inspire his disarming. Officer Hall moved in closer and he trained his weapon on the prone men. Suddenly, the lot was a wild scene as it was filled with policemen. Both plain-clothes officers arrived along with uniformed officers, sirens, flashing lights, and law enforcement officers with guns drawn, all while yelling for everyone to stay put. An officer ran and checked on Bruno Crookarelli, who appeared to be unconscious.

Seeing the situation now under control, Officer Hall turned his attention to his fallen comrade, as did Officer Mendez. Officer Hall holstered his weapon and ran over to where Walter P. Thrump still was flat out on the ground.

"We have an officer down! Help! Over here! Officer down."

Officer Hall, Officer Mendez, a team of policemen, and a paramedic rushed over to Walter, while the police called for an ambulance and more paramedics to tend to Bruno Crookarelli and the others . . . including Walter.

"WALTER! WALTER! ARE YOU HIT? WALTER, SPEAK TO US!" Officer Hall shouted as they rolled their friend over to check on him. Walter just laid there motionless for a few agonizing moments . . . the tension was horrendous. Then, to a few loud cheers, Walter's eyes suddenly opened as they all stared at him, while the paramedic tugged and pulled at his uniform in an effort to find a wound.

Walter waved at them to stop them from tugging at him. With some assistance, Walter sat up.

"I am fine! I am fine," Walter shouted out.

All the men relaxed, now that it appeared that

amazingly, and inexplicably, Walter was somehow unhurt.

"How? What? He shot you, Walter!" Officer Hall was stunned, and he could not determine how the bullet did not injure Walter.

Walter was feeling all over his little body, and now he smiled. "I am fine, I am not hit. I mean the bullet hit me, but I think it, hit—hit—hit, unbelievably, but it hit my watch! My wrist is killing me."

They all looked down at the wristwatch on Walter's left wrist, and the paramedic and one of the policemen flashed their lights on it. Walter's wrist was swollen and red, but sure enough, the watchband had a clear nick in the center of it! The bullet had hit dead center on the wristband. True to the word of the Substantial Industries top of the line product, the solid, titanium band did indeed deflect bullets!

"Holy smokes, you mean a damn bullet from twenty feet away hit your watch? And the watchband deflected it? I have to get me one of those suckers!" The policeman said, as he stared in disbelief at the testimony.

A plain-clothes policeman walked over to Officer Hall and said, "Looks like the little guy there, might have a broken left wrist, but he is all right, not sure what the hell happened here, other than your pal, is the bravest and the luckiest son-of-a-bitch in the world, and that is the best damn watch ever made. Nice work by you guys. You and your partners caught some really bad guys here tonight. We have been after these guys for quite a long time."

Officer Hall held out his retired police badges from the civilian world as well as the military, and the policeman studied them, smiled, and nodded.

"But it was Sergeant Thrump who really nailed 'em, not us," Officer Hall said as he pointed at Walter. "The little guy may not look like much, but he is one brave, fearless, and tough, little cookie!"

Officer Mendez looked back over at the scene where the paramedics were attending to the fallen gunman, and he shook his head while he made the connection.

"Russell, Sergeant Thrump, that is why the gunman went down so quickly, the deflected bullet hit him in the hip. His own bullet returned to him and took him out! This is unbelievable! Buena suerte, Sarge! A one in a million chance."

The men were stunned at the amazing incident, as Officer Hall, Officer Mendez, and the policemen and paramedics picked Sergeant Walter P. Thrump up off the ground.

Officer Mendez and Hall hugged their little friend and Officer Hall said, "You scared the daylights out of us. You are one lucky guy! When you reported, you were heading out on your tour, Juan and I called the police and we decided to follow along. I just had this feeling tonight, Walt. I cannot explain it."

They handed Walter his security cap, his tour clock and flashlight. Walter slowly stood up. He wobbled a bit, then gathered his thoughts and balance. While his left hand remained incapacitated, the brave man struggled with his right hand and grit his teeth as he adjusted his badge on his jacket; made sure his whistle and chain were in order, took his flashlight, and dropped it into the holster on his belt. In one quick motion, he slung the lanyard of the tour clock over his shoulder. Walter P. Thrump then stood at attention, and while the paramedic worked on his left wrist, he called for a salute from his crew and the gathered police officers.

After a smart and proper salute from all involved, Walter proudly proclaimed, "Luck it was indeed, men! I have the best luck for sure! What did you just say, Officer Mendez? Buena suerte! The Lucky Leprechaun came through! Ha! Ha! A one in a million shot, a deflected bullet, random thoughts to make you rush out here and assist me. It was all because of the Lucky Leprechaun! He came through for me!"

The men all smiled and stood in amazement at the testimony of Walter. At this point, they were not quite sure what he was babbling about. However, who was going to argue?

While the paramedic still checked and attended to Walter's wrist, the brave and fearless Sergeant Walter P. Thrump puffed out his little chest.

He smiled a wide smile and nonchalantly said, "So, we got the evil, shadowy figures, huh? I knew it! I just knew it! Nice work, men. Nice work."

Nice work indeed!

However, it was all in a day's work for the brave and fearless Sergeant Walter P. Thrump and his elite security team. Yes indeed, watching for stolen and smuggled pens and pencils, stolen notepads, and blocked fire exits and apprehending evil, shadowy figures too!

5

The Heroes' Reward

Sure enough, Walter was correct in his initial investigation and Bruno Crookarelli had fallen into some troubles with some well-known New Jersey organized crime figures. It turned out that Bruno had a bad gambling habit and rang up quite a bit of debt to some persons who handled overdue loans in a rather serious manner.

Bruno's scheme to raise money involved printing false instruction manuals, sales brochures, and other materials for products that did not exist. When the scheme proved lucrative for not only paying off debts, but for making easy money, with the assistance of the gangsters, Bruno set up a false outside company to assist him with the printing. Bruno issued Substantial Industries purchase orders to the phony company to collect huge amounts of money for the printing materials.

It was all working out well until Walter stumbled upon the operation and brought Mr. Plank's attention to the situation. Mr. Plank ordered an immediate audit of the print shop's accounting records. The audit of the books revealed a huge amount of money stolen from Substantial Industries and while the investigation continued, the executive management tightened the rules for issuing purchase orders. Since he had yet to find a workaround with the new system, it was then that Bruno fell behind on his payments, and the gangsters became angry at the loss of stolen funds. It was overwhelming how much they had stolen and hidden in false business accounts.

Bruno would print just enough false brochures that, if someone questioned the operation, he would have something to show to a suspicious person. He would then take the false material off-site and destroy it to avoid detection. Furthermore, Bruno was smart enough to make the phony products just close enough in descriptions and model numbers to actual products, to avoid detection for a very long time. Despite his evil, yet careful planning, Bruno's scheme fell apart and when the purchase orders and checks stopped, the gangsters closed in to settle the score. After a stint in the local hospital to recover from his beating, Bruno would be able to join his fellow evil, shadowy figures in prison to contemplate the error of their ways.

Substantial Industries Worldwide LLC, attorneys, accountants, and other executives, had been working overtime behind the scenes with local law-enforcement officials, while compiling the information they needed to nail Bruno and his operation. They had more than enough evidence to put them away for many years. Ironically, on the night that Walter stumbled upon Bruno and the gangsters, local law enforcement had staked out the parking lot and they, too, were closing in for the final round up.

"Say Walt, have you given any thought to what you are going to do with the bonus check that the CEO, Mr. Kingly Topgun, gave to you?" Lieutenant Russell T. Hall asked Captain Walter P. Thrump, as the two friends sat in the lobby of Substantial Industries Worldwide LLC Headquarters to enjoy their dinner break together.

Captain Walter P. Thrump leaned back in his chair, placed the plaster cast on his left wrist onto the security desk, and used his right hand to fiddle with the gold badge proudly displayed upon his chest, while he thought about it for a few seconds. While still thinking about the question, he slowly peeled open his bologna sandwich that Mrs.

Thrump had wrapped in wax paper for him, just as she had for the past forty or so years, and he looked up at Russell.

He finally seemed to arrive at a well-thought-out answer, "I think I am going to build a driveway next to the house, Russell. Yeah, yeah, yeah, a driveway, so that I can get the car off the street. Then maybe, I will put new vinyl siding on our house and install a new roof too. I am not too sure. Maybe stick some dough in a savings account to earn some interest. Then maybe, just maybe someday, I will buy a new car. I do not want to jump into anything, ya know. My old car still runs well. It has a few miles on it, but it runs well. Yeah, yeah, yeah, a driveway, siding, and a roof, and then I think I am going to buy Mrs. Thrump a new dress, and some fancy perfume. How about you?"

"I am going to give it to my grandson for his college tuition and buy a new set of golf clubs. Now that we all have this new rank and higher pay, between you, Sergeant Mendez, and me, we are quite the team. The only trouble is that I feel guilty about going out on the golf course and playing now. I make so much dough at this job. After all, I am supposed to be retired!"

Walter chuckled, and he reached in the top drawer of the security desk, pulled out a paper and read it aloud.

"In honor of his sound knowledge, keen judgment, superior investigation skills, bravery in the face of danger, and placing himself in the line of live fire, to defend his fellow employees and our property, I hereby award the brave and fearless, Sergeant Walter P. Thrump the newly minted, Substantial Industries Solid Gold Medal of Exemplary Employee Service. He also will receive a check for twenty-eight thousand dollars, a new Substantial Industries, Super Deluxe, Whiz Bang, model 2-4X13 wristwatch with an improved, bulletproof and dent proof wristband. By my order, I now promote him to the rank of Captain of Substantial Industries Corporate Security

Department, and he will receive all the compensation, honor, uniforms, whistles, badges, and benefits associated with the rank. Signed, CEO Kingly Topgun."

Walter sat up proudly in his chair, puffed out his little chest, adjusted his new gold badge, and his new whistle with a solid gold chain, and smiled.

When he heard of the incident and event, Mr. Kingly Topgun, the CEO of Substantial Industries Worldwide LLC, ordered an immediate dinner and ceremony for the security officers at the largest restaurant and banquet hall in all of New Jersey. He ordered in the best food, drink, and décor. He ordered local and national press coverage, a live feed to all stockholders, and all employees were invited (at least as many as could fit in the banquet hall) to attend not only in person but also via a satellite broadcast across the world. Never one to miss a free opportunity for worldwide promotion, Mr. Kingly Topgun, also slipped in a mention of how the R and D department of Substantial Industries had developed a new wristband that not only could deflect bullets (as Walter field-tested and proved) but now, was dent proof too. He also added how Substantial Industries had sold millions and millions of 2-4X13 watches over the last few weeks and their stock was trading at an all-time high! Substantial Industries never did anything halfway; it was always over the top! In addition to the awards and promotion for Walter P. Thrump, Officer Russell T. Hall and Officer Juan Mendez also received awards, bonus checks, raises in pay and promotions.

Walter continued to smile a wide, toothless grin, and he said to Russell, "Golf clubs are nice, Russell. Ya know . . . I sure am thankful that Substantial Industries is the world's greatest company, makes the best damn watches in the world, and that you, Juan, and I, are never late for anything. After all, we are a team. The best. Yup, Lieutenant Russell T. Hall, Sergeant Juan Mendez, and Captain Walter P. Thrump. Unbeatable! This is what I have been telling my wife and everyone else for years. Never be late for anything. Even a gunfight with evil, shadowy figures. You had better believe it, or my name is not, Walter P. Thrump!"

The old 1974 Whizzer station wagon pulled in front of 164 Maple Lane in Jersey City, New Jersey. Walter P. Thrump rolled down the window, opened his door latch, and climbed out of the wagon.

He then rolled the window back up and slammed the car door. He grabbed his trusty old lunch pail, his security cap, and made his way slowly to the front door of his home.

His eyes grew wide and excited when he spotted a large box sitting on his front porch.

"Oh boy! It must be my grand prize from the Big Bob's Special Spring O' the Year Food Contest. I knew I was a winner again this year. That Lucky Leprechaun keeps coming through for me."

Walter hustled up the steps, grabbed the box, and studied the label. Sure enough, he was correct. It shipped directly to him from the headquarters of Big Bob and his massive food empire. Walter unlocked the door and almost ran into the kitchen. He wanted to shout aloud, but he knew Mrs. Thrump was still sleeping from staying awake all night watching reruns of her favorite show, *El Paso* on the television, and he did not want to wake her. He set the box upon the kitchen table, pulled out his pocket knife, and carefully opened the seal on top of the box.

The excitement was incredible. What did he win this time? This was fantastic. Walter opened the first box and stared deep inside. There buried inside the packing, was another box.

"Double boxed for protection!" The shipping label proudly proclaimed.

"Oh boy," Walter said, "it must be a valuable prize this year!" He pulled the second box out and sliced that one open, too. "Wow! Two boxes inside." Walter exclaimed, as he was now astounded at his good fortune.

He flipped them out of the second shipping box and held them up to read both of the labels. The first box had a label, which had printed upon it in large block letters, "One box of Big Bob's Custom, Whiz Bang, Roller Tip, Black Pens." Walter then looked at the side of the other box, which was larger, and the label there declared that the contents were, "One eight-foot, inflatable, Big Bob replica balloon."

"Hmm . . . sort of the same stuff, I won last year. However, the balloon is one-foot taller," Walter said while he stared at the boxes. He then spotted in the bottom of the box a full-color, eight by twelve-inch certificate.

"Wow! A certificate too!" Walter pulled it out and read the words aloud, "Congratulations, Mr. Walter P. Thrump of 164 Maple Lane in Jersey City, New Jersey for being a prize winner in this year's Big Bob's Food Contest. While you did not win the grand prize, you are a winner of one of our special, twenty-eighth place prizes, as well as a proud holder of a suitable for framing, official, Big Bob's Food Contest Entry Certificate. Thank you for your support of Big Bob and his food empire!"

Nothing discouraged the ever positive, Captain Walter P. Thrump. He held the certificate up proudly, and even though it all seemed remarkably similar to last year's prize, he said, "Now, I have two balloons. One big one for the front porch and a smaller one for the back porch. Gertrude will be thrilled!"

About one year later, a few days before Saint Patrick's Day, Walter sat in his kitchen at 164 Maple Lane in Jersey City, New Jersey. He glanced at the calendar and realized that his favorite holiday was only a few days away.

"Say, honey, do you know where my Lucky Leprechaun mug is? I want to find it and get ready for the big day. I need to renew my luck, dear. Boy, oh boy, I cannot wait to enter the Big Bob's Food Contest this year. They are giving away a trip to Haledon, New Jersey and the grand prize is a trip to the Bahamas. Plus, just in case more evil, shadowy, figures come around, I need to have some good luck on my side!"

"Look in the cupboard where you put it last year, Walter. I sure hope you do not win any more of those stupid pens and another dopey balloon. Never heard of a place called Haledon. Why the hell would we want to go there? I gave the pens away for trick or treat to the kids in the neighborhood and we still have about four thousand of them left. Those stupid-ass, Big Bob balloons, give me the creeps, but they do keep the pigeons off the porch." Mrs. Thrump shouted from the other room. "I also rather not hear of you investigating any more evil, shadowy, figures this year."

Walter thanked his wife, grabbed a step stool, and set it up next to the cupboard. Walter climbed up, opened the cupboard door and peered into the rear reaches of the cupboard, and sure enough, there it was in the back corner of the cupboard. Walter grabbed the mug and carefully secured it, then climbed back down the step stool. He smiled as he set the prized mug on the kitchen table and studied it. There he was again. The Lucky Leprechaun! Walter stared at the slightly faded, cartoon-like imprint of an Irish leprechaun.

"Hello! What is this? Are my eyes playing tricks on me or not?" Walter shouted out as his wife came running into the room to see what her husband was shouting about in the kitchen.

Walter pointed at the mug, studied it for a long time, and mumbled, "Say, honey, do you remember if the Lucky Leprechaun was always winking at us with his right eye or not? And, I could swear, there were always six golden coins at his feet, not eight!"

Mrs. Thrump studied the mug, and looked at her

husband while she said, "I am not sure, Walter. I think it is just that his eye is fading away from age. He is not really winking. Maybe, I should hand wash him this year and not put him in the dishwasher. The heat might have faded him a little. The coins, well. . .."

She picked up the mug and studied it again.

"Then again, I am not too sure." She placed the mug back on the table and smiled at her husband.

Walter hugged his wife in the kitchen, and she puckered her lips up, presenting a very rare request for a kiss from her husband.

While Walter leaned in to kiss his wife, his eyes quickly caught a glimpse of the mug on the table.

Mrs. Thrump whispered, "Ya know, Walt, you do have the afternoon off and it is nice to get lucky once in a while."

It may have been the moment, or his eyes playing tricks on him, but Walter swore that he saw the Lucky Leprechaun close, and then open, his right eye and tip his cap to him. Then again, it might be just that the mug is becoming a little faded. Or the kitchen light required replacement, or yes, maybe, just maybe, his eagle-eyes were playing tricks on him. He needed to see the eye doctor; it had been a long time since he had his eyes checked. He vowed to do it next week after the new driveway is finished and Shady Joe's Roofing Company installs the new roof. Maybe it was his eyes, or maybe it was something else. Oh well, Walter leaned in and enjoyed the kiss and whispered back that his wife was indeed quite correct. He did have the afternoon off. Oh boy, his luck sure was changing. He was suddenly getting used to being a bit on the lucky side, and it surely felt nice. After all, even the brave and fearless Captain Walter P. Thrump was not ever going to doubt the immense power of the Lucky Leprechaun!

THE END

Homage to Pussface the Cat

It was a relaxing Saturday evening in late March, and I sat in my easy chair in the living room, glancing through a hockey magazine, when I heard our daughter, Heather Sarah, screaming her lungs out as she tore through the house towards me.

"Dear Father! Please tell me a story about Pussface the cat! Did he really drink beer and was he really Grandpa Henson's best friend? Tell us, dear Father. Fritzie and I need to know."

Heather Sarah came running into the living room, jumped into my lap, and waved her stuffed doggie "Fritzie" in my face.

"All right now, little girl. Wow! What brought this on, eh?" I hugged her and kissed her as she sat on my lap in my favorite easy chair.

Heather Sarah looked at me with the utmost seriousness and said, "Well, dear Mother, Paul William, and I were researching the best pets for us to have, and a kitty cat is the one that we think may be the best." She then nodded in one of her best nodding rounds that I have ever seen. I wanted to grasp her head to make sure she did not become too dizzy.

"I thought about your stories of Pussface. Now, we all want to hear more about him."

She smiled that little smile that could melt her father's heart every time. My lovely wife, Binky, came wandering into the living room, along with our son, Paul William.

Binky was carrying a Martini that I had made earlier for her, (shaken not stirred) and Paul William promptly sat on the floor and stared at me, while my wife smiled a wide smile. The clear assumption was that they would like to hear a story too!

As I gathered my thoughts, it occurred to me that storytelling as a family has become such a lost art. Perhaps it is something that has gone the way of so many other things. Out of style, out of fashion, out of vogue. And why not? You can flip on the television and tune countless channels, a computer and, the internet has put the world at your fingertips, and a video game can destroy the entire universe with the push of a button, all in the name of entertainment. Therefore, it is so easy to become lost in a maze of electronic madness.

I cleared my throat; at least it had yet to be lost in this house.

"So, you are thinking about a kitty cat, eh? And you would like to hear about the world famous Pussface the cat too?"

The three of them; my two children as well as my lovely wife, set off into an aggressive round of their famous head nodding in an epic display of continuous and fervent affirmation of my questions.

I found my own head bobbing along as they all nodded, until I finally managed to encourage them to stop by saying, "Well now. I guess you want to hear some stories, eh?" Our two children had inherited their nodding genes from their mother. Binky sat in her own chair next to mine, while she sipped her Martini, Paul William sat on the floor in front of me, and Heather Sarah snuggled in tightly next to me on my other side with her precious Fritzie held tightly in her arms. They had dug in for the long haul.

"Well now, Pussface was one ugly cat. . .." I began to tell the story of the world famous Pussface and his decision to share his wonderful life with the Henson family so long ago.

I returned home late on a Saturday afternoon from a road hockey game. I bumped and banged my equipment bag in through the back door of our house at 182 Belmont Avenue in Haledon, New Jersey. It was somewhere in or around late March in 1979 or thereabouts, and the noise that I was making while I struggled to carry all my equipment into our home alerted my dear Mum to my arrival. The door to the kitchen swung open, and it took me a bit by surprise.

"Shh, please be quiet, Paulie. Pussface is sleeping in his new bed that we got him," Mum signaled me to be quiet as she pointed down to where Pussface the cat currently laid, all snugly curled up and sound asleep on our back porch.

"Here, let me help you with your equipment," Mum said as she took one of the bags out of my hands, while I looked down quite puzzled at the sight of Pussface the cat curled up in a brand new, soft bed lined with fluffy fur. A luxurious, furry blanket covered him, and three empty dishes sat next to the bed. It seemed as if Pussface had suddenly been elevated to the level of "King Pussface."

"New bed, Mum?" I asked. "What happened to the old Big Boulder beer carton and his blanket that was his bed for years and years?"

Mum, for some strange reason, ignored my questions and instead, she focused upon my hockey career.

"Oh, how I wish you did not play that horrible goalie position and have all of this equipment. I am sure you brought me home some more of those sweaty and smelly jerseys of yours too! Did you need any stitches today?"

"Oh, hi Mum. How are you?"

I thought about how I would try a different approach.

"No, no, no cuts today. I am sorry, but yeah, there may

be a few stinky ones in there. It was a rough practice and game too. We won. I only let up one goal. It was a screen from the point and there was. . . ."

"That is nice, Paulie." My dear mum cut me off. "Now please close the door so that Pussface does not wake up." Hmm . . . very strange behavior from Mum. It seemed as if not disturbing Pussface the cat, was of paramount concern to her. Now, please do not misinterpret my meaning here as implying that Mum did not care for Pussface the cat. Mum generally did go along with and tolerate his presence, along with his begging for an occasional beer and his hanging around the house and back porch all these years. She even tolerated his habit of bringing "offerings" of various dead or almost dead "things" that he had captured and dropping them off as gifts to her and my father. It just seemed that this evening, Pussface's status and well-being were elevated somehow. It was intriguing to me.

Pussface was our adopted pet cat. He was in all honesty, and there was no real way to sugarcoat the facts because he was one ugly cat! He was an orange tabby cat, or at least at one time, he was. His head seemed as if it was at least three sizes too big for his body, his tail was just about gone, he was all full of battle scars from endless fights with dogs, other cats, rats, and various other encounters, including some with vehicles in the streets. His body displayed the hazards of a lifetime of living on the streets of Paterson and Haledon, New Jersey.

At one time, Pussface was just a neighborhood stray, who wandered into our backyard a long time ago on a terribly cold and snowy Christmas Eve. He almost froze to death in the extreme weather conditions, and my father found him, brought him in from the cold and nursed him back to health on our back porch. Ever since then, Pussface sort of became our pet cat. He loved the old man for saving his life and hung around him all the time. Pussface was my old man's best buddy. He would follow the old man around when he worked in his garden, or just sit and watch as he did battle with some repair on our old faithful 1964 Putter Classic model 200 automobile in the driveway of our home.

Pussface would, on occasion, disappear for days on end, but he would always return, begging for food, and sleeping on our back porch. Mum would never allow him in the house, and our pet fox terrier, Skippy, made sure of that!

When they first met, Skippy and Pussface were mortal enemies. Over the years, though, as Skippy and Pussface both grew older, they each mellowed. Skippy and Pussface, while not exactly friends, grew to tolerate each other. They moved from being mortal enemies to being semi-social, and even on very rare occasions, interacting without a fight and even playing together.

The other unique aspect of Pussface the cat, was that he loved beer. The old man stumbled upon this fact by accident on the night that he rescued him. Typically, you would hear old Pussface letting out a few loud "meows" as he begged at the back-porch door on a cold evening. We would let him in for the night to sleep on an old blanket thrown inside an old cardboard beer carton that we kept on the floor of the porch. The old man or Mum would put a small dish of beer out; the old alley cat would happily lap it up, eat a few handouts of whatever we had for dinner, then he would curl up and go to sleep and he was the happiest cat in the entire neighborhood. Pussface the cat, was a typical New Jersey tough guy, mooching his meals, and stealing a few beers here and there.

He fit right in with the rest of our neighborhood crowd.

Still puzzled by the elevated status of Pussface, I started to inquire as to why he had a new comfortable bed and blanket thingy, but I became diverted by hockey and I lost my thoughts. I followed Mum from the back porch, through the kitchen, and towards my bedroom, babbling endlessly about this save that I made, and this shot that an opposition player took on me.

Mum occasionally would acknowledge my drivel, with an, "Uh, uh, that's nice, Paulie," but it appeared as if she only half-heartedly listened, while she helped me with my gear. Once we arrived in my bedroom, I dropped my bag on the floor. I unzipped it, and searched around for the most gruesome of items, which consisted of sweaty, disgusting, and horrible hockey jerseys, socks, and my undergarments that I wore close to my body to not only absorb sweat, but to keep some heat in my muscles, in an aid in keeping me loose and flexible in the cold, ice hockey rink.

Mum stared into the bag, cowered in fear, and turned her nose up at the sight of the dreaded items.

"Oh my, Paulie boy. Pull them out, and I will start the washer. We will drop those bloomin' stinkin' clothes in there. Come along and bring them with you."

My mother deserved a special, "Greatest Hockey Mum of All-Time Award" for all the disgusting and horrible hockey clothes that I had brought home for all of these years for her to wash for me. She always supported me. No matter what the current disaster or trouble happened to be, through it all, dear Mum was there for me. My hockey career was in a great part, due to her support, from the first chest protector she sewed into an old sweatshirt for me, to helping ice down my latest wound, or dragging me to the doctor to check on my latest injury or receive another stitch or two. Mum was quite the first aid attendant, and although hockey was not high on her hit parade, Mum knew hockey was my love. For that alone and for many other reasons, I told her often, but never enough, how much I love her, and I could never repay her, ever!

"Where was this game? You were gone for so long."

"Cherry Hill, New Jersey, down near Philly. I was only gone for two days. I think we can play for the championship. It will be a race with the New Jersey

Rockets right to the end."

I handed my mother the horrible clothes as she added water to the washing machine, tossed in some soap, and she signaled me to drop them in the tub. My longtime faithful fox terrier, Skippy, made a guest appearance as he heard my voice. I bent down and greeted him while he wagged his tail and jumped up and down on me to say that he missed me, too. He was old now and had slowed considerably, and thankfully, in his old age, he had mellowed quite a bit too. He used to be a bit on the wild side!

Mum was nodding while she carefully handled the edges of the disgusting hockey jerseys and other assorted messes.

As she turned up her nose she said, "That is nice, Paulie. I am sure you will be down to the wire with that crazy, O'Malley. It seems to be a destiny that if he is not in jail, then you two will end up battling for the championship. Your father, the guys from the shop, Harry and the rest of the Redmonds, will be lining up for tickets for that one. O'Malley seems to be everyone's favorite scoundrel. I swear that chap is crazy."

"Yeah, yeah, yeah, Mum, it looks that way. The Colonials are in first place in their division and we are first in ours. It will be a battle for sure."

The washer machine made some swishing noises, and Mum closed the lid.

She smiled at me while she piped up, "Would you like some tea? I have some cookies and a lemon tart or two, left from a batch of tarts that I baked a day or so ago. I forgot you had an away game, so I saved a few on the side before your father ate them all."

Yes! I could always count on my dear, English born Mum to come through with some fantastic, home cooked lemon tarts!

"Oh yes, and please call Harry. He called and was

babbling something about a double date he had set up for you two for tonight. He told me that you have to call a gal named Renee, or maybe it was Glenda or something like that. Or was it, Janet?"

Mum put her hand to her chin while she pondered the name.

"Oh phooey, well, do come along for a spot of tea. I can never keep track of Harry. He is still speaking with that silly western drawl slang these days and wearing his big hat. He came by the day you left, to see you. I think he forgot you had an away game too. Nowadays, I cannot figure out what he is saying half the time. He had his big hat on, he was wearing fancy sunglasses even though it was raining, and he scuffed up my wax on the kitchen floor with his fancy, black cowboy boots. Oh my, I love him dearly but he is quite the character. Your father will be home soon from the shop. He is working a lot of overtime."

Skippy and I followed Mum back towards the kitchen and I had to laugh at her description of my best buddy, the world-famous Harry M. Redmond Jr. He was certainly one of a kind.

"Thanks Mum, I will give him a call. I think it is Janet, Glenda seems to be a gal of the past now. The tea and tarts sound great."

"Oh my. I think I remember, Glenda. She was cute and if I recall correctly, it was a short-lived romance, but she was nice. I do not know about any, Janet. I hope you go out with Harry. I am happy to hear you have a double date. You need to date more young ladies, Paulie. You are so obsessed with hockey. How I wish, you had not played so much hockey and dated Maureen Zipperelli more seriously. She was crazy about you, Paulie. She would have married you in a heartbeat. I always thought she was so nice, even if she talked your ears off, and she smelled like garlic and red wine. I do think she is the one who got away from you."

Mum was rambling a bit now while we walked. I did not answer my mother, but I smiled at her matchmaking advice to me. I put my arm around Mum and hugged her while we walked towards the kitchen. I towered over her now, and I bent down to hug her. Mum smiled at me. I stopped and thought how it was good to be home, and that you should always take the opportunity to thank your mother and make sure that you give your dear Mum a hug. If I have one piece of advice to anyone, then that would be it.

"I will make some tea, and heat up the tarts. Please take care not to be too loud. Pussface is sleeping so soundly on the porch."

"Thank you, Mum." My mind suddenly reverted to Pussface and his lofty status on the porch.

"Say, Mum," I said while pulling out a chair to sit at the kitchen table, "I could be wrong, but it sure seems as if Pussface is living the high life. Now, I know he has been around forever, but I am a bit confused. He has a new furry bed, a fantastic blanket, and warnings to be tiptoeing around as not to wake him. Wow! It seems as if he is now, King Pussface."

Mum turned and smiled at me while she slid a tray of lemon tarts into the oven to warm them up a bit. Skippy sat on the floor next to me and looked up lovingly. He was going to lure a bit of lemon tart his way once they were ready.

"Oh, I need to tell you what has happened, Paulie. I have forgotten that you have been away."

I thought about how I had only been gone for two days and how my own home was not unlike Harry and the rest of the Redmonds where two days could translate into a cavalcade of adventures. I leaned in while dear Mum sat opposite me at the table. I could tell that she had something of vital importance to tell me. She had a look of reverence upon her face. It was a look of kindness mixed with appreciation.

I had to say that it was unique indeed.

Mum began to speak while she smiled broadly, “While I have always sort of enjoyed having Pussface around, and I have to admit he was not my favorite, but your father loves him so much that I went along with him. It was as if we had an agreement that Pussface stayed on the porch, drank leftover beer from the bottles, took care of some troublesome food scraps, kept the mice out of the garden, and he was in his place and I was in mine. He is not too handsome to look at, but he had his place in my life. Sadly, I must admit that until now, I just tolerated him. I could do without him bringing me back gifts of disgusting things that he had captured, and then we had the horrible, Fluffy the parakeet incident.”

I nodded my head at that now legendary incident in Henson family history that was indeed an entirely different story.

“You know how much I love dogs and how I do much prefer them over cats.” Skippy wagged his tail in response to Mum’s proclamation. Our old family dog was very smart.

Mum shifted back in her chair. And she must have sensed my confusion, since I had a stupid look on my face. Let me clarify that statement, in that I looked more stupid than I usually did. This conversation was making no sense at all to me.

“You see, yesterday, it was a beautiful, early spring day. It was cold but above freezing, with crystal clear blue skies. I thought how nice it would be to wash all of our bed linens and let them dry on the clothesline outside in the backyard. You know how fresh they smell when they dry like that, eh?”

I nodded my head slowly while I secretly wished dear Mum would quickly tell me what had affected her in such a manner.

"I washed all the linens and was hanging them out on the line in the yard, when I heard a terrible noise and spotted a horrifying sight. A large, growling dog—some type of mixed breed of some sort, came barreling through the hedges on the other side of the garden. The dog came from the vacant lot where the restaurant used to be. He stood there growling and barking at me with his terrible teeth showing. His lips turned back, and he slowly came closer to me. I was frightened out of my wits and did not dare to move! I had no idea why he was so angry, or where he came from. I think he may have been sick or that something or someone had the dog terribly frightened. All that I could do was to think that I should try to calm the dog down, so I tried speaking to him in a comforting voice, and a low tone, telling him it was going to be all right and that he was a nice doggie. It was not going to work, and I feared that this was not going to turn out so well. The dog was coming after me and running would be futile. Your father was at work, you were away, and Skippy was in the house. I am not sure poor Skippy would have fared so well since he has grown so old and slow now. When Skippy was younger, he would have been a typical fox terrier and provided the fearsome dog with quite a battle. Even in his old age, Skippy must have heard the growling and sensed the dog, because I could hear him barking inside the house."

Skippy, who had now returned to waiting for the tarts to arrive, and was curled up under my feet waiting for the magical moment, sat up when he heard his name, and looked over at Mum with a bit of a sad look on his face. He might have been doing his best to convince both of us that he still was a tough guy, well, maybe in his heart he still was. I sat in horror now, listening to this terrible situation that had confronted my dear mother. I felt terrible that I was not there to help.

Mum continued the horrifying tale, "How I wished that

by some remote chance of luck that Harry would have come by, or someone else to help me, but I was on my own. I decided the best thing to do was slowly inch my way towards the door and then make a quick break for the door when I was close enough, but it was not looking good. The dog charged me and I screamed and ran!"

"Oh, geez, Mum!" I shouted out at the thought of the situation. "Thankfully, you seem to be okay. Did you make it into the house in time? You must have. I am so sorry that I was not here!" Mum waved her hands in the air as a signal for me to stop talking until she told me the rest of the story.

"Yes, Paulie, it was terrible! I dare to say that it was the scariest situation in my life! Just when the dog was inches away from me and the door was still three or so feet out of my reach, I could feel the hot breath of the dog on my leg . . . I saw a flash out of the corner of my eye, and, and, and, it was Pussface! Pussface jumped through the air, and he landed on the neck of the dog! Pussface let out with a shriek and a terrible cry! It was a sound, unlike any sound that I have ever heard before. It is not easy to describe, but it was almost for lack of any other description . . . a battle cry, and the dog stopped in his tracks. The dog tried in vain to shake Pussface from his neck and back. Pussface held on, and I could see him digging his claws down into the dog, and biting his ears! I ran and made it into the back door while I watched from the porch window. The dog shook his head violently back and forth, and cried in pain. But Pussface would not let go. Then Pussface looked up, and I swear to you that he saw that I was safe, and he let go, jumped in one long leap onto the picnic table by the maple tree, and then he leapt into a lower tree branch. The dog was a mess. I am sure he was hurt, and scared, and he half-heartedly ran to the tree and barked, but he must have not wanted anything else to do with Pussface. Eventually, while I heard the poor dog still whimpering in pain and pawing at the injuries on its ears, the dog finally ran and took off. Pussface the cat saved me, Paulie! He saved your dear, old mother from harm!"

I stood up from my chair, walked over to Mum, and hugged her. She was crying now, and I kissed her cheek and held her hand.

"I am so sorry that I was not here, Mum. Thank God for Pussface the cat. It is somewhat amazing, Mum. Pussface protected you. He is amazing."

My mother hugged me back, and she whispered, "Yes, thank God for him and for his incredible courage. He is very smart, you know. Extremely so." Mum leaned back in her chair, and I stood there with my hand on her shoulders, while she reached into the pocket on her apron, pulled out a tissue and gently dabbed at the tears in her eyes.

"I brought Pussface inside, and gave him some beer and food, while I called the police to report the terrible dog. Later on, in the day, they returned my call to report that animal control had captured him. It appears as if the poor dog was very sick. When your father came home from work, and he heard the amazing story, we both went to Scruffy's Pet Store and we bought the best bed and a warm blanket that we could find. I cooked Pussface a fish dinner for a reward, and he then curled up for two days or so, enjoying his new bed and blanket, and a full belly of fish and beer. It was the least we could do. After all, he earned it."

I smiled and slowly walked back to my chair. Skippy jumped up and sat on my lap. He knew the tarts were near.

"That explains King Pussface status, eh?"

"Indeed, it does, Paulie, indeed it does. I think the tarts are warm and the tea is ready, Paulie."

Mum stood up and walked over to the oven. She turned and said with some tears still in the corner of her eyes, "I know that God sends us special things in our circle of life. You know, he sends us people to love, he sends friends such as Harry for you, even animals arrive, to make our lives better. I believe that it is part of his plan. I am sure that he sent Pussface to us years ago, for your father to save the old cat's life, and for him to love us, as we love him. Pussface may not be the most handsome cat in the world, but he surely is the bravest!"

I smiled and said, "I think you are correct, Mum. All of it is God's plan and I think sometimes, we just have to understand that everything happens for a reason."

Little did I know how situations such as this one would guide my life later on, but that again, is a whole other story.

"As far as being the bravest cat, well, I surely will not argue with that fact. He surely is the bravest. Indeed, he is." In an effort to divert her emotions, I decided to bring us back to where we had started.

"Say, those tarts smell wonderful."

"Oh yes, I bet they are. Maybe Pussface, when he wakes up, would like to try one, or, ah, King Pussface that is." Mum laughed at her statement and I smiled at her genuine fondness for her feline hero.

It was the fall of that same year and I was sleeping soundly in my bed when I awoke to my father shaking me violently.

"Hey, Paulie, wake up! C'mon, wake up will ya?"

I rolled over and opened my eyes to see the old man standing above me. He had his hat and coat on, and even in a sleepy haze, I could tell by his voice and body language that he was serious.

"C'mon, get ya lard-ass up. We have a problem and I need your help right away. Stay here, Skippy." The old man waved at Skippy to stay on the foot of the bed. Old Skip had looked up and actually started to stand, but he sank back down and curled up once he heard the old man's instructions.

"What is going on, Dad? What kind of trouble? I am out

of it here. I am sorry. I was sound asleep. It was a rough game last night and Harry and I went out with some ladies after the game. I missed what you said."

The old man was intense and serious as he waved his hand for me to follow him.

"I know. Staying out late and playing grab-ass with the ladies is fun, and I am sorry to cut into your nightie-nights, but I need ya. C'mon, I need to show you, hurry up! Throw a pair of pants on and a shirt. You will need your vest and hat because it is cold out."

I nodded, jumped out of bed, and pulled on my clothes, found a hair tie in my pocket, tied all of my long hair behind my head, grabbed my vest, a ball cap, and I was ready for action. I looked over at my alarm clock and it was not even six in the morning. I could not imagine what had the old man worked into such a frenzy, but I met him in the kitchen, while still rubbing my eyes.

"Out on the back porch, we need to move fast—before your mother wakes up."

I followed the old man as we walked out on the porch and he pointed down to where Pussface was sleeping in his bed. Or at least, I thought he was sleeping. I looked at Pussface curled up in his bed with his special blanket over him, as usual, then back to the old man. The old man stood there with an intense look on his face, and he stared at me. I swore even in the darkness of the pending dawn. There were tears forming in the corners of his eyes. I then looked closer and knelt down next to Pussface's bed.

I stared in and looked closely at the old cat, and then I realized that his chest was motionless.

He was not moving or breathing at all.

Pussface, the ageless cat, had passed away.

"Oh my, Dad, he is gone. Old Pussface is gone."

"Yeah, yeah, yeah, it musta happened last night."

The old man took his hat off, as did I.

"He ate last night and had a dish of beer, too. I guess

that he just came to the end of the road, Paulie. There is no telling how old he was, ya know."

I stood up, walked over to the old man, and placed my hand on his shoulder. The old man covered my hand with his, while he sadly looked down at his longtime pal and mumbled, "Best damn cat that ever lived and the bravest too. Saved your mother's ass ya know, he saved her . . . and I sure am going to miss sharing a beer with him. At least he died happy. He went away while sound asleep, with a belly full of beer and a good meal. We all should wish for such a thing when our times come. Say, I need your help to bury him. I want to bury him in the corner of the garden. He always sat there and watched me and he would clean his fur while I worked. Old Pussface knew when I finished working and weeding that we would have a beer together. He was smart too!"

The old man looked at me and put his hat on.

"I do not think I can do it alone, Paulie. Say, can, can, well, can ya help me?"

I smiled and gripped his shoulder tightly.

"Sure thing, Dad, I understand. I will take care of it."

The old man nodded, and he walked out the back door into the yard.

"I will get the shovel and a flashlight and meet you in the garden," my father said as he disappeared into the early morning light. I knelt down and carefully scooped up Pussface's body and wrapped the furry, special blanket around him. I carried him out and walked into the yard, to find the old man standing off in the corner of the garden, with the shovel and flashlight. He pointed to me as I set Pussface's body down carefully on the ground.

"Over there in the corner near to that post, where the cucumber trellises will go. That is near where we buried the parakeets too."

With the onset of the cold weather, the garden was now void of plant material. There were just a few rows of lettuce and one or two rows of radishes still hanging on. I nodded, took the shovel and plowed it into the earth in the spot the old man had directed me to. As he held the flashlight, I dug and dug until the hole was round and deep. It was easy to dig in the loose garden earth and when I thought the hole was deep enough; I dropped the shovel and looked up at my father.

"Whadda ya think, Dad? Good enough?"

I sensed that my father was having a difficult time with it now, as he did not answer me, but he simply nodded his head. The sun was coming up now; it was going to be a clear, cold morning. The leaves were falling, and a smattering of crisp spent leaves danced around our feet, and moved into corners of the garden propelled by a slight early morning breeze. I walked over to where I had laid Pussface's body, scooped him up in my arms, and hugged him tightly.

As I went to walk over to the hole, my father grasped my shoulder, and he softly said, "Wait, Paulie."

I stopped as he held his hand on the blanket covering the old cat. "Goodbye, my old pal. May all your mugs be forever frosty and filled to the brim with joy." He then nodded to me. "Say, Paulie, you know all those prayers and stuff. Can ya say something nice for Pussface?

"Sure thing, Dad."

Little did I know then that this was my first funeral service, but that is an entirely different story, best left for another set of words somewhere down the line.

I walked over to the hole and carefully and reverently laid Pussface the cat to rest. As I shoveled the first round of dirt into the hole, I took my hat off and tossed it onto the grass. I stopped and bowed my head, and I spotted the old man remove his hat too.

I prayed aloud in the cold air, "God, here today, in this cold morning air, as we watch the dawn of another day on your wonderful creation, we lay to rest our dear friend,

Pussface the cat. He lived a long life, and it was a blessing that you sent him to us. For all of us to share in a lifetime of adventures and enrich our lives with his love, indomitable spirit, bravery, and presence. I am sure he is enjoying a well-deserved dish of beer in your kingdom. Some people would say, he was just an old, alley cat, but we know better. In actuality, he was Pussface the cat. And that, Lord, for everyone who knew him and enjoyed his special life and company, just about sums it all up. In Jesus' name, we pray. Amen."

I heard the old man sniffle and mumble, "Amen. Thank you, Paulie. Thank you for those words."

Only a handful of times in my life did I ever see my father cry, and this was one of them. I mounded the dirt up and climbed out of the garden, while walking over to the old man. He was just staring ahead, and when I reached his side, he reached out and shook my hand.

"Thanks, chief, I appreciate that. Ya would not think an old tough guy like me would become so fond of some, old alley cat. Ya know, from the day I saved his old ass . . . Pussface the cat never forgot it. I guess he felt he owed me, but the truth is that he paid me back a million times over with his friendship."

The old man looked away from me. I caught his eyes in the early morning light. He looked down at the fresh grave and then he looked towards the light of the sunrise peeking just over the drab city, which lay sleeping just beyond the boundaries of our backyard.

The old man wiped his cheeks of his spent tears, and he turned back to look at me as he spoke once again, "You know all about the Bible and God stuff. I still think someday you will have something to do with the church if ya ever have a hockey puck knock some sense in ya thick skull. Do we get to see pets, you know . . . on the other side? Do you know . . . if . . . ya know . . . I will see Pussface the cat again someday?"

I put my arm around the old man and smiled while I told him, "The Bible does not really say, Dad. But it does tell us that Heaven is full of joy, and all the things, and people that we enjoyed and loved, so yes, I have a feeling that old Pussface the cat will be a part of it."

That seemed to lift his spirit as he put his New York Bugs hat back on top of his head and he laughed.

"Well, sounds good to me. I sure hope they have some Big Boulder beer too. Those Dingleberries are way too damn sweet. Say, let's go tell your mother. No sense in us putting off that conversation. This is not going to be a lot of fun." I nodded, shook my father's hand and together we went back into the house, and yes, it was not going to be easy to tell, dear Mum.

A week or so later, I returned home from a road hockey game and wandered into the backyard. Something had caught my eye in the corner of the garden. I walked over and saw a brass plaque mounted on Pussface's grave. It was obvious that the old man had made the plaque in his machine shop.

I read the words aloud, "Buried here is, Pussface the cat. Born, who the hell knows, died in October 1979. He was the best damn cat who ever lived."

Yup, the old man had a way with words, but you know something. No one could have ever said it any better.

I looked up and realized that I had been rambling on and on for a long time. The story had captured my thoughts and emotions, too. It did not take very much for me to return to my childhood home at 182 Belmont Ave in Haledon, New Jersey. Heather Sarah looked up at me, and I saw that she had tears in her little eyes. I then looked at Binky and Paul William and they were crying too.

"Oh my, I am so sorry! I did not want the story to make

everyone so sad. Pussface the cat lives on! He lives on in these stories, in all of our hearts, and in Heaven too. Please do not cry." I felt terrible, as I first hugged Heather Sarah, and then I hugged my wife and son tightly.

"But, dear Father, Fritzie and I are so sad. We did not want Pussface the cat to die. He was the bravest cat of all time. He saved Grandmum Henson from that mean doggie! We want to go out tomorrow and get a little kitty cat and name him Pussface. That way, he will still be alive." Binky shook her head to agree while Paul William rushed over and the three of them conducted another incredible head-nodding round of agreement. Once they finally finished nodding, we all hugged one another as I emphatically shouted in agreement.

"Well now, a kitty cat it is!"

As I sat there smiling, I had a very strange thought. I wondered if the little kitten would enjoy a dish or two of beer.

Probably not, but you never know.

Please Lord, forgive me, but I just have to say it. Yup, Pussface the cat, the best damn cat who ever lived.

THE END

The Show

1

A Disaster of a Date

"Easter and Spring Fashion Show!"

I read the words to the advertisement in the newspaper, in which I was reading on a late March afternoon.

Hmm . . . those words sparked a memory. . ..

I put the newspaper down and stared out the window next to my chair. I felt the presence of those now too familiar ghosts that haunt me for all time. They were about to float into the air, and chase my memories into every corner of the room. It happens all the time to me.

It was late March in 1984, and I had been passing time in my little apartment in Norfolk, Virginia, and the bold printing of the advertisement caught my eye. I was not a big newspaper reader, a quick glance or two at the sports page, some headlines or two, and that was it. I only received the local newspaper since some weepy-eyed kid came by a few weeks earlier pleading for me to take a subscription. I felt sorry for the kid and signed up, but most of the time, the paper went unread and tossed into the trash can. Life on the road, playing professional hockey, had brought me to Virginia, and to be very honest, it was not my favorite place. Number twenty-seven was now the property of the Boston Bears and one-step or so away from the big leagues. And I was lonely as lonely could be.

I missed my home in New Jersey, the cold winter air, the

snow, the hopes and dreams left behind, my friends, my best buddy Harry M. Redmond Junior, and the old neighborhood.

Most of all, I missed a woman. Not any plain, ordinary woman. No, it was so much more than just that because I missed . . . her.

Ms. Binky Hobnobber and her memory chased me into every corner of the room. She was contained in a misty shadow hanging here and there, she was a constant whisper in my mind, and I never could forget the look in her eyes. She had left without much more than a spoken word. All she left me with was a handwritten letter and it shattered my heart. It was not the first time that my heart suffered a serious blow from the loss of love from a young woman; there were a few other gals along the way who also delivered some pain.

One other special woman in my life left me too, and that loss tore me up even more than I could have imagined. Indeed, maybe as much, if not more, than when Binky left me. But that was another story. That woman was still in the back of my mind, but buried quite deeply now.

However, right now, for some reason, Binky was in the forefront of my mind. I just could not let go of the memory of Binky.

Her memory tore at me endlessly.

However, as it had so often been for me in my life, hockey was there. The haven in the storm, the place I could hide, where I strapped on my pads, hid behind a fiberglass goalie mask, and no one could find me.

Or so I thought.

The only trouble was, I had mirrors to the inside of my soul in my apartment, and they revealed the truth to me every single time.

The proverbial icing on the cake was this horrid stretch of playing in Norfolk, Virginia, waiting for the call to come from the Boston Bears hockey club. The dream of making it to the Boston Bears was the only thing that drove me, kept me going, and held me up.

It was my dream.

In pursuit of my dream, my hockey career took me to places that I never dreamed about while wandering the gritty streets of Paterson and Haledon, New Jersey.

I knew that I should be thankful, but sometimes, I could not see the silver lining through the clouds of loneliness. My mind wandered back in time, and I picked up the newspaper and reread the lines.

This time, I read them aloud to the ghosts, "Easter and Spring Fashion Show! Come to the Norfolk Spring Fashion show at the Norfolk Concord Hotel and Convention Center. See all the latest spring fashions for both women and men! All the most popular and famous designer's work will be on display, with the most beautiful women and handsome men modeling them for your enjoyment. Champagne, wine and beer, food, spring flowers, and fashion. A wonderful and unbeatable combination!"

I put the newspaper down, chuckled, and tossed it on the pile next to my chair with the rest of this week's collection of printed drivel.

Oh boy, that headline sparked a good memory now. I now laughed harder and harder until tears came down my cheeks. It was quite the memory, and it felt good to laugh. The laughter helped to purge the pain. I recalled a time when my best buddy Harry M. Redmond Jr. arm-twisted and roped me into another one of his wild ideas and maniacal schemes. As was usually the case, this scheme involved money and attracting young women. To be honest, the raising the money part was in order to attract the young women, but at this time in our lives, other than hockey and cars, it was all about attracting the young women.

Harry roped me in good this time around! This time, he convinced me to be a part of a spring fashion show that led to another one of our famous and wild adventures.

It was the middle of March in 1976, or some year thereabouts. I had just picked up my date for the evening, the very lovely Miss Glenda Flabbergaster to take her for some pizza and then enjoy a movie. It was a rare occasion for me to be heading out on a date alone.

Let's recap how I finally ended up with a date with the lovely Glenda.

Generally, I did not have much luck with the women, certainly not in comparison to the luck my best buddy in the entire world, a certain Harry M. Redmond Jr. had. We usually double-dated, when Harry introduced me to his current young woman's best friend or some other wild scheme. Harry usually worked hard to connect me with a woman that somehow always served his best interest in the primary pursuit of a woman he was "after." He had a seemingly endless entourage of the young women to pick from that were chasing after him. He had to purchase a bigger wallet to keep all of their telephone numbers handy, and I had to keep a scorecard to sort them all out!

Now, I did have a few dates here and there and I had my pen pal and sort of, kind of, girlfriend of many years, a gal named Debbie Boatwright. I had not heard from Debbie in quite a few months. The main trouble with my relationship with Debbie was the fact that she lived way up on Christmas Tree Mountain in Sussex County, New Jersey. My unreliable transportation and the continuous lack of funds to purchase a more reliable set of wheels forced us into a long-term, long-distance relationship. I really enjoyed Debbie's company, and we had shared a memorable night the previous summer when Harry and I accompanied Debbie and her best friend on a date at a dance, but that would be an entirely different story for another time and place.

Then, I had my sort of steady girlfriend, Maureen Zipperelli. Now, I had known Maureen for years and years, in fact, since we were just little kids together. Growing up, she was the best friend of my sister, Dottie. I really did like Maureen. She was beautiful, and in fact, she was gorgeous! She was a first generation Italian-American (her parents were straight from Italy) she was alluring; in fact, she was downright sexy, with a voluptuous and perfectly shaped female figure. Maureen had long brown hair, a wonderful personality, and although Maureen was a bit on the talkative side, to say the least, she could talk the ears off an elephant, but in addition to her beauty, she was a ton of fun. She always smelled a bit like garlic, and when she grew older, a bit of red wine too!

And therein, I could easily feel where the root of the trouble was, and why I felt this underlying apprehension of pursuing a full-blown relationship with Maureen Zipperelli. Maureen was about three years and a few months older than I was, and it was that fact, which always stayed in the back of my mind. No matter how much I enjoyed her company, I had this terrible hang up about our age difference. Everyone, even my dear Mum, told me that I was being foolish, Maureen was the perfect gal for me and that three years was nothing in this day and age. In my heart, I knew everyone was correct. It was just my own hang up and whether it was right or it was wrong; it was my own.

Maureen was a wonderful gal, and we did date here and there, it was just that on occasion, and to some extent, on purpose, I made it clear that I was not ready to commit to her as being my "only" gal. I told her many times, sometimes to her frowning at me, that she should feel free to date other guys, and I would date other gals. I told Maureen how much fun I had with her, how I thought she was a wonderful gal, but I was staying loose and somewhat free and would date some other gals from time-to-time.

It did not go over very well with her.

Maureen, on the other hand, took no effort to conceal her feelings for me and she pursued me endlessly. We actually grew a bit more serious as time went by, but once again, that is a whole other story. I find myself saying that quite a bit nowadays. Someday, maybe, I will run out of either time or stories.

I am not sure which one will come first.

Miss Glenda Flabbergaster was a young woman whom I had met at one of my hockey games. She hung around the ice rink one day after the game and approached me as I walked out of the locker room. Glenda asked me some obviously staged questions about the game, asked about my background, and made a point of explaining how she wanted to meet me for a long time. Glenda also told me how she was a huge hockey fan. Now, I knew she was stretching the truth a bit on that one, because so far in my career, I had met very few young females who were huge hockey fans. She giggled a bit, and her friends, who were with her at the time, giggled along too. She dropped many hints to try to provoke me into asking her for a date. First, she told me all about the college she currently attended, and the hockey team that played for the college. Then Glenda went on and on about what she enjoyed about the hockey game, and then to top it all off, she then rambled on a bit about her favorite music artist.

"Do you enjoy music?" Glenda asked me.

"Well, yes, in fact, I do. Very much so. Music is a big part of my life. . .."

She never allowed me to finish. Instead, Glenda ran over the top of my usual long-winded words and enthusiastically, told me all about a chap named Zippy Starlight, and his famous backing band, The Starlighters. Glenda was gorgeous, but she seemed to be a bit on the aggressive side, especially for some random chick that approached me after a hockey game. Glenda babbled on and on about Zippy coming to the big city across the river and how she would love to attend the concert. The hints for me to ask her if she wanted to go to the concert with me were overwhelming. Glenda was certainly a beautiful gal, and I surmised that she was a lot of fun to be with and to spend some time together. However, the major trouble that rolled repeatedly, in what Harry would constantly remind me of "my too logical mind," was that I despised Zippy and his type of music. Zippy came from the genre that next to disco, was most disliked amongst us progressive rock fans, and that was glamour rock-and-roll. He wore big sunglasses, giant boots, had outrageous makeup, wild hair and acted as if he was a lunatic with his acts on stage.

I was, and still am, a huge music fan, listening to many different genres of music, but I did not know one song, in which Zippy had recorded that was even remotely appealing.

Of course, wanting to appeal to the young gal, I fudged it when she asked, "Do you like Zippy's music? I think he is fantastic! I would love to go to his big concert in a month or so in the city!"

"Oh, a big concert, huh? As far as his music goes, I honestly never listened to his music all that much but sure, I will give him a listen."

While studying Glenda closely, her beauty overwhelmed my hormones, and I suddenly found myself embroiled in a testosterone-induced haze.

Glenda, sensing my aloofness, dropped the ego bomb on me for a final blow, "You know, number twenty-seven, I have to admit that I have been only coming to these hockey games to check you out. All the ladies think you are mega-hot, but you never seem interested in any women, ah, but I bet you would be interested in what I have to offer."

Oh, oh, that was it! Glenda had pulled an ace out of her deck and I folded like a cheap tourist camera. I took the bait, but remained slightly noncommittal. The current thinness of my wallet overcame the testosterone-induced haziness.

"I think going to a Zippy concert might be a great time. Yeah, yeah, yeah, great."

Even I was stunned at the fraudulent nonsense spewing out of my own mouth. Doing what all good young men of my age do, I weaseled my way through the rest of the conversation, planning to study up on him and his band when I had the chance to do so. In the back of my mind, I knew that I needed to check out how much the tickets were going to cost for the upcoming concert before committing to the dates. It was all part of the strategy when in pursuit of the young ladies.

At the time, I was playing here and there in organized and unorganized leagues, goalie clinics, and holiday tournaments. I found myself being a hired gun or "ringer" playing the position of goaltender, wherever I could and for whatever team needed a goalie, in a desperate attempt to attract the eyes of some scouts and managers from the nearby semi-professional leagues.

Glenda continued the conversation, and I finally had a chance to escape her, when one of my coaches came by, excused himself, and asked to speak with me about an upcoming game. I told the coach that I would be with him in a minute, asked Glenda for her telephone number, which she had already handy, and bid her good night. I watched her walk away and my goodness, she surely was attractive! Wow! Glenda had long red hair, wore tight bell bottoms, hip-hugger dungarees that showed off a perfect female figure, and she wore a loud, printed, tie-dyed shirt that was so common in the 1970s! I took the paper with her telephone number on it, stuck it in my pocket and then became busy as usual and I never called her.

I told Harry about the encounter at the ice rink and, of course; he knew of Glenda Flabbergaster. Long before every person in the world had a personal computer on their desk, in their home, and in their office, and one or two mini-computers hanging on their waists or in their pockets, Harry M. Redmond Jr. had a database of every attractive female in New Jersey, New York and Connecticut. How he did it remained a mystery, even to me, and we were as if we were brothers. All we had back then were the famous "black books" along with pencils and pens. Harry's black books were very thick. . ..

"Let me get this straight now, twenty-seven." Harry tried hard to understand the situation. He asked me for a recap after I told him of Glenda approaching me. "Ya know, make sure we are on the same page. This here, Glenda Flabbergaster comes up to ya after a game and spews all of this at ya? Now, let's make sure that it is the same Glenda Flabbergaster we are talkin' 'bout here!"

I stood there in front of Harry, feeling very much like an idiot. Figuring in my mind that I have nothing to lose at this point anyway, since Harry was ultimately going to lambast me, I interjected some of my famous logic into the conversation, "Harry, now I am sure of one thing, that I doubt very much there are any other gals named, Glenda Flabbergaster around here."

Harry clapped his hands in the air; he jumped up in the air and feigned some phony shock and awe at my logic while yelling, "EXACTLY MY POINT! *The* Glenda Flabbergaster that all males around here know of and lust after. Okay, let me describe her. Let's see, long red hair, perfect body, soft voice, the greatest, wiggling ass in the tri-state area! Yes in-deedy, I know of her and so does every male human being from the age of two years to one hundred and ten! She is gorgeous! She is a famous fashion model, you dodo!"

"Oh, I did not know that was her job. She left that part out of the conversation."

Harry was going to run a ramshackle over me on this

one. I did not stand much of a chance now.

"At least, I think she is a famous model. Who the hell cares? Famous or not, she is a knockout. And because of your affliction with the dreaded Old Lady Syndrome, you have to determine if you like Zippy two shoes or whatever the hell his name is, to see if you should go on a date with her or not."

When listening to Harry repeating the chain of events, I had to admit that I did feel like an idiot.

Harry laughed at me, walked a few steps away, turned around and waved his hands in the air towards me.

"I swear, I love you like a brother, twenty-seven, but you are hopeless. I am gonna call the center of sickness control there in Atlanter, Georger and see if they are working on a pill that you can take to cure you of being an old lady."

"It is the Center for Disease Control, Harry." The Old Lady Syndrome forced me to correct Harry. I *was* out of control and hopeless.

"Whatever! Who the hell cares if she wanted to go on a date to watch paint dry on walls? Just call her and go! Men have fallen over and died while trying to get a date with her."

Harry, in his typical, dramatic, Harry M. Redmond Junior fashion, faked pondering about the situation by crossing his arms and supporting his chin in his hand, as if to mimic that he was deep in thought.

"Okay, let's take four micro-seconds to analyze this situation and remarkable display of doofussiness. Miss Glenda Flabbergaster just happens to stroll and wiggle up to you after sweating your ass off after dodging hockey pucks. She tells you how all these chicks have the hots for you and she does too and, let's see now—you are not too sure about the music that she wants to go and listen to at a concert! For the love of Pete! If she wanted to go and listen to some guys playing tubas, while passing gas to the melody of Christmas songs, and simultaneously banging trash can lids together, then read my lips! JUST FRIGGIN' GO! For such a smart man, ya act like a doofus! Must be too many blows to the head from hockey pucks that now has all ya brains all scrambled."

"Well, Harry, I am kinda seeing, Maureen. And I like her a lot. It is just that. . .."

"Did you not tell Maureen that she should date other guys and you were gonna date other gals?"

"Well, yes, I did."

"Well, Mr. Old Lady, there ya go! What the hell are ya waiting for?"

After the severe verbal scolding by Harry, a brush up on the music of Zippy Starlight, and wasting three bucks on his latest recording on an eight-track tape to play in my van on our potential date, I did finally muster the courage to ask Glenda out for a date.

That is the history of the adventure behind the date.

And so, it goes and here we are in March 1976, driving in my bomb of a set of wheels, which was a reworked 1968 service van. The van did not look too bad. Recently, I had the van painted for fifty bucks, which was another horrible adventure.

The old man helped me tinker with the engine, which had a tremendous number of miles on it, I fixed up the interior a little as we did in the 1970s, and thought overall, considering my limited funds that it did not look too bad.

I dressed in my best clothes for the date, consisting of a 1970s-style pair of black bellbottom slacks, with a wide collar black shirt. Currently, these were my only "nice" clothes other than my suit and white shirts for my "church" clothes. Around my neck, I wore a gold chain that my sister had given me for the previous Christmas.

My hair was still very long, way past my shoulders now, and most folks thought I was just a hippie, not an athlete. Generally, I tied my hair behind my head with a hair tie, however, tonight my hair hung long. In the interest of looking my best for this coveted date with a famous fashion model, I did attempt to comb my hair back a bit. As of the last few months, as my old man commented on, "That ya musta lost ya razor, Paulie," I had grown a blonde beard with red highlights all over my face. For two reasons, I kept the beard trimmed and close to my face. First, I did not like the look of long, scraggly beards, and two, wearing a fiberglass goalie mask with a long beard was not too swift of an idea.

After drowning myself in some after-shave that my old man allowed me to use, I was off to pick Glenda up for the date. I thought that I actually looked good, or so I thought. In the back of my mind, I was a little miffed at myself for selecting this particular Saturday night for a date, because, my favorite hockey club, the New York Rovers were fighting for a playoff berth, and the game on television tonight was important in the final standings. The old man gave me his usual good-natured ribbing about the date, and my dear Mum came to my defense, but I think even Mum was surprised that I picked a date with Glenda over an important hockey game. Maybe she chalked it up to the evolution of her son's life.

We were ready for tooling off for a "hot" time in the old town. This was as much a date to prove to myself that I was not going to be stuck on Maureen as much as it was a date to see if Glenda was as nice as she initially seemed. It was going to be a wonderful night.

Pizza and a movie and a prelude to a Zippy concert. Maybe. Now this was high class.

Ah, no . . . not exactly. The best plans often go awry.

After picking Glenda up at her fancy home in a nice section of the fancy suburb of Wayne Township, meeting her parents, and stinking up their home with my overzealous application of after-shave, we set off on our date. She was indeed the proverbial rich gal from the other side of the railroad tracks. The area in which she lived was the high-rent district. I tried hard not to dwell on the fact that most areas of the world, when compared to our old neighborhood, we could classify as high rent districts.

I held the door open for her, gently closed it while absorbing her glorious compliments on how nice I looked, ran around to the driver's side, jumped in and turned over the engine. Just to further impress the lovely Miss Flabbergaster, I popped in the tape of "Zippy Starlight Sings to the Solar System" in the eight-track player, and turned the music up. She looked wonderful while wearing a tight pullover sweater that enhanced her lovely chest and she smiled seductively at me, with her long red hair flowing all around her.

Oh my, what a gorgeous chick!

Off we went. Well, not exactly.

We made it about a mile down Alps Road, and that was it.

Yes, the sad end to a potentially wonderful night.

You see, my old van had a tricky water pump, and it decided that this was just the night to let loose and overheat the engine. Tricky water pumps in old 1968 service vans did not care about hot twigeons in tight, hip-hugger pants, wearing a glorious pullover sweater, on a March night in 1976. When those suckers let go and decided not to pump, it was not pretty. Steam and the pungent odor of hot coolant billowed out from the mid-engine cover in the center of the van, filling the interior of the van with what you could say was an atmosphere not very conducive to romance.

Even Zippy and The Starlighters could not save us.

I pulled off to the side of the road, jumped out, and confirmed the coolant pouring out from under the engine was going to be troublesome, and sadly told Glenda that our date appeared to be over. I apologized up and down, and repeatedly told Glenda how sorry I was, but it was about to fall upon deaf ears. She showed her true colors.

And after I mumbled a few hundred or so humble apologies, scrambled to control the situation and minimize the coolant spray, I realized that the water pump explosion turned out to be a blessing in disguise.

The lovely Miss Glenda Flabbergaster, well, she turned out to be a bit of a prissy pants and a boring snob. She howled and complained about what a hunk of junk truck that I owned, how the steam messed her hair up, and stunk out her best clothes, and how she did not realize when she first met me that I was just a "loser hippie" from poor, old, Paterson city and Haledon town. On and on she rambled, about how she thought that I was a fancy athlete, a famous goaltender with tons of money.

Ah, sorry, there Glenda, but you are shit outta luck. Hockey goaltenders are many things, but we surely are not the handsome shining star quarterback for the football team. It is more, as if we are the tiny light bulb hanging from a short-circuited cord in your basement.

She proudly stood aloofly on the side of the road, impatiently tapping her toes on the asphalt shoulder of the road and folding her arms across her ample breasts. While I desperately tried to cool my engine down and explain the situation to her. Glenda proclaimed to me, somewhat unabashedly, that my long hair, hockey skills, and good looks had blinded her and how I was just a poor bum in disguise. She insisted that I do something to bring her home immediately! On and on she went, repeatedly crabbing at me for taking her out on a date in such a wreck of a vehicle.

My patience now had worn thin. She looked good, but not *that* good. Tight sweaters, nice backsides and big chests could overcome many things in a young man's world, but not this time. I still had some pride left, and this chick was now a royal pain in my ass. I had no time for her at the moment. My wheels and my world, just so happened to be melting before my eyes. She was a beautiful woman, but her attitude more than neutralized her attractiveness.

I quickly determined that she was just not worth it. Within a few short minutes of disaster assessment, I reached my maximum limit of Glenda Flabbergaster's jaw flapping. Number twenty-seven was no longer going to apologize, nor was I going to be humble and stand mumble-mouthed and apologetic, like some dumb ass, while broken down on the side of the road.

It is what it is.

I might be an old lady sometimes, but right now, Glenda had pissed me off, and I lost patience with her. I decided that I no longer would listen to her insults and witness temper tantrums from a fancy chick that did not have a clue of what real life was all about.

I reminded her that, "She was only a mile or so from her home, and that loser hippie bums such as I happened to be, well, we were so far beneath her that I could not possibly be worthy of accompanying her any longer." While standing in front of my truck, covered in the sweet smell of coolant, which thankfully finally drowned out the horrible aroma my after-shave, I suggested rather boldly, "If your feet work as well as your lip flapping does, then I suggest that you turn around and march your pretty little ass on home. Have a nice walk home there, Glenda. It is a fabulous night for a bit of a springtime stroll and you can keep your tight, little ass really tight with some exercise," was my overt suggestion.

She folded her arms across her chest again and asked me, "Well, aren't you concerned for my safety? You are going to allow me to walk down this dark road and walk alone all the way to my house. Don't you want to escort me?"

"No, I am not concerned about your safety. You will be fine. The walk will do you good. Besides, I rather escort a fire-breathing dragon."

Off she stormed in a huff, wiggling her fantastic figure

in those tight dungarees with her rather alluring rearview, fading away into the cool March evening. At least she looked a lot better walking away than she did when you really knew her face-to-face.

"Good riddance. Here is your crummy tape of Zippy. You can keep him because his music sucks!" I yelled to her while tossing the tape in her direction. To her credit, as miffed as she was, she did at least catch and take the tape as she stormed off in anger. I turned on the emergency flashers, locked the van up, and began a jog about a mile or so down the road to where I knew there was a service station. This was the 1970s; no cell phones or fancy wireless devices existed, in order to save you when you broke down back then. When you broke down, then it was shoe leather time until you found help or a pay telephone.

I was in good shape, and a mile run was just another daily workout to me. I kept an optimistic viewpoint and thought about how this workout would save me from having to run tomorrow.

As I ran along, I thought about how Maureen Zipperelli would have climbed under the truck and attempted a repair with me. Maureen's dad was a stonemason and her mom was a seamstress. To earn a few extra baubles and trinkets, they sold homemade bootleg wine to the Italian-American community. Mr. Zipperelli and his brother made the wine in their basement, and they all worked hard to earn a living as best as we all could in the old neighborhood.

Maureen completed hair stylist school last month, and she was excited about now having her own chair in a local hair salon. Her plan was to start to earn money to pay back her school tuition loans and start out on her own. One thing I knew about Maureen was that she was not shy about hard work. Once again, dear Mum was correct in her assessment of my limited gal pals. Maureen Zipperelli was the real deal, and I had to admit that I could easily fall head over heels in love with her.

Perhaps I already had, and I was too stupid to admit it.

Oh well, maybe I will call Maureen up this week. I thought, yes, I would take her to the movies and we would enjoy a pizza together. Maybe I would tell her that I wanted her to be my only woman, and me to be her only guy . . . well, maybe. Once I got my truck fixed and figured out a way to pay for all of this.

On the bright side, at least I could cross off my list, saving my pennies to take Glenda to that stupid concert.

At this time in my life, I was quite far from the image that Glenda envisioned in her silver-spoon enhanced mind, with barrels of money rolling into my bank account. It was quite the opposite, as I had this immense trouble of limited funds. My regular job as an electrical and electronic serviceman did not pay too much and the hockey gigs, as of late, were a little lean on the old coins too. I did rake in a whopping seventeen bucks for a shutout the week before this little adventure. I had tucked that dough in my wallet along with a few extra dollars that I intended to use for the date this evening.

It was not much, but at least I had something.

I made it to the service station, stopped my run, walked up to the door of the station, and entered. A loud buzzer sounded a harsh alarm to alert the employees of the station that a customer had entered their establishment. It was a typical New Jersey gas station for this day and age. A few gas pumps out front with two service bays inside. The office area had oil-stained tile floors, and a dirty, greasy sales counter with a cardboard display of dusty air fresheners sitting on top of the glass counter next to an ancient, push-button brass cash register. The fresheners were not exactly selling like hotcakes.

I could look through a window in a door in the counter area to see inside the service shop. There were belts and hoses hanging on all the walls in the service bay, one car on a lift, and toolboxes lining the sides of the shop. There was a black and white television with rabbit ears sitting on a table next to the front counter. It had a snowy picture on the screen and the image was fading in and out, yet I could see and hear the New York Rovers hockey game playing out on the screen. There also was the distinct odor of a strong cigar filling the air.

I stood at the far end of the front counter and from where I stood; I could see a man sitting in a chair at the other end of the counter. He did not immediately acknowledge me, but eventually, I heard the creak of the springs of the old chair that he was sitting upon as the man leaned back in it. A middle-aged man with a greasy cap on his head and a cigar stuck in his mouth took his eyes off the screen, stood up from the chair and looked at me. He was short, round, and bald and greasy, yet I felt that I was in luck, because he was a hockey fan!

"Whadda ya want ya hairy-ass, hippie freak?"

Oh no, so much for my luck, because this did not seem as if it was going to go so well. My appearance had stereotyped me once again. I thought to break the ice that I would try the hockey angle!

Yes, indeed that will work.

"Say, what is the score? The Rovers need a few more wins to make the playoffs since the season is down to the wire now. Is Rumblehowser in the net? He is a solid goaltender and my favorite player."

The greasy man puffed his big cigar and rolled his eyes while he said, "Rumblehowser is a bum! He sucks. His old ass has a hard time stopping a beach ball now. I swear he is blind. What does a hippie, freak, weirdo like youse is, know about hockey anyway? Once more, whadda ya want? I doubt ya hairy ass came in here to talk about hockey."

I would have liked to explain the hockey connection, and for a fleeting moment, I felt the old fire rise up inside of me. It came from growing up on the gritty streets of our old neighborhood, and fighting my way around a few hockey brawls too, but it was not worth it. The cigar would look very good sticking out of his ear, and at six feet five and a little more, and in prime shape, I was just the hippie to do it too.

Back to reality, "Ah yes, thank you, sir. My van broke down about two miles up the road. I was hoping to get a tow back to Haledon. I live on Belmont Ave near Burhans right on the north edge of Paterson. It is the water pump."

"Ha! I do not tow hippies who protested about the Vietnam War. And if I, did it, 'wud be three hundred bucks to get ya ass to Haledon down near the Paterson border. I would have to add a few bucks in case my truck was machine gunned, and they tore the tires off of it!"

I frowned. This was just my luck of all the gas stations around; I had to pick one with a certified jerk in it. This evening was turning out to be a mega-disaster. In mere seconds, we had jumped from the subject of hockey, what I might know about the game, all the way, to me being a war protestor.

"What the hell does the Vietnam War have to do with this? Where did that come from? By the way, in case it actually matters, I did not protest against the war. I have my draft number. If I had to go, I would have, and I still will, if they call the number. One of my best friends fought in Nam . . . just because I have long hair. . . ."

I waved my hands in disgust at him to indicate my frustration.

"You know, chief, thanks for nothing. Up your ass. Guys like you are not worth it. Do you know where there is a pay telephone?"

"Nope. Get lost hippie!"

For a second or two, I felt the fire burn harder and my muscles twitched, but I relaxed. This jerk was not worth the effort or the time of the day. He seemed to sense that with one quick movement, I could turn him upside down and shake all the loose change out of his pockets that I required to make the phone call. The greasy man sensed that he might have crossed the line. He looked me up and down and suddenly realized that I may be a hippie, but I was big, strong, sweaty, and most likely a little imposing now.

"Down the corner to ya left, about another half of a mile down the road," he said, while pointing and sitting back into his chair. I turned, left, and in short order, found the pay telephone. I knew calling my old man for a rescue mission was not going to be the best solution at this point, so instead, I dropped a dime for Harry's house. He had mentioned a date with his current steady gal, Joyce, but maybe, just maybe, he was still home. One ring, two rings, and a voice. It was his brother-in-law and my friend Ronzo who answered.

"It's your dime! Talk fast, the hockey game is on, and the beer is cold!" Ronzo bellowed into the phone. I could tell that old Ronzo had been dipping rather deeply into the Dingleberry beers this Saturday night while enjoying the hockey game.

"Hey Ronzo, it is Paulie. Is Harry there, or did he already leave for his date with Joyce?"

I heard Ronzo chuckle, swig a sip of beer, and he said, "Hey, Paulie! Nah, sorry, he is gone off with Joyce already. By now, he is probably deep into necking and tearing up the upholstery in the back seat of his Sonicmobile, or even a little more."

Ronzo was telling it like it really was.

"Say, why are you not watching the game? You can come over here if ya want. Rovers are ahead three to one in the first period. Rumblehowser is standing on his head!"

"Ronzo, I would love to, but I went on a date with Glenda Flabbergaster, and my van broke down on Alps Road just past Osborne Terrace here in Wayne. The water pump exploded. Some bozo guy here at a gas station says he will not tow me because I am a hippie, and even if he did, he said he would soak me three hundred bucks because our neighborhood is so bad!"

Ronzo laughed aloud, "Oh boy, a bad scene, Paulie. Bad! Ha! Maybe we need to pay him a visit and kick his ass."

"No, Ronzo, he is a jerk and is not worth it."

"You are probably right, twenty-seven. A bad neighborhood, huh? Shit, he should have tried schlepping around the rice paddies in Vietnam, with bullets whizzing around your ass. Now, that was a bad neighborhood, this is just children's play. Ya are a victim of prejudice there, twenty-seven. Say, Glenda, okay, wow, old Harry told me about her. She has quite a caboose towing the end of her line, or so Harry described. She stuck with you?"

"No, Ronzo, she turned out to be a bit of a dud. Her greatest attributes did not really pan out to be worth it. She is a stuck-up, snobby, chick who stormed off in anger when the van broke down and to be honest, I am glad to be rid of her."

"Oh yeah, yeah, yeah, twenty-seven. Too bad, tough break for ya. I hear that you do not get many dates these days. Especially, with chicks with dynamite backsides. Oh well."

I sighed, as even Ronzo knew about my poor luck with the young ladies.

"It could have been an exciting night for ya. Ya should stick with Maureen Zipperelli, now that twigeon has it together, Paulie. In more ways than one! She is the real deal. Say, I have to be honest, I am a little half in the bag, but Bill Porter is here, and he is still sober. The period is almost up, and Bill, Pop, and I will jump in Bill's big Galaxy Super Glide 500 with the Substantial Industries rope and haul ya ass on back to John Street!"

"Oh no, Ronzo. I will call my old man. You are enjoying the game. Geez, I feel bad for bothering you."

"Ha! Call your old man! No way. His 1964 Putter Classic

model 200 could not pull a toy wagon, let alone that van of yours! Let him relax. He works on Saturdays, and he is watching the game too. Knowing you and your lack of funds, ya most likely only have twenty bucks on ya anyhow. We will be there in a few minutes. You are only a little up the road. Hang tight. We will listen to the game on the radio, and we can catch the end on the television once we pull that pile of junk back here for ya. Bill will saddle up the big car in a few minutes. You hang out there, we are on the way."

"Click." The line went dead.

Despite Ronzo's statement, I was not broken down, "just up the road." Ronzo minimized the distance in an effort to make me feel as if it was no big deal. They all were the best friends in the entire world. I could never repay them for anything. I can only say how much they made my life better for knowing them. Back then, people stuck together, helped one another, and worked for a common cause. Ronzo knew that if he were broken down that we all would do the same for him too! With a tug at my belt line, I jogged back up Alps Road the mile or so and waited by the van.

Mr. William H. "Bill" Porter was a wonderful man. He was the Redmond's long-time neighbor, and the father of our other boyhood friend, Jeff Porter. Jeff was always out with Debbie, his steady girlfriend of many years now. We did not see so much of Jeff these days because Jeff and Debbie had become quite the steady item. Mr. Porter always hung with Ronzo and Harry's dad, drinking beer, watching sports and shooting the breeze.

Sure enough, I heard the roar of the big engine of Mr. Porter's huge Galaxy 500 Super Glide with giant steel bumpers, and a welded steel chassis that had hauled everything from the swimming pool parts to lifting car engines. The car was legendary in our neighborhood and a veteran of many jobs.

Once more, an entirely different story.

Ronzo, Mr. Redmond, and Mr. Porter pulled in front of the van, backed in close, and put the car's flashers on.

"Hey, Paulie! Bite the bullet!" Mr. Porter popped out of the car with a big smile on his face. He had pulled out from his pocket his famous signature key chain, which was a large brass bullet from his World War Two days. He drilled a hole in the end and put his keys through it. As long as I knew him, it was always the same greeting! Even to this very day, I can still see his face and hear his always happy voice.

Mr. Redmond always directed missions such as this one, and in short order, he waved to Ronzo and instructed us, "No time to waste, men! Let's get the rope around the van. Paulie, you jump on in, turn your flashers on and we will be back home before the third period! Go Rovers!"

He came over to me and put his arm around my shoulder while Ronzo and Mr. Porter tied the rope around the bumpers of the vehicles. Mr. Redmond was like a second father to me.

"I see and hear that it was a tough night, Paulie. Oh well, twenty-seven, remember that the beauty is only skin deep on these young gals. Someday, you will find the right one, and years later when her figure has changed, and her face is wrinkled and old, and you are too, you will have known that you made the right choice. A good woman is hard to find, it is worth it to keep searching for one. Seems to me that Maureen Zippawhooey gal is a good one. I lost my eyeballs and had to take an extra blood pressure pill when she wore that bikini to our pool party a little while back!"

I nodded my head and said softly, "Zipperelli, Mr. Redmond. Her name is Maureen Zipperelli."

He smiled at me and said, "Oh yeah, yeah, yeah, whatever ya call her! Please, just take my advice and call her. Let's go! Hockey and cold ones are waiting." I smiled, thanked him for his wise advice, climbed into the van and watched as the big Galaxy engine roared and I felt a tug as it easily pulled me along. Soon, we had pushed the van into the driveway at 182 Belmont Avenue. Tomorrow, I knew that if I asked for the help, that the old man would help me pull the water pump out of it and begin the repairs on the van, but that was tomorrow.

Tonight, I spent the rest of this Saturday night sitting in the living room at 20 John Street, drinking beer and watching the end of the New York Rovers hockey game with Mr. Porter, Mr. Redmond, and Ronzo. We had a great time, while occasionally cheering and leaping from our chairs and spilling a little beer on that fancy black shirt of mine. Looking around at some of the greatest bunch of guys that I ever had met, and had the pleasure of hanging out with, I did not miss Glenda Flabbergaster one bit.

Her tight dungarees and her view from the rear. I might have missed those, but that was about it!

I still severely lacked the funds to fix my van, but for now, I tucked that away and enjoyed the rest of the night and the hockey game.

The night did not go exactly as I had planned, but hey, the Rovers won! Yes, Mr. Greasy Jackass guy at the gas station, you were wrong, because Rumblehowser won the game with a last-minute stick save, and it was a beauty.

2

The Great Sofa Adventure

Harry M. Redmond Junior and I sat on the front steps of my house at 182 Belmont Avenue. We sat there, sipping some water while the two of us observed the fact that grease covered most of our exposed body parts. My old man had just returned to the house; he went to wash up after helping us work on the engine on my van. The news was bad. Not only did the van have an exploded water pump, but it also had a blown head gasket from the engine overheating. Then, for good measure, the old man mentioned the present condition of the van's tires. They did indeed look as smooth on the tread side as a bowling ball did. No, that is not true. Bowling balls were a little rougher in texture. The old man was correct that the tires were a safety hazard.

Now, I had no wheels, and no way to get to the hockey rink, unless I bummed a ride with Harry, or the old man, would let me use the 1964 Putter Classic model 200. At least I could take the city bus to make it to my job, but needless to say, this, for sure, put a major cramp in my lifestyle.

Harry put his big arm around me and pulled me close in an attempt to cheer me up a little. I knew the big guy well enough to know that the words he was about to say meant well, but chances are they would be of very little comfort. In fact, they might be quite the opposite!

"Well, twenty-seven, we both have the same trouble. No dough. There is a little different spin on our individual troubles though. Ya see, I make a lot of money, but very sadly, you are merely a pauper!"

Yup . . . I knew it. Another wonderful chat with my best buddy.

"My current trouble is that I am soaking all my dough away for a down payment to replace the Takajunky Model 10 car that I have been rolling around in for way too long now. I have my eye on a fancy sports car for this next go around."

Harry poked me in the side as he offered, "Ya know, now, that I am hot stuff, I need a chick magnet. I also had to shell out some major dough for a fancy necklace that was a birthday present for Joyce, so it has been a little rough. I would loan ya some jingle for the parts to the van, but I am flat broke, too. I need to limp along to my next paycheck and then I will be all right. I vowed not to touch my down payment dough and I am sticking with that. I hate to say it, but your old man has a point. It just may be time for you to spend the dough on something else. The van may be a bad investment at this point, there number twenty-seven."

Harry looked at me, frowned a little, and then he chuckled as he said, "Ya just don't get paid too much, twenty-seven, not like me. And that is the bottom line why you are virtually a pauper and never have any money."

Harry always had a way of making me feel so much better.

"Now, your van needs major work, and that leaves us with the Takajunky as our primary means of twigeon and cruising transportation. It is a little tricky with the doors that fly open when ya hit them bumps, but overall, it ain't a bad car, it is just time to make a change. I cannot allow my image as the coolest dude around here to suffer, cuz of a shitty set of wheels. Right now, for both of us, our lives are full of crushing defeats!"

I had to agree with Harry. His Japanese Takajunky

Model 10 had a new engine installed a few summers ago, we worked on the exhaust, patched and painted the rust spots, put new tires on it, and while it would not win any awards for being the coolest set of wheels around, it did successfully bring us here and there. The main trouble with it was the unusual trouble that the door latches had. When you hit a hard bump, the doors would randomly fly open. One cool thing about the car was that the radio had an awesome auto-selecto feature where it would find stations for you, and once you were used to the doors, and kept your hands on them, it was not so bad. It was a bit of a pain when we always had to explain to people why Harry had a rope tied on the rear door handles to hold the doors closed.

"Harry, I am thinking of making an offer to Vince for that M-17 jeep on the corner there. If I could round up five hundred bucks or so, Vince might just go for it. He is asking six hundred, but maybe we can talk him down a little. The body has a couple of dings on it here and there. I sure would like to have that jeep. It would be cool."

Vince Barroni, who was the owner of the corner gas station a few doors down from my house, had rolled the old jeep out on his lot last week or so, and put a "For Sale" sign in the window. It had caught my eye for sure.

Harry nodded at my comment, but at first, he did not say anything. He then looked at me out of the corner of his eye and slyly asked, "Really, twenty-seven? That old relic of a jeep has caught your eye?"

I nodded to confirm that it had.

"Really? Five hundred bucks?"

I nodded again and Harry gently shook his head before he suggested, "Ain't that sort of frying pan into the fire type of shit?" I shrugged my shoulders and heard Harry mumble, "That I was an old lady."

We sat there for a while, pondering our fate and sipping our water. Two lifelong friends sitting on the steps of my home, forlorn and down to their last nickels, watching the busy traffic fly past, up and down the main drag in front of my home. A bunch of lucky stiffs who have reliable vehicles were my cold, hard thoughts while I watched them zip along on Belmont Avenue. We were not going to be down too long—no, not these two guys. It was not part of our makeup, not part of our character, not the way of the old neighborhood. It was time for one of our famous action plans!

We just could not think of one right at the moment!

Then, just when you think you have no options, and have hit a dead end in life, a golden opportunity suddenly pops up!

Or something like that.

Harry and I decided to walk back to his house, and we picked ourselves off the front steps and made our way down Belmont Avenue towards John Street.

While walking halfway across Cook Street, right in front of the liquor store, our luck changed. We ran into the famous Charles "Cricket" Boozer. In an old urban neighborhood, as you can imagine, there is always a vast collection of colorful characters. We had them all jam-packed into a few blocks, the colorful, the wacky, the eccentric, the unusual. Cricket Boozer was included in the mix and in fact, he might have been right near the top of the whacko list.

We had a complete selection of very curious characters who all resided within our few city blocks, ranging from the world famous, Mr. Cliffy McWhiffy and his incomprehensible, chronic mispronunciation and obscenity laden language, with his signature "HA, HA, HA," after every, single, sentence, all the way to Ronzo Boatmann, Mr. Porter and his famous bullet, Harry's dog Cocoa, who was the world's smartest dog, Joe Hink and his chronic criminal tendencies, to the seemingly endless supply of Nit-Nat kids.

Ah, yes, the Nit-Nats. . ..

Of all the unusual and vast collections of characters and residents in the old neighborhood, the Nit Nats had to be at the top of the list.

We called them the Nit-Nat family, as everyone else in our neighborhood did. Their actual name, if I do recall, was Nitnatirellilini.

I may have that wrong, but it was something close to that. Regardless, I know that it was a really long Italian name that no one could either remember or pronounce it, hence, it simply became "New Jerseyized" and we shortened it to the Nit-Nat family. The world-famous leader of the Chronic Mispronunciation Gang, Mr. Cliffy McWhiffy punted, and never even tried to pronounce their actual name. This was not surprising, since he had trouble with his best friend, Mr. Porter's last name. He would often call him "Bill Order," but we all knew whom he meant.

The Nit-Nat family lived across the street from the Porter's house on John Street. There had to be at least forty-seven Nit-Nat kids, and they owned at least twenty dogs, ten cats, fourteen hamsters, a canary, and a pet snake.

One time the snake got loose. . ..

All of them resided in one house. Equally divided between boys and girls, they remarkably seemed as if they never grew up; they always seemed to, on an average, be around seven years old! There were, on occasion, a few smaller Nit-Nat kids produced in the baby production line. Occasionally, you would see a toddler sized, Nit-Nat kid. The toddler sized, Nit-Nat would be running around mostly naked and barefoot in November, with only a diaper hanging off their little backside, while in futile pursuit of the older and speedier Nit-Nat kids around the streets. The smallest available version of a Nit-Nat kid seemed to be a toddler size. I never recall ever seeing Mr. or Mrs. Nit-Nat ever appear while holding an infant or newborn, Nit Nat. I thought how that was very strange, but perhaps they kept them in the house and concealed them, while undergoing Nit-Nat terror training, until it was time for them to be unleashed on the world.

Mostly, the Nit-Nat kids just all ran around screaming and hollering, riding bicycles in the street, hanging in the trees up and down the street, never wearing overcoats in the dead of winter, sometimes, they barely had clothes on at all! They would break windows with baseballs, footballs, and rocks, tip over garbage cans, destroy everything in sight, trample flower gardens, run all over the street at all hours of the day and night and scream and yell like fog horns. They were as if they were miniature hurricanes.

The Nit-Nat house was actually the second house that I recalled being in that same city lot. The first home was some long since abandoned, old dump, which burned to the ground one night when Harry, Jeff, and I were only ten years old or so. The fire was so intense that it melted the steering wheel on Ronzo's car, which he had parked in front of the house. In fact, to be honest, it melted Ronzo's entire car. Once more, that is another story.

The owners of the lot bulldozed the house after the fire, and it was a vacant lot that we called "the woods" for many years, until they built a beautiful, two-level house on the lot. For our neighborhood, it was quite a nice home. It had fancy doors, an actual garage with a door that rolled up automatically, a brick front, and fancy metal trim. It had something we had never seen except in the rich neighborhoods in Wayne Township, and that was a mailbox out by the street, on a post.

In the old neighborhood, we had mailboxes mounted directly on our homes, and the mailman had to climb up your steps to put the mail in the box, or in some cases, through a slot on the front door. Yes, we always called the mail carrier, the mailman, even if the carrier was a woman. It was another weird New Jersey nuance along with the milkman and the garbage man.

The new house was quite the place! It had fantastic

roses, shrubs, and flowers planted in the front yard. The builder also planted a wonderful little maple tree right in the front of the house. The house was nice; it was new, and that alone made it something special in our neighborhood.

Then, shortly after they finished construction, the Nit-Nat family bought the home, and they moved in. Within ten or fifteen minutes of their arrival, they decimated the home. It looked as if it had gone through an atomic blast.

Scorched Earth.

They tore the windows out, threw toys, trash, and general junk all over the front lawn. The doors hung by one hinge, they tore the mailbox out of the ground along with the post, and tossed it in the shrubs. They tore the window screens apart within minutes and now, the screens hung precariously from the windows by wires, and the Nit-Nat kids covered the fancy brick front in spray paint and chalk. Dogs ran all over the place, tearing up the grass, and the constant stream of Nit-Nat kids trampled the rose beds, the shrubs in front, and annihilated the small maple tree planted in the front yard. They broke the trunk of the tree in half and used it as a seesaw for years.

The Nit-Nat kids could easily destroy a military tank. It would take them about twenty-five minutes, but they could reduce it to a pile of rubble.

We seldom saw Mrs. Nit-Nat. She would on occasion open a window, and yell down to the kids that it was time to eat a supper, or to stop hanging in the trees, or breaking windows, or destroying the neighborhood, but I guess she was so exhausted from producing children, that she stayed inside most of the time. Mr. Nit-Nat would leave for work very early and arrive home late at night. He worked forty-seven jobs to support all the family. Since there were so many children, we had to surmise that he did come home occasionally.

What a gang. And there was no doubt that we had quite a collection in our old neighborhood, and I have only touched the surface of the people who lived there. I even have to include my own father and his legendary status as a patriarch of the neighborhood. The old man was the anchor, and, in the end, he and my dear Mum were actually the very last of our gang finally to leave the old neighborhood.

I would not trade meeting and living amongst any of them for anything in this world. The neighborhood and the people there made us all what we were.

Cricket Boozer was also unique, to say the least. Short, skinny as a rail, a pug-like nose on his face, a thin mustache above a zipper-like mouth, and he had a round head with a wisp of hair remaining on top of his head that swirled around similar to the top of a whipped ice cream cone. Mrs. Boozer, in stark contrast to her husband's small size, was an immense woman. Wide, tall, and large, she had a hairdo that towered above her head as if it was a skyscraper. On and on, it rose above her head, touching the very stars while she strolled along. She was by nature quite jolly, and constantly encouraged her husband to whistle his trademark chirp.

Interesting people, to say the least. . ..

Cricket did have a terrible habit of swigging gallons upon gallons of rye whiskey, which unfortunately caused his early demise. I guess that might not be completely true, because; he seemed as if he was at least eighty years old forever, but besides that fact, he was unusual for his ability to whistle and be able to mimic the sound of a cricket. When I mean that, he could whistle just like a cricket, I mean it! You would swear that you were standing right on top of a cricket. Then when you add to the mix that at the end of almost every single sentence that he spoke, he whistled the cricket chirp, well; you do have a bit of a unique character.

He would finish the sentence; purse his lips and whistle, "CHIRP! CHIRP! CHIRP!"

"Say, how are youse guys doing? You two birds look like ya took baths in grease. CHIRP! CHIRP! CHIRP!"

"Oh hey, Cricket. We are hanging in there. We need a little dough. Paulie's van blew a head gasket, and a water pump, and I bought Joyce a birthday present and spent too much dough on her. How ya doin?"

Harry always gave people whom he met his current life status and story.

"I am good. Need a bottle of hooch here, though. Say that Joyce is worth it and I don't mind sayin' if you do not get mad at me for that, she is quite the looker. Poor Paulie here, geez ya, ought to stick with Maureen Zipperelli. Now, that gal's chest is nothing short of spectacular. Even half in the bag and as old as I am, I can see her coming from the next block over! Who cares if she is a little older? Maureen should be your steady gal. CHIRP! CHIRP! CHIRP!"

Even Cricket Boozer knew of my poor track record with women and thought I was foolish not to make Maureen my steady gal.

"Yeah, yeah, yeah, thanks, Cricket. I agree that she is a pretty gal for sure, say, we will see you. . .." I pushed Harry along, not wanting to receive any additional romantic advice from Cricket Boozer.

Cricket stopped, turned as we waved goodbye and yelled out to us, "Say, do youse guys want to earn thirty bucks? CHIRP! CHIRP! CHIRP!"

We both spun around simultaneously, and without hesitation, concurrently answered, "YES!"

We did not even worry about what the task would be for us to tackle.

"Watcha got for us, Cricket?" Harry asked as we anxiously ran over to his side. Thirty bucks would keep us afloat for a full week, give me a few bucks towards the parts for the van, and sounded like it was just what we needed. After all, this was the 1970s and gas for the Takajunky was only thirty-four cents a gallon!

"I have this old sofa coming over from my son's house. He has a bad back and cannot lift a thing. Mrs. Boozer wants it moved upstairs into our living room. My son's buddies are dropping the sofa off in front of the house, but they said they did not want to move the sofa up the stairs to our second-floor apartment because it is a little heavy. It would be a piece of cake for you two guys. You gotta get that grease off of ya, so youse don't mess the sofa up, but youse can handle it. You two guys are big and strong and those guys are wimps. CHIRP! CHIRP! CHIRP!"

Cricket stood back and smiled as he licked his lips. He had baited us, but deep down, I had a bad feeling that the other guys knew a little more about the job than we did at this point.

I piped up with my usual logic and conservative suggestion, "Well, we would like to take a look at the job first before we. . .."

Harry slapped me on the back and cut me off in mid-sentence.

"We will do it. We are on our way right now, Cricket. Paulie is just a hapless victim of the Old Lady Syndrome. Do not pay any attention to him. Look at the size of us! We can move mountains!"

I sighed and frowned. But there was no real defense when dealing with Harry when he shifted into blowhard mode. Somehow, someway, I knew deep down that this was a trap. It sounded too easy and therein was the trouble.

"Yeah, yeah, yeah, thirty bucks is a lot of dough for ten minutes of work. Paulie is a nice guy, maybe the nicest guy in the entire neighborhood, but man, I see what ya mean about him acting like an old lady. That must be why he is not chasing Maureen all around town. CHIRP! CHIRP! CHIRP! Let me go to the store here and I will meet you in front of my house."

Off Cricket walked and wobbled with a big smile on his face, chirping the entire way into the liquor store. I always enjoyed some conversations that people had, as if I was invisible and not standing there listening. It really boosted my self-confidence.

"C'mon, twenty-seven. Oh boy, thirty bucks for just moving a sofa! You almost blew it by acting like an old lady!

Harry stepped up the pace. I opened my mouth to protest, and then I stopped. The words would not come out. I only shook my head and followed along. I knew it was coming; the words had to be on the tip of his tongue; it was just a matter of time. Those fateful words that always are muttered when one of our wild schemes or adventures was about to go wrong.

"After all, how bad can it be, twenty-seven? It is just a sofa and some stairs!"

Yes! There we go! Good, because all is well now. The level of premeditated doom is comfortably in place. I felt a lot better now that Harry sealed our fate with his ever-confident words. When we rounded John Street from Belmont, we trekked up to Cricket's house. The entire way, Harry preached to me as to seeking a cure for the Old Lady Syndrome. He then moved on in the conversation, to staying positive, how I should date Maureen on a steady basis, grab and hold Maureen in certain places of her body that would most certainly get me in a good deal of trouble, and how paupers could not be fussy when it came to taking odd jobs. At one point, he stopped and put his big arm around me, and squeezed me as he often did when he wanted to sell ice to an Eskimo. His speech was not going to work because I was not an Eskimo.

Waving his free arm over the entire face of the Earth he said, "The world is your oyster twenty-seven, you need to realize that Harry and Paul can do anything. First, we need to stop at my house and get this grease off of us, but after that we can do anything."

"Sure, Harry, it is just that I felt we should have scouted

the job out first. I know where Cricket Boozer lives and that staircase up to his second-floor apartment is a little on the narrow side."

We stopped off at Harry's house, washed up, and made our way to Cricket's house. Cricket lived on the other side of the Porter's house, in a narrow, brick front, row-type dwelling that was amongst the oldest, if not the oldest house on the street. It was a typical two-story row house with two very small apartments stacked on top of one another. Nothing was very fancy here, just a bedroom, living room, a small dining room, one bathroom and a narrow kitchen at the rear of the home. I felt slightly optimistic, because I remembered that the front staircase leading to the second floor was very tight and narrow, but the rear porches and stairs were wider and wide open. Hmm . . . that would be the obvious way to bring the sofa up.

We approached the front of Cricket's house and stopped in our tracks. Our mouths dropped and our eyes popped out of our heads. The sofa was sitting on the sidewalk in front of Cricket's house and it only slightly resembled a sofa. A better description was that it more closely resembled a steam locomotive. It had to be ten feet long, about five feet high, it had solid wooden legs, a curved fancy back, and it looked as if it weighed twenty tons.

"Oh, . . . shit, twenty-seven . . . it is kinda big," Harry said, while he held me by the shoulders as we scanned the view of the enemy.

About ten of the Nit-Nat kids were sitting on the sofa. Ten more were bouncing up and down on it as if it was a trampoline, and ten more were underneath it while it sat there on the sidewalk. Cricket rounded the corner with his bottle of hooch tucked under his arm, yelled, and chased them off.

"Hey, youse pesky Nit-Nat kids . . . get lost! Get the hell offa my sofa!"

Immediately, an entire battalion of the Nit-Nat kids scattered in every direction, the Nit-Nat kids, who were stuck underneath the sofa, took longer to slide out and run away. They had been trying to pry the springs out of the bottom of the sofa to use as Pogo sticks.

Mrs. Nit-Nat opened the upstairs window of the Nit-Nat home, and screamed out, "STAY THE HELL OFFA CRICKET'S SOFA KIDS! STAY THE HELL OUTTA OF THE DAMN STREET AND STOP ALL THE SCREAMING!" She slammed the window closed and then suddenly, threw the window open again, stuck her head out and screamed, "AND JIMMY, WIPE THE DAMN SNOT RUNNING OUTTA YA NOSE." She slammed the window shut, and she was gone. Mrs. Nit-Nat never even asked why there would be a sofa sitting on the sidewalk. I guess she figured it was somewhat normal for our neighborhood.

While Harry and I stood there scanning the scene, one of the older Nit-Nat boys came up to us, stood there with no shoes on, no coat, wild, twisted hair on his head, and all kinds of goo running out of his nose.

"Youse stupid jerks are going to carry that thing up the stairs?"

Harry looked at him and frowned, "Listen to ya mother. Wipe your nose there, Jimmy Nit-Nat. That is disgusting. Yes, we are big and strong, this is no trouble. Now, stay out of the way!"

The little Nit-Nat looked at us, wiped his nose with the sleeve of his shirt, and instantly, more replacement goo oozed out of his beak, while he laughed and said, "I am Johnny. That is Jimmy over there. His nose runs worse than my nose does. He's got-a-cold. Youse guys can't pick that up. We watched six men take it off the truck and drop it there!"

I stepped in with some old lady advice, "Thank you, Johnny, that is good to know. You are very helpful. You should go inside and clean your nose. Your brother should be inside too if he is feeling poorly."

Johnny Nit-Nat looked up at me, sniffed, and wiped. It did not help. A long string of dangling nose goo immediately reappeared.

Harry grew ever more impatient, and he gently eased me aside while saying, "Let me handle this, Paul. Ya gotta know how to handle Nit-Nats. Get lost Johnny! Beat it, kid! Would you please, go and run, scream, and destroy something over on Geyer Street? Better yet, why don't you and the rest of your fellow wild maniacs, go and pull the wheels off, and strip the hell outta the abandoned car sitting on the corner of Geyer and John Street? That should keep you and your fellow Nit-Nat kids busy for about ten minutes or so."

Johnny enthusiastically nodded his head, took off like a rocket in the direction of Geyer Street, as waves and waves of previously hidden and now screaming, Nit-Nat kids appeared from concealed enclaves and followed him on his destructive quest.

Harry saw me staring at him and shaking my head at his behavior and suggestion.

He shrugged his shoulders and feigned innocence, while justifying his actions with Harry's unusual logic, "What? It will save the city tow charges and the taxpayers some dough. Don't give me that old lady look, will ya. Ya just gotta guide them along. Give 'em a mission. Ya know, give 'em something to do."

"Sure, Harry. Sure. Anyway, back to the sofa. Little Johnny Nit-Nat has a point. You heard him too. He told us six men dropped the sofa off on the sidewalk."

Harry looked at me, waved his hands and discounted the testimony, "He is a Nit-Nat! What does he know? His nose runs like a faucet! Now, do not go spinning off into the old lady universe! You and I can lift this . . . it is a little big, but let's go. You're the strongest guy around. Ya can break people's hands with that grip of yours."

Whenever Harry knew that I was about to be proven correct, he shifted gears and turned into the world's greatest "minimizer" of overt situations.

The big galuk tugged at his belt and puffed out his huge chest while he confidently strode over to the sofa. He bent down, placed his hands under the edge of the sofa, and bent his legs, exhaled, as he picked up the end of the sofa. Harry staggered. The big guy twisted and turned, and his face immediately turned beet red as his heart pumped every ounce of blood in his body into his head. His legs buckled and then recovered as his massive leg power kicked in. He managed to lift the sofa about four inches off the ground, then he dropped the sofa down and smiled, while he did his best to minimize the weight, "See. Piece of cake. There is nuthin' to it, twenty-seven."

"Sure, thirty-five that is why your face is ten different shades of red and your eyeballs almost popped out of your head. Let's go take a look at the back stairs. The front stairs will be a beast."

Cricket had been standing silently on the sideline, watching his evil plan unfold, and finally, he decided to offer some profound advice.

"The back stairs are not going to work there, Paulie. I will show ya why. Say, ya had better tie all that long hair back. You will not be able to see in front of your eyes, and you will drop my sofa. CHIRP! CHIRP! CHIRP!"

I took a little hair tie out of my pocket and tied all of my hair behind my head.

Sure, he was happy. He had just snookered two poor dopes into carrying the titanic sofa into his living room. We followed Cricket into the backyard, up the steps, and climbed the two levels of staircases and porches. This sure seemed the logical way to go. It was a long climb, but it was wide and clear. A few twists and turns, but doable. Maybe.

"See youse guys, we fancied up our kitchen here and had my son put in this fancy cabinet and counter. Ya will never make it past this counter here in order to clear through the back door and kitchen. Too bad, because it would be straight in from here into the living room. CHIRP! CHIRP! CHIRP!"

Between chirps, Cricket pointed out the unfortunate obstacle, and he was correct. Although the back porch and steps were easier to maneuver, the kitchen had a new countertop and island cabinet added in a wrap-around style, and it blocked the path a few feet into the kitchen. We would have to pick the sofa up and over the counter, but there would not be enough room between the countertop and the ceiling to squeeze it over the top. I had to admit; it was a bit unusual for a kitchen design, but it did look nice.

I was about to ask how he intended to move his refrigerator out of the kitchen when he moved, or it required replacement, when Harry walked through the apartment and into the living room.

Harry confidently opened the front hallway door, took a few random looks around and he magically proclaimed, "Oh, this is not so bad, twenty-seven. It is a little steep, and has a turn or two, but it is not so bad."

I knew that tone of voice and the actual translation from optimistic, sugarcoated, Harry language would be, "This is the worst staircase on the face of the Earth. The pitch and angle of the staircase is close to one hundred percent straight up vertically, and the vertical climb equals the slope of the Matterhorn. The staircase is barely wide enough to clear the width of the sofa. You have a better chance of seeing Santa Claus than you have of actually getting this sofa up these stairs."

Four and one-half hours later, we were still stuck at the top of the stairs. Sweat covered every square inch of our bodies, my long mop of hair was drenched and sweat ran off the ends of the strands like a river, our backs were throbbing, the blood vessels in our heads were ready to burst, and every, single, muscle in our bodies screamed in agony.

In addition, we now had a crowd of spectators gathered to watch the saga of the sofa.

Everyone from four or five city blocks around arrived on scene to watch the drama unfold. Everyone, from the Nit-Nat kids, to the guy who lived in a box on Geyer Street, to Joey Hinky Doo and little Joe Hink (freshly released from their latest stint in prison) to Anton "Andy" Grindirini the head sausage-making guy from Andy's Provisions on the corner of John Street and Geyer. Even Mrs. Nit-Nat, who we later learned was in the early stages of pushing out another Nit-Nat kid, took a timeout from early labor screaming to come and watch. Joe Hinky Doo and his son were taking bets and making the cuts on which one of us would drop dead on the staircase first. Some of the spectators had set up lawn chairs to watch, and they were smoking cigars, while they all offered up key advice.

If one more person had suggested, "Hey, youse guys, try to turn it on the right side, and flip it at the same time, while you lift it straight up over the railings," then Harry was going to execute them all.

We also could have done without Anton the sausage maker singing in his Italian accent with some new lyrics to the melody of a famous Italian song, "When, youuuu unzippppp the door and your stuff hits the floor . . . that's . . . a rupture!"

Thank goodness Mr. Porter, Harry's old man, and Ronzo were not home from work yet, or we would really be in trouble!

There we were stuck at the top of the staircase, and no matter which way we spun it, lifted it, or turned it; we could not make it to the top and over the railing.

"Look Cricket, we have no choice here, man! You have to saw the top of the railing off, and these legs on the sofa, to get it in. We can glue and screw them all back on, but it is the only way that this piece of shit is getting in there!"

Harry screamed for the four hundredth time to Cricket to try to convince him that a strategic cut here and there was the only solution. Harry was at the top of the stairs pleading his case with Cricket. While I desperately tried to prevent my back, internal organs, and legs from exploding out from underneath me, while holding the weight of the sofa up from the bottom.

"Harry, nothing for nothing, but this is a little heavy down here." I pleaded in vain. I was in good shape, big and strong, but this was a little over the top.

"Yeah, yeah, yeah, twenty-seven, I can tell. . .."

I was about to explain the rules of gravity and point out the fact that Harry was at the top when I heard Cricket say, "Oh all right, I guess it is the only way. But, youse guys have to fix it just like new for the same thirty bucks! CHIRP! CHIRP! CHIRP!"

"Great! Twenty-seven, hang on down there. I am running to my house to get the saw and tools. Are you okay?"

"Oh, sure Harry. Not as if, I have a choice here. To quote you . . . this is . . . nothing. A piece of cake!"

"Yeah, yeah, yeah. I told you that it was no big deal. Good, I will be right back."

Twenty minutes later, I was feeling my pulse beating in my little toe on my right foot. I had prayed to every single saint that the Lutheran Church recognized and I created a few more on my own, just for good measure. I was still holding the sofa when Harry cut the railing free, he cut the two legs off, and we mercifully carried the sofa into the living room.

The gathered crowd cheered at the top of their lungs, and the Nit-Nat kids dashed off screaming, "THEY GOT IT INTO CRICKET'S APARTMENT! THEY DID IT! PAULIE IS PURPLE AND RED, BUT THEY DID IT!"

Joey Hinky Doo moaned and groaned.

He mumbled something about, "They did it, but for those interested in some longer-term bets, I will take some bets now that Paulie will never be a father!" Joey Hinky Doo continued to work the angles, as he had to pay out on the fact that neither Harry, nor I, keeled over and croaked.

It was such a wonderful feeling knowing that we had provided everyone on John and Geyer Street with such cheap entertainment and a chance at some illegal betting activity on this March afternoon.

I collapsed on the floor in Cricket's living room. Gasping for air and praying to the Lord for salvation and mercy. I relived memories of my life in fleeting, newsreel-like moments. Harry leaned over me while beads of sweat running from his forehead dripped on me. He patted me gently on my shoulder in a vain attempt to humor me.

"You okay, twenty-seven? I told you it would not be so bad. Well, it may have been a little worse than I thought, but we did it!"

"Harry . . . once I regain the circulation in my body and I can pick my arms up again, then I am going to kill you."

Harry frowned and said, "Yeah, yeah, yeah, well, that will be about three weeks from now and you will have forgiven me by then. Just stay down there, relax and suck in some air while I get to these repairs. Ya look a little blue."

I rolled over while Harry hustled to glue and screw the legs back on the sofa and repair the railing. Cricket poured us some glasses of water, and I sat there sipping water, recovering and watching, while Harry made the repairs on the railing and legs. I started to feel my feet, legs, and hands again, and rubbed at the huge red mark on my arm where I had nestled the sofa on my body. Harry strategically reassembled the railing together and in doing so, he devised a system, so that a mechanic could at some time in the future take it apart again, when some other poor suckers had to carry the sofa down from the apartment.

We finished, and Harry gathered up all of our tools and supplies. I slowly stood up from the floor, and felt every single muscle in my body expand and contract as if they were rubber bands, when Cricket said, "Well, thanks youse guys. Let me pay you for the work. Oh, hi, honey. Look, Harry and Paulie got the sofa up here. CHIRP! CHIRP! CHIRP!"

Mrs. Boozer had returned home from a shopping outing, and she walked into the living room. She put down a little shopping bag she was carrying and waddled over to where we were standing.

"Oh, thank you! It looks so nice. I bet it was easy to get it up the backstairs and up through the porch too. Since our son, Jerry devised that fantastic system, he made the kitchen countertop, and cabinet to unscrew from the floor, and move out of the way with those four bolts . . . I bet it was easy. Right?"

Mrs. Boozer smiled widely. And she first looked at me, then at Harry, and then at her husband. I imagined that the incredible looks of horror on our faces, and the fact that our eyeballs were set for an explosive launch out of our heads, told her to probe a bit deeper into how the sofa arrived in her living room.

She sensed some type of "bump in the road here" but she continued with her positive and upbeat supposition of the events, "I bet you came straight into the living room. Right guys? Our kitchen looks so nice with those new cabinets and countertops. Don't you think that was a brilliant idea? Jerry, he has a bad back, but he is so smart! Otherwise, you would have to move things up and down that front staircase and that is nearly impossible." Mrs. Boozer rather gingerly smiled and thanked us once more, while Harry and I glared at Cricket. The look on our faces, and the lack of an immediate agreement with Mrs. Boozer's testimony, caused her some pause, and she sensed that something had gone awry with the system.

She stood there asking, "Easy? Wasn't it easy? Right?"

"CRICKET!" We both screamed in unison while he fled off towards the kitchen.

We heard him yell out, "SHIT! Oops! Sorry! I forgot about those bolts! All right, here is your fifty bucks, youse guys! Thanks again! CHIRP! CHIRP! CHIRP!"

"YEAH, I AM GOING TO CHIRP YA ASS!" I held Harry back; we took the money and left. While we carefully and slowly walked down the staircase, one painful step at a time, we could hear, behind the closed doors of the apartment, Mrs. Boozer screaming at Cricket.

It was something about being a "Drunken bum."

The extra dough for forgetting about "Jerry's method" was a nice touch. Still not worth the pain, but it was a nice touch. Over the next few days, we recovered with some heating pads, some ice packs here and there, and a few hundred or so bottles of aspirin. Before we knew it, we perfectly healed. We were young, and in good shape, and between that adventure and the unexpected run-on Alps Road, I had my workouts covered for a few days.

It could have been my imagination, but my arms, once the feeling came back into them, sure felt stronger! The wounds opened again, when a few days later, while hanging out and shooting the breeze with Anton, he kidded with us and started to sing that stupid song again.

We stopped him rather quickly.

Harry, now that he could actually walk normally without looking as if he was riding a camel, actually relished the adventure. He felt that it simply contributed to his "world famous" status, and it was just another notch in his belt as he continued the climb up the mountain, which will someday bear his name.

I never asked Cricket Boozer what his plan was going to be if we had not come along to help him. I guess it did not matter, in the end; we did earn twenty-five bucks each. It was the hardest earned fifty bucks in our lifetime, that was for sure, at least, until now.

The great sofa adventure became a legendary event in our neighborhood for years and years. Old Harry sure knew how to work us into corners, but once more, somehow, someway, we did it.

That was always the amazing part!

My share of the money for the work was enough for me to buy the water pump for the van. Now, I just needed to save for the gasket and the tires to get the old clunker back out on the road. It sure would be nice to have that old jeep, but I guess that will have to wait. Even if I fixed the van up and sold it, I still would be a bit short of the cash for Vince's asking price on the jeep.

The old man thought that we could handle the repairs, and my father remained the best backyard mechanic in the entire neighborhood. That way, I would save the labor on the repairs. All I had to do was buy the tires, and Vince could mount and balance them for me at his station.

Now, if I could somehow or someway just come up with the rest of the money.

Although it was a bit unnerving and creepy for a guy to sing, especially a guy who grinds random, unquestionable origin meat up and makes sausages for a living, now that we could safely look back at the great sofa adventure, we had to admit that tune of Anton's was rather catchy.

You know . . . now that we survived with our "stuff" intact.

"When youuuu unzipppp the door and your stuff hits the floor. . .."

3

An Inspirational Invitation!

These were the days that made you what you were. Or so my old man told me. I would think that if he had the extra dough to give me that he and my mother both felt sorry enough for me to loan me the extra jingle to buy the jeep. However, my parents scraped by during these days just like everyone else in the old neighborhood did. In our world, you learned about some of the hard lessons in life, and one of them was by earning your own money.

Handouts did not come easy in our old neighborhood, and you learned hard lessons all about personal responsibilities.

"Paulie, it is Maureen on the telephone! Geez! Please, will ya just take her out on a date! Man, oh man alive. I would think, if not for the fact that you can see a hockey puck from ten miles away that ya must be blind," the old man was bellowing for me to come and pick up the telephone, while commenting on my current love life.

I was sitting on my bed, reading a hockey magazine, while passing a Saturday away with my faithful and now very old fox terrier, Skippy, when I heard the old man bellowing for me. I had worked until noon at my job at the electric shop, and now I was down to city buses, my old bicycle, and good, old shoe leather in order to make it to my job.

"All right, on my way, Dad!" I turned to old Skip, who looked up at me. "Say, what do you think, Skippy? Should I just concede defeat, and admit that I love her and make

Maureen my only gal?" Skippy looked at me, sat back down on the bed, sprawled out and seemed to go to sleep.

Hmm. . .. No help whatsoever from my faithful dog.

"I will be back in about two hours."

I knew how Maureen could talk.

Two hours could have been conservative.

"Thanks, Dad," I said as I took the telephone from him. I held my hand carefully and fully over the receiver and whispered to him, "Say, if I am still talking on the phone here in an hour, could you come in and yell really loud that you need to use the phone? It might be my only chance to get away."

The old man nodded and said, "Sure, sure, sure. Please stop being an old lady and take the woman out on a date. My goodness! Geez, look at her man! I will say it again that I do not know how you see hockey pucks at a hundred miles an hour if you cannot see the size of that gal's chest and those glorious curves." His voice drifted away as I took the telephone from him.

"Hello, Maureen, how. . .."

"I agree with your father. You should listen to him. Come and chase me down, shower me with gifts, and passionate kisses. I will be sure to make it worthwhile for your efforts and repay you in ways that you could not imagine. I can tell you that some of them involve those glorious curves!" Maureen had obviously overheard the comments from the old man.

I hoped and prayed that she did not hear all of them.

I chuckled a little at her forthright comments regardless of how tongue in cheek that they might be. I knew they had some very strong elements of truth associated with them.

Maureen was always very aggressive. Fun, gorgeous, talkative, but always very aggressive.

"Hey, Maureen. How is it going?" I decided to ignore her comments. The truth was that her aggressiveness embarrassed me at times.

"Oh, you are such a cutie. I can see your face right now turning red."

I flinched even more, since she had pegged me right away.

"I heard from a reliable grapevine source, known as a certain Harry M. Redmond Junior, whom I met wandering in the Foodworld frozen food aisle that your van broke down."

"Well, yes, that is true, but I am close to. . .."

Maureen ran over the top of my long-winded ways. It happened quite often to me. I never seemed to be able to speak many words or put together complete sentences as of late.

"Okay, well, that sucks. So, you need to raise some cash to buy the parts to repair it, or maybe, just maybe, you are going to decide to buy something newer."

"Well, honestly, I do have my eyes on a jeep. . .."

"I thought that I would offer up my assistance to see if you need a ride to a game or hockey practice. I also have not heard from you in a little while, so I am being rather aggressive, and not hiding the fact to use this excuse in order to see you and lure you into a date of some sort. You know, sometimes a gal has to take matters into her own hands."

Oh, boy. Thanks, Harry.

"Well, Maureen, that is very nice of you."

I now stammered and stuttered a little. I knew that what I was about to say would come out sounding anything but cool. Despite Harry's constant coaching of me, the dreaded "Old Lady Syndrome" would never stop following me around.

"Ah, ah, yes. It really is nice of you, but the old man is lending me the 1964 Putter Classic model 200 to get me to the rink tomorrow. I take the bus to work and walk between bus stops. I bum a ride with Harry, you know, Maureen. I am working through it. To be honest, I well, rather think that a guy should, you know, pick a gal up for a date. Not the other way around. I am too traditional, I guess."

"I knew that's what you would say!" Maureen shouted out over the receiver. She was famous for her talking ability, and once she got rolling, there was very little to stop her once she began talking. Perhaps an Earth tremor or nuclear attack would cause her a slight pause, but I assure you it would be only a momentary delay. Therefore, I sat in the chair next to the telephone and prepared for what was going to be, inevitably, a very long conversation.

She continued to chuckle, until she cleared her throat and continued, "Yes, you are, and in many ways, that is why you are so special. Traditional and old fashioned, really stuffy at times, but oh, my oh my, you are such a cutie and you drip in pure sexiness. Those are just some reasons that I love you so much!"

She then said something in Italian and she let out a long, almost alluring, sigh. I did not want to know what the words meant and decided to stay away from asking. I think I knew the general gist even if my Italian language skills were severely limited.

Maureen continued, "So, now, my darling Paulie, I cannot feel guilty at all. You see, I offered, even though I knew how that would not fit the Paul John Henson mode of gallantry. Maybe, I had another reason for calling too."

"Oh, well, thanks again, Maureen. I do not want to seem unappreciative. I am just . . . well . . . I guess I am just a bit on the stuffy side. What is the other reason that you called? Does your dad need electrical work on the old house again?"

From the other room, I could hear my father deeply sigh; he was obviously listening to the conversation and despite his coaching and his dropping of strong hints, he knew that I was blowing it.

I heard him mumble, "Electrical repairs. Shit, this here

son of ours is a thick-headed dope. Too many blows to the head from hockey pucks. She don't need no electrical work. She needs something else from ya, but it sure as hell ain't no electrical work. Wake the hell up, Paulie."

Visions of Harry wagging his finger in front of me and lecturing me as to my deep and now hopeless affliction with the Old Lady Syndrome floated through my mind. I guess, in the big picture, that I was hopeless.

I continued to babble, like some stupid fool, "Now you have me on an edge and just a bit over to the curious side. What is the other reason?" Once I spoke the words, I shuddered, as I suddenly felt pangs of regret as to what might be the next thoughts that Maureen Zipperelli actually had on her mind.

She was so aggressive.

"No, electrical work. No. I need other things from you, but it sure as hell is not going to be electrical work."

I thought about how there seems as if there is an echo around here.

"I would like to invite you over to our house for Easter dinner. You know, we have a big Italian celebration for Pasqua at our home. It is a special holiday for our family. I have the inside scoop as to how this will all shake out. My father already called your dad to invite your entire family over, but your dad explained that they are going out of town to visit your uncle, and you have a game scheduled the next day, so you are staying in Haledon. Now, I know you could go over to Harry's house, but I thought I would take advantage of the situation and invite you here. I do not want you to be lonely and believe me. I will keep you company!"

"Well, that is nice of you Maureen, but. . .."

Once again, Maureen cut me off and turned it up some more.

"I thought we could attend the Easter sunrise mass on Garret Mountain together. Father Mark is holding mass and I know you enjoy hearing his services and homilies. I know that you are Lutheran, but it seems as if between the Redmonds and Zipperellis, you have become at least an honorary Catholic. Plus, I have to say, natale con I tuoi. Pasqua con chi vuoi."

"Ah, what? My Italian is somewhat lacking these days, Maureen."

She chuckled and softly said, "Oh, Paulie, that in English means, Christmas with your family. Easter with whomever you like. Since you begged out on me for Christmas, and there is no one that I rather spend Pasqua with other than you, I am striking early and digging in deeply to get what it is that I want."

"I am quite flattered, and honored, Maureen. Thank you for the compliment, but I do need to defend my net here just a bit. I did not actually beg out on Christmas. I had made a commitment with church services and needed to stick with a promise."

"Oh, I know, Paulie! That is only one of the many reasons why I am so hopelessly in love with you. You are so committed and conservative. I have to tell you that you invade a woman's soul. You need to understand that, yet, I can never seem ever to get through to you."

Oh, geez . . . there she goes with that love word again!

Maureen paused for a mere half of a nanosecond, and I attempted to speak, "I do enjoy listening to, Father Mark. He and I have become quite close, and my. . .."

Not quick enough, old lady Henson!

Maureen was off to the blabber races once more, "Good! If you are not careful, then I will take that as a yes. Mama and Nonna will be cooking up a storm. Roasted lamb chops will be the main meat dish. Then we follow it with piles and piles of ziti, meatballs, antipasto, Mama's famous gravy, mountains of salads, wine, beer, cannoli after homemade cannoli, biscotti, you name it, we will have it."

I felt my mouth open and my taste buds drooled.

Roasted lamb chops! Sweet water of life! Mama Zipperelli was the world's greatest Italian cook. To add the gravy on the pasta, Maureen's grandmother, or as she called her, "Nonna" will be in the kitchen too, coaching and running the show. Another Italian cooking legend!

The wonderful English cooking of my dear mum filled our lives with wholesome food and tasty delights. Until now, and my relationship with Maureen, homemade Italian food, (other than pizza from Sunray Pizzeria in Paterson or the Greek Joint's pizza, which Harry and I enjoyed all the time) was something rather foreign to us. The Zipperellis introduced my family and me to the wonders of Italian food on one legendary Thanksgiving when our dinner plans went astray. Now, my dear Mum had adopted a lot of Italian food in her own dinner menus, and she was now quite the adopted-Italian food cook herself.

Once more, an entirely different story!

Visions of heavenly meatballs chased me around in circles in my mind. I ran as fast as I could, all to no avail, as they rolled over me as if they were runaway boulders chasing after me, enveloping me in rivers of tomato sauce.

I mean, gravy.

In my daydream, I ate and chomped my way to survival. It was the only way to live. I stood there like a dope, with the receiver in my hand, not saying a word, while smiling at the thought of it.

"Paulie, Paulie . . . ah . . . Paul. Are you there? What do you think? Will you come over? Do I take your comments as meaning, yes?"

Maureen, using my actual name, forced me back to reality.

No one ever called me by my actual name.

I arrived back to reality, and I left the world of Italian food behind. To the continued agony of the old man listening in the other room, I still rather persistently, yet precariously, hung on to my Old Lady Syndrome.

"Well, I dunno, Maureen. It is very nice of you to invite me, but. . .."

I heard her sigh for just a second, then she cut me off abruptly and said, "Oh shit, you are a pain in my ass. I love you dearly, but man alive!"

Maureen said something very fast in Italian, but I did not follow a single word. Given the circumstances, perhaps, it was best that I did not understand anything of what she was saying.

Maureen switched over to English, "What is it that Harry says when you are stuck in the mud? I think he always yells out, for the love of Pete! Damn, you *are* an old lady! Geez, let's give this angle a try. Paulie, listen the hell up now. Listen care-full-y. I just bought a new spring dress for Easter. It has a flower print on it, and it fits me rather tightly with a plunging and extra revealing neckline too! My breasts bulge out of the top of the dress and they are barely covered. I can hardly even breathe in the dress, and if I am not careful, even with wearing a special brassiere to lash them in place, when I bend over just a little, then, my huge and fantastic breasts will pop out of the damn thing and fall right into your hands! Now, does that plant a vision in your mind, or are you still gonna be an old lady?"

Maureen had lost patience with me, she quit messing around with me, and she had brought out the big guns.

In more ways than just one.

Sweet water of life! Roasted lamb chops, mountains of ziti, and Maureen wearing a dress with a plunging neckline that is trying in vain to contain her bulging breasts!

I folded like a cheap tourist camera.

"I will be there, Maureen. I promise!"

I heard the old man shout from the other room, "Finally! Holy shit! Thank friggin' goodness! I swear that I am gonna take ya to the doctor to get ya eyeballs and brain checked out! Geez, look at her son. Maureen will never drown!"

I almost laughed at his reaction, but recovered nicely to hold my conservative line, "But, we have to go in my van." I still desperately clung to my traditional, conservative, and rather boring behavior. After all, despite dresses with plunging necklines, a man has to have *some* principles.

"I will get the stupid van fixed. I promise. Sunrise service is, at what time? Five, six, or whatever the hell time it is—I will be at your house at four in the morning!"

"Now ya talkin' there, Paulie," the old man shouted in joy.

Visions of spring dresses, Italian food, meatballs, ziti, and plunging necklines on Maureen's incredibly shapely female figure had inspired me to new heights.

Old Lady Syndrome?

Never heard of it.

What Old Lady Syndrome? Hallelujah! I am free!

So, she is a few years older than me. In reality, it is really no big deal.

Maybe.

Maureen was laughing hysterically at my change of heart. She continued to ramble on, saying something in Italian, and I answered her in Welsh.

I laughed and said in Welsh, "Fenyw'n bert," which means pretty woman. I picked up quite a bit of Welsh these days, from Mum and my conversations with my Grandfather, and his sister, the world famous; Aunt Alma. I also did some more studying on my own.

Maureen stopped laughing for just a second and said, "What did you just say?"

Oh, oh! Maureen nabbed me.

"Nuthin'. I did not say anythin'."

"Yes, you did, Paul John Henson! Put Mum on the telephone! She will tell me. I heard you say something in Welsh."

Oh boy, now I felt nothing except for wicked

embarrassment.

"Well, you were going off in Italian and I just kind of sorta was thinking of you in that spring dress, so I said, pretty woman."

Silence ensued on the telephone.

Very rare and unheard-of Maureen Zipperelli silence. However, not for long.

"Oh, you are such a cutie! That was so romantic of you to say. I am so excited. We are going to have such a good time, blah, blah, blah, blah. . .."

I wiggled in the chair to settle in for the long haul and practiced my "Uh huhs."

I was going to need them.

The old man finally rescued me, but not until I had withstood about two hours of Maureen babble. She talked right through a salesman ringing our doorbell selling magazines, Mum running her vacuum, Skippy barking at Pussface the cat, and the old man screaming at the news report that the New York Bugs just announced that in a preseason trade, they had traded, Saggy-Pants Tommy Wompers, who was one of the old man's favorite players. The old man took the telephone from me, (because he said that I was too nice) and told Maureen that he had an emergency breakdown with a machine at the shop and he had to use the telephone to check on the status.

After surviving the conversation, I was back in reality. Where would I get the dough to fix the van? Easter was only a few weeks away; and so was the big day with Maureen. And now, I had put more pressure on myself to fix the old relic. I went back to my bedroom, sat on the edge of the bed, and picked up the hockey magazine. All I could think about was Maureen wearing that dress.

Fenyw'n bert.

Oh, yes, and I thought about some lamb chops and meatballs smothered in Italian gravy, too. But mostly, I thought about Maureen wearing that dress. Time to shake out of it, twenty-seven. C'mon, now, you need to think about something else. Think about hockey. Yes, hockey! Just keep telling yourself that you are not falling in love with the gorgeous Maureen Zipperelli. There is always hockey, put the love aside for now.

Concentrate on hockey.

I fingered a large welt on my leg from a slap shot that I took a few days earlier. It was sore and a little nasty. I should try to ice it, but I was too lazy to go make a pack of ice. Hockey was slowly taking a little toll on my young body. The scars were starting to add up a bit. With a long sigh and drifting thoughts, hockey faded away. Maureen had cast a spell on me and she captured me with it. I leaned back in my bed, propped up a pillow, and that was it. Dresses, slap shots, meatballs, ziti, ah no, back to Maureen and tight dresses.

I drifted off to a nap.

"WAKE UP! GET YA ASS OUTTA THE RACK! Harry is on the telephone. Geez! I am going to install a switchboard to handle all of these calls." The old man was in typical exaggeration mode, while he shook me from my lazy Saturday afternoon nap.

"When are ya going to cut off all of that hair? It looks like a mop on ya head!"

Huh? Where did the hair thing come from? I staggered out of my sleep, wandered into the dining room, where we kept our telephone in a corner and picked it up.

"Hello."

"WHAT THE HELL ARE YOU DOING BY SLEEPING A SATURDAY AWAY?" Harry screamed at me.

Geez, this was some afternoon. Everyone was blasting me and all that I was trying to do was to take a little nap and dream about Maureen in that dress. I mean, dream about hockey.

"Huh? What? Well, I . . . just actually. . .."

"Wake up. Knock the sleep outta ya eyes, stop thinking

about Maureen in that tight dress, and come over to my house right away. I have the adventure and the deal of a lifetime for us!"

"CLICK!"

The line went dead.

How did he know about the dress? Another typical four-second-long Harry conversation.

I grabbed my vest and went out the back door while I stopped and told Mum not to cook anything for me. I told her that Harry and I would grab a little something over at the Redmond's house.

She nodded, requested a kiss goodbye, and said, "So I hear you finally woke up and are going to spend Easter with Maureen and the Zipperellis, eh?"

"Yes, Mum."

"I hear that she has a new Easter dress to wear that she bought special for you."

I thought about how the news about this dress had now circled the entire Earth.

"Well, I am not sure that she bought it special for. . .." Mum shook her head and cut me off, while wiping her hands on a dishtowel.

"Oh, Paulie. You are such an old lady. Of course, she bought it for you. She is hopelessly in love with you, and I can't blame her. What woman would not be in love with you? I hear it is rather revealing, eh?"

She winked, and I turned a little red.

Mum grabbed me and she whispered to me, "I love you too, dear Paulie. I am happy for you, after all, it is springtime and young love is all around."

"I love you too, Mum. I guess that it is springtime and you are correct."

I kissed her cheek, and I was on my way. I paused for just a moment to stare at my broken-down van in the driveway. It appeared to be so ominous and imposing. I swore that the tires looked even balder than they did before, and I knew that the van had not even moved in a week or two. As I walked the two city blocks to Harry's house, I shuddered at what potential scheme or adventure Harry had conjured up for us now. Those words always meant some sort of wild idea, crazy, convoluted, plot or wacky situation for us to become embroiled in.

I would soon find out. I noticed, as I walked by Vince's gas station, that the jeep that had been for sale had now moved to the back of his lot, and now sat neatly in a corner. The sign was gone from the window. Maybe someone had bought it. Too bad, I would have tried to make an offer for it, if I could have come up with enough money.

Upon arrival in the wild Redmond household, I met Harry's dog, Cocoa, at the door, holding his ever-present rubber toy, Piggy in his mouth. After greeting Cocoa and making my way through the maze of screaming nieces and nephews sprawled across the floor, watching the famous Dinky the Orange Teddy Bear cartoon on the television, I made my way into the kitchen.

"Hey, twenty-seven. Sit down. Sit down." To my surprise, I ran straight into Harry's brother-in-law, the legendary George "The Big Spike" Pinia. George greeted me and he was waving me in for a landing.

Harry appeared from the back door. He was smiling from ear-to-ear, and he wildly congratulated me, "Way to go, twenty-seven. I have to say that I am slightly impressed. Finally, shaking off the lingering afflictions of the Old Lady Syndrome and snagging a big date for Easter Sunday with Maureen, a new tight dress, with a low neckline, whoa, whoa, whoa. Magic, pure springtime magic!"

"Yeah, way to go there, Paulie," George said while patting me on the back. Even for Harry and the Redmond hotline and news wire, I had to say it was amazing.

"Wait! How did you know already? Did she really tell you about her new dress? Geez, I only just spoke with

Maureen a few hours ago."

Harry pointed at the refrigerator and asked me, "Big Boulder or Dingleberry?"

"Big Boulder, those Dingleberries are too sweet for me." Harry nodded, grabbed me a Big Boulder beer from the refrigerator. He took a soda and we popped the tops off and took a few swigs. I felt it was a stall tactic on his part and a diversion to avoid answering me about how he knew of my date with Maureen.

"Well?" I asked.

"Oh, I met her in the Foodworld. Over in the frozen food aisle. She told me all about it. I did not let Maureen know, but I knew 'bout the dress already, cuz, my sister, Linda, knows some chick in Meyer Brother's Store in downtown Paterson that sold it to her. The store clerk chick said that Maureen looked like a Hollywood movie star in the dress. Maureen showed the store clerk chick a picture of ya, and told her the dress was to lure you into a date and perhaps, a little more. If ya know what I mean! Man, she is going to knock your eyeballs out of your long-haired head in that dress. She is a knockout!" Harry whistled low while shaking his head.

I thought how Foodworld must sell an awful lot of frozen food, and how hard it is to keep something under wraps around here. Harry had a reconnaissance network that would rival the British M.I. spy operations.

Harry waved his arms and hands in the air in typical dramatic fashion as he commented, "About time twenty-seven that you were finally able to shake the Old Lady and Mr. Nice Guy Syndrome. I was starting to worry about ya. Say, suck that beer down, sit down there at the table, and listen up. Man, oh man, do we have good news for you."

Harry pointed at a chair at the side of the kitchen table, George sat down at the head of the table, and Harry pulled the other chair out and sat down.

"Tell him, Big Spike. Tell him about the job you have for

us to do." Harry was very excited, and I leaned in hard now when I heard the word, "job" because jobs equal money, and money equals Italian food, and low-cut, plunging necklines. I knew my Algebraic formulas from paying attention in the electrical shop class. Hmm, let's see, yes, money over the job, divided by meatballs, gravy, times antipasto, equals spring fever and Maureen Zipperelli in tight dresses!

The Big Spike explained the potential gig, "Okay twenty-seven, as you know, I recently landed a new job a few weeks ago, managing tuxedo and suit rental stores for the Bickerson Company all over New Jersey and New York," the Big Spike started to explain, while I nodded my head.

"This Saturday, we have a huge fashion show and Easter show at a fancy hotel and conference center over in Wayne, in that big joint. The Majestic Wayne Hotel and Conference Center or something like that. Anyway, we need male models dressed in our best suits to walk down the runway and accompany beautiful women dressed in fancy, schmancy, dresses. No tuxedos for this one, only the latest in cool, modern suits. I have collaborated with the woman who runs the dress end of the show, to have you two bananas be two of the male models. I showed her a picture of youse two guys, and for some reason, she said youse guys were hot, and would have the ladies eating out of your hands. She is very excited and thinks that she will sell a record number of dresses!"

Harry leaned back and clapped his hands in joy. His eyeballs were spinning with excitement in his head, and smoke was pouring out of his ears, "Oh yeah, yeah, yeah, hot chicks on the runway, and hot, drunken, gals in the audience. It is like Heaven on Earth!"

I moved uneasily and frowned at not only the thought of the work but also the thought of letting the world-famous womanizer, Harry M. Redmond Junior, loose in a fashion show filled with gorgeous ladies. It was a nightmare for the world, but Harry's dream scenario. This somehow had disaster plastered all over it.

"I do not know about this gig, Big Spike. It is not exactly my cup of tea. Walking around with some women that I do not know, you know, they would all be strangers, all of them wearing fancy dresses and me in one of those fancy suits. I just landed the date with Maureen. If she got wind of it, she may just flip her lid."

I saw Harry rolling his eyes to load his cannon to blast me when the Big Spike cleared his throat and said, "The job pays three hundred dollars. I just need to measure youse guys."

I saw Harry lean back and smile as he saw the look on my face change. Three hundred dollars for walking around with the strange but beautiful ladies!

Once more, I folded like a cheap tourist camera.

It was becoming a pattern with me.

"I suppose I can wear one of them fancy suits there, Big Spike. Where do we start? Did you bring your tape measure?"

"Oh yeah, yeah, yeah! Nuthin' like a little dough and big breasts hanging out of dresses to cure twenty-seven of the Mr. Nice Guy and Old Lady Syndrome!" Harry jumped up from the table as George motioned for us to stand up. He had the tape measure in his pocket.

While George was measuring us for our suits, Harry's sister Linda returned from Foodworld and she placed a bag of groceries on the table.

"Hi, boys. Hi, twenty-seven. Say, congratulations on the big date with Maureen for Easter. I also heard that her new dress is going to knock your eyeballs out, Paulie. That is going to be a wonderful holiday, and with youse two guys earning the three hundred dollars with the Big Spike, you can even get that heap of junk van repaired to pick her up with now."

I looked over to the groceries that Linda was now unpacking and putting away and most of them were frozen foods.

I didn't even ask, but I smiled and said, "Hey, Linny. Yes, it sure is exciting. It will be nice to get the van back on the road."

George finished with his measurements, and while we discussed the details of the event and standing around the kitchen table, the front door opened. Immediately, we watched Cocoa run off with Piggy stuck in his mouth to check out who was there at the door. The barking of Cocoa, combined with the screaming kiddies, told us that Harry's father and Ronzo had returned home from work. Ronzo worked with Mr. Redmond on weekends at his metal shop to earn some extra part-time money. Work and party. It was the old neighborhood way.

After the commotion of their entry died down, Ronzo greeted me with a big slap on the back, "Hey there, you, old sly dog there, twenty-seven. A big day is coming up, a very big day. We heard today that Maureen has a dress that is cut so low you can see Florida from her front porch!"

I smiled, but I did not say a word, while I watched as Mr. Redmond set a Foodworld bag on the kitchen table, along with a case of Big Boulder beer.

Now, it was Mr. Redmond's turn to tell me all about the upcoming date, "Oh boy, yes indeed, we heard all about the big date. Maureen is a nice gal. She smells a little like garlic, and a little touch of red wine, but man, oh man, ya need to hold on tight when she walks on by. She told Ronzo and me how she is very excited about the big day. Now that you will have earned enough dough by walking around like a bunch of penguins, you will be able to fix your junky van. Wow, life is good." Mr. Redmond looked at me, and he smiled while he lifted a gallon of ice cream out of the Foodworld bag.

"Say, I picked up this gallon of Dingleberry Beer flavored ice cream in the frozen food section of the Foodworld. I thought we could all try it. I thought it might be better than the beer, and not quite as sweet as the beer tends to be."

Trying to keep something secret around here was impossible. I guess Maureen must have had an awful lot of shopping to do this afternoon, and it must have all been in the frozen food section. All I needed now was for Harry's other sister, Patty, to arrive and tell me all about the date, too. Indubitably, she must have been in the Foodworld in the frozen food section this afternoon, along with the rest of the city of Paterson and town of Haledon.

Ronzo and Mr. Redmond slid into their usual chairs at the kitchen table while Harry came over and put his big arm around me.

"Three hundred smackers twenty-seven. Your van is as good as back on the road, thanks to me and the Big Spike. Plus, we will be escorting fantastic women who are all dressed to kill, combined with cheering and drooling gals in the audience, all fueled with champagknee-a-roo-ski and cheese tidbits, throwing their telephone numbers at us! Unreal, it really is unreal."

"I guess, Harry. I am going to explain it to Maureen just in case, though. Are you going to tell, Joyce?"

"No, Paul. Nice guys, who are hopelessly afflicted with the Nice Guy and Old Lady Syndromes, confess these types of things to their gals. Wild maniacs, who are living on the edge such as I am, do not even give it a second thought. Go ahead and knock yourself out twenty-seven, just remember that someday, you will thank me and eventually listen to me."

It seemed as if I now had another affliction to add to my ailments, with Harry recently adding the Nice Guy Syndrome to my array of various diseases. I shrugged my shoulders and smiled. There was not too much else to say.

Harry had summed it up in my opinion.

Ronzo waved to his wife while saying, "Linny, please hand me a Dingleberry beer, would you? Pop, do ya want one too?"

Mr. Redmond shook his head, turned to his daughter, and said, "Nah, please, Linda, let me have a Big Boulder. Those Dingleberries are way too sweet."

I felt a pat on my back as I stood in the doorway between the kitchen and the dining room while casually sipping my beer.

"You big long-haired, sexy, lover boy, there, Paulie. Here, I thought I could slip away from the Big Spike, and run off to some Caribbean island with you!" I recognized the voice as Harry's other sister, Patty's voice.

I turned; Patty was smiling, and ready to grab me for one of her famous, jealousy-induced hugs, which she would perform in front of George. As she grabbed me, and crushed me in her powerful grip, while faking a wild love scene, I could see that she held a Foodworld bag in her hand. The freezing cold temperature of the bag against my leg, while Patty gyrated around with me, told me that it contained frozen food.

As everyone broke into laughter at Patty's good-natured antics, I thought how, yup, I just knew that bag came from the frozen food section of Foodworld.

Indubitably.

4

The Show

The Majestic Wayne Hotel and Conference Center was indeed a pretty, fancy joint as far as our circle of life went. First off, anything that had a Wayne, New Jersey address; we considered upscale. We passed the facilities often in our cruising here and there, but of course, never ever dreamed that we would someday set foot inside of the place. It was on state highway number twenty-three, which was one of the world's worst roads. They held weddings, conventions, big shindigs, gatherings, and so on, and so forth, but it was not really a place that we ever had a reason to frequent. These types of joints in northern New Jersey usually were run by, how shall, we say, "Organized operations."

The day for the big show arrived, and I met Harry and the Big Spike at 20 John Street, and we set out towards the hotel. Testosterone-induced madness enveloped poor Harry, and he babbled like a lunatic during the entire ride.

Of course, being hopelessly addicted to my ongoing afflictions and ailments, I had called Maureen and let her know about the gig we had landed. She immediately wanted to attend, but she had a conflict with some key customers, who had their hair done regularly by Maureen in the hair salon where she worked. Saturdays were big days for her and between the tips and the dough she made on these days, it was something that she could not miss for attending a dopey and stuffy fashion show. She did seem upset about it at first, but then she felt comfortable. That not only was I earning a lot of money but also, I did have enough honesty to tell her about the event.

"Maybe this means that you are thinking of dating only me and no one else but me, Paulie?" Maureen had asked me.

Oh, oh! I did not answer her, but somehow managed to escape the conversation. I now was treading on dangerous ground for sure.

Mum had made me trim my hair just a little, to even out the longer ends, and I trimmed my beard and facial hair very closely and neatly. Mum checked me out, and she pronounced me good to go. The old man did not say much, just a chuckle or two at the latest wild scheme we had gotten ourselves into this time. He could not laugh too much when he heard how much we were earning, and I think if George had required an older model for one of the suits, the old man might have signed up for the stint himself!

The ride from Haledon to the hotel was only about a half an hour or so. We parked, grabbed our gear, and made our way towards the front door. The place looked as if it resembled a castle from the outside. The architecture was stunning. The front lobby area was just as ornate as the exterior of the facility was. While Harry and I stood next to George and gazed around in awe of the facility, George smiled and waved to a middle-aged woman who was hustling over towards us at a frantic pace and with a harried look upon her face.

"Oh, George. Oh, George! I am so glad you are here," she bellowed as she hustled across the lobby floor.

"Hello, Mabel. We are here. I would like to introduce you to the two young men that I showed you the pictures of and brought with me. This is my brother-in-law, Harry M. Redmond Jr. and the long-haired guy there is his best friend, and our long-time family friend, Mr. Paul John Henson. Men, I would like you to please meet my partner, Miss Mabel Rosenbloom."

George stood there smiling as the woman reached out her hand and shook each of our hands, one at a time.

She spoke in a decidedly Jewish, northern New Jersey accent, "Yeah, yeah, yeah, you two will do rather nicely. Please turn around. Will you both spin please?" I looked at Harry and Harry looked at me while we shrugged our shoulders and both spun around.

I felt like an idiot.

Mabel Rosenbloom reached for a pair of glasses that hung from a chain around her neck, and she placed them over her eyes. She folded her arms across her chest and studied us as we moved slowly in a circle.

"Hold your arms above your heads, please. I need to study your asses."

Oh boy, this was not starting out too swift.

"Nice, nice, you two guys must have the ladies chasing you from Paterson all the way to kingdom come. Big, tall, strong, nice leg and ass muscles. The long-haired one is a unique one . . . he is so tall. He looks rough and tumble with a hippie look, but somehow, he is also athletic looking too. Whoa, all that hair . . . I would like to . . . my, my, my." Mabel then whispered something in Hebrew or Yiddish; I could not quite pick up what she said. Growing up and working with quite a large population of Jewish people, I knew all the keywords, but that one slipped by me.

Mabel Rosenbloom was short, with obviously dyed black hair, with just a touch of gray highlights. Her hairdo was beautiful, in fact, it was impeccable, and not a single hair on her head was out of place. She wore a very nice, low-cut neckline, black dress, which was knee length, and looked as if it cost a fortune. The dress fit her shapely female form tightly and attractively. She wore an expensive pearl necklace around her neck, pearl earrings in her ears and all types of rings that glistened and twinkled on her fingers. I would have guessed Mabel Rosenbloom to be in her early fifties or thereabouts. She was very attractive, and she presented the appearance of being quite the high roller. This might have been a bit of supposition on our part, but her appearance gave you the impression that she was very successful in her business endeavors. George had only introduced her as being his partner, but Mabel seemed as if she was somehow the proprietor of the dress end of the business, or involved somehow in the fashion business. She continued with her somewhat uncomfortable assessment of Harry and me.

"Great build and some gorgeous arm muscles, very nice ass. If I was younger, I would chase ya myself there hippie kid. In fact, after I have a few drinks today, ya better be able to run fast."

I made a mental note of that fact.

Mabel walked over to Harry and pushed him a little while she smiled and said, "This fire hydrant guy here, shit, he is like a rock. Wonderful chest and fantastic-chiseled features. Very, very handsome. I love them both! Nice, good work George, we will sell a fortune today, especially when we combine these more rugged ones along with the fancier looking ones, who are really just, well, you know . . . kinda delicate flowers in a man's disguise." Mabel laughed, as we all smiled, since we got her point. I felt as if Mabel spoke of us, as if we were inanimate objects and not actual human beings. I brushed it off as being just her day-to-day business lingo.

George waved at us to calm down and play it cool, and Harry gave me the famous, secret Harry and Paul hand sign of playing it cool acknowledgement.

"Telephone call for you, Miss Rosenbloom," the hotel desk clerk was frantically waving to obtain her attention.

"Excuse me," she said, while she walked over to the front desk and took the telephone call.

"Man, oh man, she is some good-looking dish for her age. Did youse guys check out that jewelry? It might be worth more than all the houses on John Street put together.

I think ya should ditch the hockey career there twenty-seven and go into this here modeling stuff," Harry said as he nodded his head in admiration. George put his arm around Harry to calm him down before he blew his cork even more. The telephone call was not a pleasant conversation, and we could tell that Mabel was very upset at the nature of the call. She hung up the telephone, thanked the desk clerk, looked back at us, and then she looked at me.

Oh, oh! I did not like that look. Years of studying shooter's eyes in hockey while playing the goaltender position had taught me always to follow a person's eyes. She looked as if she had just had a very determined thought. She came hustling back over, her pearl necklace and ample chest bouncing along.

"How tall are you, hippie Henson?"

"What?"

"Ya friggin' deaf? How tall are you?"

"Well, six feet four, and a little more. I guess that I am almost six five, Miss Rosenbloom." I answered her with a puzzled look on my face. "Why?"

She studied me for a moment. She folded her arms across her chest and paced back and forth while the three of us stood there watching her. Suddenly, she stopped, spun around, and pointed at me.

"I will pay you one hundred dollars on top of what George is already giving you to do a special job for me today."

"He will do it, Miss Rosenbloom!" Harry immediately retorted back.

"Wait, wait, wait! Harry, please. I need to know what this special job is first."

"Are you kidding me, Paul? You are currently rubbing two nickels together in an effort to make them bleed. Look, Miss Rosenbloom, Paul suffers from terrible afflictions known as the Old Lady and Nice Guy Syndromes. I will do the special job for you." Harry smiled at the prospect of doing the special job without even knowing what the job was!

Mabel proclaimed, "You cannot do it. You are not tall enough. I need hippie Henson here. The Big Spike could do it since he is so tall too, but we need George to run the show."

Harry frowned at the loss of the extra dough.

I stepped forward and said, "Miss Rosenbloom, perhaps you could tell me exactly what it is that you would like for me to do?"

"My, my, my, such a well-spoken hunk of a hippie. I will give you fair warning and tell you that you might not want to ask me that same question after I have had a few drinks. Yes, yes, yes, you see that telephone call, was my character actor, and he has come down with some type of illness and cannot make it today. It is a tradition that every year at this show, it is a spring, and Easter show, you know, for us to have an Easter Bunny character present here. The Easter Bunny stands next to the runway, he hands out eggs with prizes hidden inside, he hops around, stupid bullshit, ya get it—he is the damn Easter Bunny! You know, wave to the crowd, get them in the mood, make them relaxed, laugh, and have some fun. They buy more stuff when they are all bombed and when they have fun! Well, the suit only fits Joe Perkins, who is the actor who has done this for years and years. It was made especially for him, and he is around six feet four or five, just like hippie Henson here."

"You want me to dress in an Easter Bunny suit and wave to the crowd, Miss Rosenbloom? No, no, no, I do not think so. Very sorry, but I am a goaltender in ice hockey and if word ever got out. . .."

"I hate this. I had such high hopes for you, and your tight ass and all that hair, uh huh, uh huh, out on that runway selling a ton of stuff for us today! Come on, hippie Henson. I will show you where to get dressed." Miss

Rosenbloom may have been short, but let me tell you that she was strong. She grabbed my arm and pulled me along and through the front lobby while the Big Spike and Harry followed behind me. I could hear them both snickering and laughing.

"No, please Miss Rosenbloom. I have to tell you that I was slightly apprehensive about the whole modeling thing, anyway. I just as soon pass this by. I can wait outside while the show is going on. . .."

"Oh, please, stop the babbling bullshit. Your fire hydrant buddy just told us how you are broke. I am offering you not only a fortune but also beginning in the modeling business. This could be your big break. We may have to cover up some of those scars on your face, from what I now know are hockey injuries, send you to a dentist to straighten some of those choppers that the puck has popped here and there, but overall, you are a Hollywood bound, hunk of meat, hippie Henson. The women will be flipping their wigs over ya. I have to admit, I might take a stab at ya too."

"No, no, no, thank you. That is very kind of you, but I rather just stay in New Jersey, Miss Rosenbloom. I kinda like it here just fine."

She stopped short, leaned over to Harry and the Big Spike, and said just over a whisper, "I see what youse guys mean about the Old Lady Syndrome! Boy oh, boy!"

Harry nodded and said, "I told ya there, Miss Rosenbloom. I am afraid there ain't no cure 'cept his gal has bought this low-cut dress for Easter and her breasts are the size of Texas. That finally got a rise out of old twenty-seven. Say, you are quite the dish, maybe after the show we could. . .."

She shook her head at Harry, and spoke out of the side of her mouth, "Sorry, ya hot stuff, but ya ain't tall enuff. I got my eyes set on the hippie here now. That gal of his better buckle in tight for some serious-ass competition."

"Ah, Miss Rosenbloom, you seem very nice, but I am somewhat committed to Maureen, and we. . .."

"Yeah, yeah, yeah, sure. Committed, huh? Guys who look as you do, hippie Henson, should not commit to anyone. Ya meant to be shared."

Miss Rosenbloom continued to pull me along at a frantic pace, as George and Harry followed, until we reached the side of a grand ballroom. She stopped, opened a door, and with a strong push, she pushed me into a room. Immediately, about forty half-naked women (or half-dressed, depending upon your point of view) looked up at us. The Big Spike and I yelled out in horror. We both turned to sprint out the door, while Harry ducked under and around us, and stood in front of the room.

"Good afternoon, ladies! I love this! Now, this is what I am talking about! Hello, modeling world, I am Harry M. Redmond Jr.!"

"C'mon, move along there, handsome fire hydrant guy! George, hippie Henson, come on, please. We don't have time for you to stand here and drool. Welcome to the fashion and modeling business. These girls do not even see you. They dress and undress so many times in front of people that they are oblivious. I can see how painful this is for hippie Henson though."

George and I were covering our eyes while we pushed the gawking Harry along.

"I am quitting the welding business tomorrow, guys. That's it. All ovah. I am hanging up my torch," Harry said as his head was on a swivel and he scanned the scene.

"Mabel, I am a married man too, you know," the Big Spike protested a bit.

"Sorry, George. I had to bring you this way. It is a shortcut to the men's side. Time is growing very short. We will go around this room when the show starts."

"No, this way is perfectly fine, Miss Rosenbloom," Harry suggested. We all ignored his comments and continued to another room, located off the first one.

"There it is there, hippie Henson. Let's get you into it. Hurry!"

Mabel pointed at a table sitting in the center of the room, which had a brightly colored costume sitting upon it. The four of us looked down at a giant pink Easter Bunny costume. It had a gigantic plastic head, with big floppy ears, a molded pair of eyes, and a stupid grin on its face. The body of the suit had a white belly, blending into pink colors along the belly, and it had "paws." The backside had a little fluffy puffball for a tail on it. There were also props sitting there on the table. A plastic molded carrot, a wicker Easter basket with plastic eggs in different colors, and a sign on a stick that proclaimed, "Happy Easter!" in large, block letters.

"Please, Miss Rosenbloom. You seem as if you are a nice lady, and I do feel sorry for you, but this is just not my style. If this gets out, or someone finds out that I wore this stupid costume, then I will be ruined on the ice."

"Oh stop! Who will ever know? You will have this big plastic head on and no one can even see you. You will get dressed in here and take it off after the show. Look, I can put you in this room over here away from anyone else and no one can ever know, except us that it is you in the costume."

"I dunno know, this is too much to handle. . .."

George and Harry looked at each other and tried not to laugh at my plight.

"Look Paulie, Mabel is right. No one will ever know it is you. You have that giant plastic head thing on. Harry and I will never say a word and think about the extra money."

Harry nodded in agreement, "The Big Spike is right, twenty-seven. Don't worry. Your secret is safe with us guys."

They all looked at me as I stood there. Why did I have to be so tall? Why, why, why?

"I am not doing this!"

"Please, you are my only hope, hippie Henson. You do not want to break a twenty-year-old fashion show tradition. Even the advertisement flyer promotes the appearance of the Easter Bunny. Look, I will add twenty-five more dollars onto the pay and maybe, later on, a few more spiffs." Miss Rosenbloom batted her eyes, tucked at her neckline, adjusted her cleavage to expose a bit of her large chest, and she posed somewhat seductively at me.

Once more, I folded like a cheap tourist camera.

"Oh, all right! I will do it! I swear Harry, between this and moving that stupid sofa, I am not going to forgive you for this one."

Miss Rosenbloom came over and gave me a big hug, pulled me down to her level, and kissed my cheek.

"Thank you, hippie Henson. I think that I am in love. That gal of yours is so lucky. When we are done here, I am going to give her a run for it and wear ya out. But right now, we have work to do. Now, go ahead in this dressing room. Unfortunately, for me, you can leave your pants on, but later on, I will sneak a peek at ya bare ass."

Apparently, Miss Rosenbloom was quite outspoken with her feelings.

"Just strip down to a tee shirt and put the costume on. It is going to be hot inside there. Do you have a hair tie to pull back all of that hair? What a shame to pull back those gorgeous locks, but we have no choice."

I nodded and pulled one out of my pocket as I pulled my mop of hair behind my head.

"I never leave home without 'em," I mumbled while grabbing the costume and dragging it over to the dressing room. The stupid plastic "paws" dragged along the ground behind me. I walked into the dressing room and stood there inside, pondering my fate for a long time. This was, without a doubt, the most embarrassing moment of my entire life. It was even worse than when I had a green bean become stuck in my nose in a restaurant when I was around eight years old.

As I peeled off my shirt and figured out how to climb into this ridiculous costume, I wondered exactly how I did get myself into these horrible situations. No matter how I pointed the question-indexing arrow, it always pointed to one thing, a person named Harry M. Redmond Junior! There was his big, old, mug of a face in front of my eyes and those words, "No one will ever know it is you . . . we promise there, twenty-seven!"

I studied a label inside the costume, which told me who the evil jerks were that would manufacture such a ridiculous thing, and it was then that I noticed that the tag also proudly announced how this torture chamber was "Flame Retardant and Fire Resistant."

"Ha, too bad! That eliminates the possibility of me burning this sucker," I spoke aloud to myself.

I slipped my legs into the bunny suit, wiggled my long legs and feet into the paws, and then stuck my arms and hands into the arms of the bunny. I pulled it up and proceeded to pull the stupid costume up and over my body.

I zipped up the long zipper and stood there in the dressing room in front of a full-length mirror. A giant, ridiculous Easter Bunny, with the head of a long-haired hippie goaltender, looked back at me in the mirror. The costume fit me perfectly. Of course, it did. There was fate once more; dealing me an unusual and devastating blow. Of course, Mr. Joe Perkins and I were exactly the same body type. I made myself a mental note to meet Mr. Joe Perkins someday and punch him in the nose. Mr. Nice Guy or not, there was only so much a fraudulent Easter Bunny could take.

I took a deep breath and put my hand on the doorknob, and spun it. I stepped out and knew what my fate would be. Why not face it after all; it was only a matter of my reputation and my honor.

We fraudulent Easter Bunnies need to stick together you know.

I stood there dripping with embarrassment as Harry, then the Big Spike, took one look at me, and they both lost it. They grabbed each other and roared with laughter. They held onto one another, their chests heaving in grand waves of rollicking laughter. Tears streamed down their faces and poured onto the floor.

"Go ahead, get it out of your systems, youse two guys," I said as I stood there—a dejected, rejected, and shameful example of a beloved holiday symbol. "I am going to kill each of you soon, very soon. It will be a slow and painful death. Sorry, but it will be. God will forgive me. He sees me in this costume too, you know."

Harry could not even speak as his chest heaved in mighty sobs of laughter while the Big Spike held onto Harry's arm and tried to recover.

Even Miss Rosenbloom struggled to hold back some chuckles as she grasped at some vague and phony words of encouragement, "You look cute, hippie Henson. Very cute. I like the tail on your ass. Gives me an excuse to pat your tight ass."

She patted the little, fuzzy tail on my backside while she reached down to pick up the giant plastic head.

"Here, try on your head." She grabbed the giant plastic head and placed it over my own head. That was the turning point, because Harry and the Big Spike could no longer even stand on their feet. Both of them fell on the floor, rolling around, and crying in laughter while they pointed at me. They were practically in need of oxygen because they could not even breathe properly from laughing so hard. It was a crippling blow to my already fragile ego and to make it even worse, I could not see inside the head.

I tried to say, "I cannot see" but the muffled sounds of

my voice sounded to Miss Rosenbloom, Harry and the Big Spike as, "Mmmmmmcccccccc."

"What did you say, hippie Henson?" Miss Rosenbloom asked me.

"Mmmmmmcccccccc."

I realized that no one could understand me and pulled the stupid head off my own head.

"I cannot see a thing! How do you walk around if you cannot see?" Harry and the Big Spike still were rolling around on the floor, their chests heaving in great waves of laughter, so I ignored them.

The Big Spike was now apologizing between heaves of laughter, "I am so sorry, twenty-seven. I am so sorry for laughing at you. I just can't help it."

Miss Rosenbloom grabbed the plastic bunny head and explained, "There are little shutters in here. Ya just pull them down to open them up and you can see. There is also a shutter for your mouth so that you can speak and people can hear you. I have to get out there and start the show. I will coach you on how to be a proper Easter Bunny. Once the show starts, just wander over to the side of the stage and stand there waving." She then reached over to the table and grabbed the sign, plastic carrot, and the Easter basket.

"Here, do not forget your sign, carrot, and basket. I will put notes inside some of the eggs that will announce the prizes, and you can hand them out to lucky winners."

She handed me my sign, carrot, and basket.

Harry and the Big Spike had almost recovered from their initial round of hysteria, they were wiping the tears from their eyes and desperately trying to compose themselves, but when they saw me holding the basket of eggs, my sign and my carrot, it started all over again. They fell on their knees, holding onto each other, roaring with another round of laughter and pointing at me.

I felt total and complete humiliation.

It was utter devastation in the ego department. There I was, all six feet five inches of me, sadly transformed into an Easter Bunny with a basket of plastic eggs, a stupid sign that said, "Happy Easter" and a plastic carrot.

It was unreal.

"C'mon, hippie Henson. Ya had better leave now, so that George and the handsome hunk of man can recover. As long as you are around, they will not stop howling with laughter. You two had better get ready, too. We do not have much time."

I pulled my shutters open, put the head back on, and followed Miss Rosenbloom into the world of Easter and spring fashion show wonder. As I walked through the door into the hallway, I hit my bunny ears on the top of the doorway and almost lost my head. I grabbed it in time, and I thought, wow, this is great, two seconds into the public eye, and I had already almost revealed my secret identity! I needed to do a better job in judging the height of my bunny ears. I left my two friends rolling in laughter and gasping for oxygen. Serves them right if they choke from no air. At least I will survive inside my Easter Bunny costume.

But maybe I would not. It was fifty-two bijillion degrees inside of the head and now, to top it all off, I had to go to the restroom. Oh boy, I had a few too many cups of tea before I left the house today. I did not even want to think about how I would go to the men's restroom with this stupid costume on, but I had to pee before I went out there. Mabel helped me find the shutters, but where the hell was the zipper? There was no way that I would ask Mabel where the zipper was! She would have her hands all over me to "assist."

I think I was better off with the green bean stuck in my nose.

Miss Rosenbloom instructed me on how to stand next to the main stage, wave my stupid sign, and make believe that I was chewing on my plastic carrot. I also had to wave to the models as they flaunted down the runway and I needed to dance around like a happy ding-dong at the sight of them. On and on she went, in the finer points of being an Easter fashion show character bunny. When she finished the coaching lesson, Mabel told me to stand and wait in the doorway here until she gave me a signal to make the grand Easter bunny entrance.

Looking around, I spotted a set of restrooms down the hallway from where I was standing. I thought this might be my only chance to make a dash to the restroom, and to hope and pray that I did not run into someone and reveal my secret identity. With a quick glance up and down the hallway, I saw that it was all clear. While holding my head onto my body to make sure that I did not lose my bunny head, off I went, making a mad dash towards the men's restroom.

I was in luck because it was all clear!

For a very brief, fleeting second, I glanced at the urinals, and quickly determined that the use of them would be one of the most ridiculous scenes in the entire world. Besides, even if I could find a zipper, I could not bend my head over far enough to see down there.

Not wanting to risk exposure (in more ways than one) I quickly slipped into a stall, pulled my head off and tried to set it on the floor of the stall. Geez! The stupid head was so big that it took up all the room in the stall. I opened the door, poked my head outside the stall, and seeing that it was still clear, I set the head on the floor outside the door of the stall. While praying that no one came into the restroom, and saw a giant Easter Bunny head sitting on the floor, I decided that rather than waste more time in finding a zipper, I just removed the costume and made the entire process easier.

Oh no! Geez. . ..

I heard the door to the restroom open, some footsteps, then I heard the voice of a man speak, "I guess even the

Easter Bunny has to do what we all have to do!"

He then burst out in a rollicking round of laughter, and soon, he was laughing so hard that I heard him say, "I can't even pee, I am laughing so hard! I am gonna whiz all over my own leg."

More footsteps. Then the door opened and closed behind him. I thought, perfect, please, go ahead and leave, ya jerk because it serves ya right. I hope you take a leak in your pants.

I cannot even explain the level of stupidity this all measured in my heart, but once the room was clear, I carefully opened the stall door, grabbed my head, dashed out of the room, back up the hallway, and stood once again in the doorway.

The event was close to the kickoff, and I studied the floor of the grand ballroom, and spotted Miss Rosenbloom speaking with some wait staff, while standing next to the main stage. Good, she did not miss me while I dashed off for my restroom break.

People now packed the grand ballroom; tables spread from one end to the other. The tables were set with elegant tablecloths, full candelabras with lit candles, and flower bouquets in golden vases sat upon each table. The room had cocktail bars and food tables set up in the four corners of the room, and the drink and food stations all had wait staff standing at them, all of whom were dressed in impeccable black suits. The fashion show, runway and stage sprawled along the front of the grand ballroom. The runway for the models to walk upon extended just past halfway out into the middle of the ballroom dining area. Fantastic chandelier lights glowed overhead, casting an exotic and captivating glow upon the room. Music thumped quietly in the background. A disc jockey sat in a station next to the stage, and he worked a bank of record players and audio equipment. I stared at the disc jockey and recognized that it was the world famous, or at least famous in northern New Jersey circles, Disco Dan!

Oh no! I needed to be very careful. Disco Dan knew both Harry and I quite well, from his stints at playing music, and providing entertainment at the very popular Friday and Saturday night stints at the public ice-and-roller-skating sessions at the local rinks. Oh geez, just my luck that out of all the disc jockeys in New Jersey, Miss Rosenbloom had to have hired Disco Dan! He was the resident celebrity disc jockey at nearly all the ice and roller rinks and other venues in New Jersey. He was in our circles, about as famous a celebrity as we ever got close enough to in order to say that we actually knew him.

Disco Dan had a thick, black beard, with black hair teased up in a wild-style that went almost to the ceiling, and he wore thick, soda bottle glasses with huge lenses that covered most of his face. His glasses were typical for the era, in addition to the large lenses; the glasses also had those 1970s-style heavy black frames. He was, however, a fantastic disc jockey, with great musical knowledge, and a loud, booming, frantic voice. He was a master showman and I am sure he would put on a great show here this afternoon. My only fear would be that he recognized Harry and somehow connected the dots, since we were very seldom apart. In my heart, I knew that a more likely scenario would be that Harry opens his big mouth and spills the inside scoop, but he promised to keep this under wraps.

A cold shudder went up and down my spine at the mere thought of the leakage of my secret identity. What would Maureen think? Then there was Glenda Flabbergaster, who I was not high on her popular list anyway. She would flap her jaws and tell everyone at the next hockey game! That could ruin me forever if she wanted revenge for the van incident. The guys in the hockey circles, the opposing teams would tee off on me as they shot head shots to try to take out the nice, little Easter Bunny.

My heart sunk. The things young men do in pursuit of the young ladies!

It was horrifying.

I stood in the doorway, waiting for the signal from Miss Rosenbloom. While I stood there, sweating my brains out inside the plastic bunny head, I scanned the growing audience. Young women dressed to kill; older gals dressed in somewhat dated fashions but still decked out in what they felt would rock their particular worlds. Bored looking husbands, brothers, or boyfriends accompanied some women, but it was difficult to tell what the various relationships were. All I knew was that most of the men, unless they were checking out the ladies, looked bored stiff. I surmised that once the women modeling the attire paraded out on the stage and runway, their collective moods would brighten up significantly.

They all stood there sipping cocktails, downing glass upon glass of as Harry called it, champagknee-a-roo-ski. All of them living the high life, and here I was, sweating worse than I had ever sweated in any hockey game that I had ever played in. All of this nonsense, just in order to earn enough dough to fix an old relic of a van, to take a young woman out on a date. The heat inside this bunny suit made my goaltender equipment seem colder than a well digger's ass in January. I was lost in the thoughts of my misery when I realized that Miss Rosenbloom was frantically waving at me to enter the ballroom!

Oh, oh, I was blowing the grand entrance! Disco Dan had announced my arrival to the crowd of pompous, rich folks, and I was daydreaming and blowing it. I moved reluctantly into Easter Bunny mode and walked into the grand ballroom amidst cheers and loud jeers.

Miss Rosenbloom was now running over to me and shouting, "No, no, no! Ya gotta hop, hippie Henson! You are a bunny, you're supposed to hop, not walk!"

A newspaper reporter and his photographer rushed

over to me and snapped a bunch of pictures.

"Say something to the loyal readers of the Paterson Evening News, Mr. Easter Bunny!" The reporter bellowed to me as he held his pad and paper and the flashbulbs went off.

I pulled the shutter open for my mouth and said, "Happy Easter!"

"That's all ya got, bunny?"

"That's all I got, ya ding-dong. How about this? Get lost and up your ass, pal," I said.

No more, Mr. Nice Guy.

"Geez, I can't print that! Ya a testy bunny."

"Hop along, hippie Henson! Hop!" Miss Rosenbloom screamed out.

Oh, for the love of Pete! This is too much! I gave a few half-hearted hops, which caused my head to wobble on my head, so I reverted to a skip or two, and the already half in the bag majority of the crowd broke into loud roars of laughter. I was a laughingstock fool. I gave up on the skipping and instead reverted to waving the stupid sign and a little fake chomping on my plastic carrot. In some strange way that actually seemed more reasonable than the hopping thingy.

Disco Dan was blasting the song, *Here Comes the Easter Bunny*, and he started screaming into the microphone, "Here he is! The star of the show, and folks, those plastic eggs that he is carrying, all have raffle prizes inside of them. If you are nice to the Easter Bunny, then he may toss an egg your way!"

I will give them nice. If I only had my goalie stick, I would wrap it around a few heads here and there, and cram the plastic eggs down their throats and stick them up their asses.

I made my way to my post next to the stage, and waved and carefully, hopped occasionally along the way. Folks cheered, some clapped, and a half in the bag woman ran over to me and hugged me.

With my one free paw, I held my head securely, so that I did not risk losing it while she assaulted me and screamed, "I LOVE THE EASTER BUNNY!"

Quickly opening my mouth shutter, I told her as she in jest, rubbed her huge breasts on my pink belly, "Well, honey, the feeling is not mutual."

She stepped back and waved her hand at me while saying, "You are no fun! Geez, I just wanted to rub my big juggies on ya."

"Yeah, well, you ought to treat the Easter Bunny with more respect. Go rub your chest on someone else. Besides, you are not going to love that hangover tomorrow!"

A team of security officers that lined the runway for protection of the models moved over to assist me. They led the drunken, juggie-rubbing woman away, and continued to escort "the star of the show" to my post. There I stood, hopping, jumping, and waving in place, just as Miss Rosenbloom asked me to do.

"Nice work, hippie Henson, you did great! The crowd loved you. Even the juggie-rubbing-drunken fool. Now give me your basket and I will load the eggs with the prize notes. At various breaks in the show, you need to signal Disco Dan, and he will announce you to make an egg drop to someone in the crowd," Miss Rosenbloom had met me next to the stage, and she explained more duties to me.

"An egg drop?" I asked.

"Yeah, yeah, yeah, ya have to go out in the crowd, work it up with some fun, and pick out someone to award an egg to. Geez, hippie Henson, you are the damn Easter Bunny! You are a smart guy . . . work it out!"

She patted my tail, and then squeezed me on the backside, tore my basket out of my hands, and she quickly ran off with my basket. She soon returned and handed me the basket, and then she hustled off to some other task. Miss Rosenbloom was a tad uptight now that the show had begun. I imagined that the pressure was on now and money was at stake.

The lights dimmed and Disco Dan took over, "Welcome to the twentieth annual Rosenbloom and Bickerson Easter and Spring Fashion Show! Here we are, displaying all the latest in fantastic new fashions for the men and women in your life. All of them, modeled by the most beautiful woman and handsome men in all of New Jersey! Let the show begin!"

Therefore, it did. After an appearance on stage from Miss Rosenbloom and the Big Spike explaining the fashions, the names of their companies, where you could obtain the attire, and so on and so forth, the show began. I wondered where Harry was hanging out, but then again, I had a vision of something that I did not want to surmise or dwell upon for very long.

A beautiful woman waltzed out onto the stage as Disco Dan babbled from a script that described the dress and attire the young woman was wearing. The model paraded across the stage and then down the runway to the oohs and ahs of the crowd. Soft background music would change to thumping and wild music if the dress was a bit racier, then Disco Dan would tone it down for the classic evening gowns or more subdued styles. They had created a well thought out and superbly orchestrated atmosphere for selling their products.

"Miss Poppy Hornblower is wearing a spring patterned mini-dress with spaghetti straps. . .."

Oh, oh, Miss Hornblower was going to lose that one if she was not careful. I hope Harry was not any place close by!

I grew a bit bored standing there sweating my brains out, when Disco Dan suddenly changed the music up, and a new tune blasted out of the loudspeakers. Hmm . . . that song sounded a bit familiar to me, but even my usually sharp musical knowledge brain could not place the song right away.

I stood there pondering when it hit me!

That is the horrible Zippy Starlight and the Starlighters! What was that tune now, 'Off to the Moon' or something like that?

"And now, wearing the latest spring fashion in the twenty something age group, and walking to her favorite song, it is New Jersey's most famous fashion model, the lovely and gorgeous, Miss Glenda Flabbergaster!"

I almost lost my bunny head because I whirled around so fast. It bounced and tumbled along my neck and only a quick effort on my part saved it!

MISS GLENDA FLABBERGASTER! OH NO! I AM RUINED!

This is unreal. No wonder she was such a stuck-up gal! She *is* a professional model. Harry was correct when he told me that, and for once, he was not just blowing off drivel with his usual exaggerations. The crowd was going crazy, and the men in the audience were drooling right and left. She did indeed look gorgeous wearing some pink-colored, sleeveless party dress, dancing and prancing along the runway, her long, red hair blowing alluringly from the fans set up next to the runway and her backside wiggling all around. Photographers scrambled and jumped over each other as they crammed the sides of the runway, snapping their shutters endlessly, in an effort to capture the moment and beauty of Miss Flabbergaster.

I just could not believe the cruel blow that fate had somehow delivered upon me today. If she spots Harry, then it will be downhill from there. My only hope was that the ever alert and vigilant Harry M. Redmond Jr. would blow so much smoke that Glenda would never suspect who was hiding in this stupid costume. I sat on the edge of the stage; thankfully, all eyes were now on Glenda, not on some stupid jerk dressed up as the Easter Bunny.

Oh well, she turned out to be a prude, anyway. A

fantastically, gorgeous, stuck-up prude! I just kept telling myself how much of a pretentious chick she was, but my goodness, that was some dress.

On and on it went, until suddenly the lights went up, and the crowd grew silent. Miss Rosenbloom appeared on stage. Mabel explained that it was now time for a change of clothes, some scenery changes, and that the next phase of the show would begin shortly. She motioned to me for me to entertain the crowd during the interlude, so I turned and gave Disco Dan a hand signal and held up my basket.

Disco Dan nodded at me and bellowed into the microphone, "While we adjust the stage and the models change into the next round of attire, it is time for the Easter Bunny to make his rounds. Some lucky people are going to win all types of prizes. The magical bunny has prizes hidden within his eggs. Let's see . . . we have free tickets to the premiere of 'Cruisin' starring Crystal Zirconium, we have passes for free massages at Sexy Marlene's massage parlor. There are many coupons for free dinners and drinks at Kyle's Greasy Spoon, and fifty-dollar discount coupons for the You Stab 'em and We Slab 'em Funeral Parlor on the north end of the city of Paterson. There are discount coupons for Dingleberry Mint Ice Cream, courtesy of Big Bob's Food Empire. We have a grand prize ticket for a round-trip, all expenses paid, family vacation for four, to Newington, Connecticut and many more prizes."

I waded into the audience of drunks and whackos in attendance when one drunk guy pulled my fluffy tail.

"Nice bunny tail! I bet you're a cutie inside, with a nice tail too!"

I leaned over, opened my mouth shutter, held my head and whispered to him, "Bug off ya jerk. I am a man, six foot five, about one hundred and ninety pounds, trapped inside this stupid suit, and when this is over, I am going to find you, seek you out, and knock your teeth clean down your throat. You will need to eat ice cream for six months!"

He leaned back and nodded his head fervently to show that he understood.

"Don't mess with the Easter Bunny, cuz he ain't happy today!" I warned him as I slid the shutter closed.

I was not in a benevolent bunny mood. No more, Mr. Nice Guy. I tossed a few eggs here and there, skipped and hopped along. Posed for a few pictures with people, and on my way back to my post, I picked the drunken tail-pulling guy off with an Easter egg that I threw. Nailed him right in the head!

The crowd went nuts, they loved it, and one of the security officers leaned over and said, "Nice shot, Easter Bunny. He deserved it. Hope it was the egg with the coupon for the funeral parlor inside of it."

Soon, I was back at my post. The stage was set, the lights dimmed and the music started. I recognized the movie theme music of the famous British secret agent, Ian Leadfoot, playing loud and hard over the speakers.

"Now, modeling the famous black suit worn by Ian Leadfoot himself, and accompanied by the lovely, Miss Glenda Flabbergaster, is the world-famous hockey player, welder, sports car driver, womanizer, and part-time secret agent, Mr. Harry M. Redmond Junior! Yes, youse guys can look like Ian does too this year! Just check out how great Harry looks!"

I jumped off my seat and shook my head (carefully) while I watched Harry appear with Glenda wrapped around his arm. World famous hockey player, sports car driver, and part-time secret agent! Where did that bullshit come from? A part-time secret agent! Oh brother! So much for him not running into Glenda!

He was hamming it up big time, snapping his fingers to the music, stepping and dancing around in time to the beats and blowing kisses to the crowd. The women were going wild, and for good reason, because Harry looked better than Ian did! The suit fit him perfectly. He had a dark pair of shades on, his hair was perfect, and he was a superstar on stage! The women rushed the stage, and some fainted at the sight of him. The women who remained upright had to have security hold them back, as they yelled and threw pieces of papers with their telephone numbers written on them at Harry's feet.

This adventure was one for the ages; even in our wild adventures, this one was a little rough to take. The money was just not worth it. I would take Maureen to Easter sunrise service on a Pogo stick. Here I am, sweating to death in an Easter Bunny costume, Harry is showering in an avalanche of papers scrawled with single (and maybe not so single) women's telephone numbers, and he is working the crowd like a fine violin! Harry reached down, scooped up all the papers, and stuffed them in his suit pocket. He gave a little whirl, twirl, and bow, right before he entered the stage left door. He suddenly reappeared, and he now held a bouquet of flowers. As he stood there, working the women into a mad frenzy, he was tossing the flowers individually to his adoring fans.

An obviously drunk young woman, who had stars in her eyes, and was hell-bent on grabbing a piece of Harry, ran across the ballroom floor in the direction of the flower-tossing hockey player, part-time secret agent and whatever the rest of his titles might have been.

This chick, who obviously had enough alcohol in her veins to start her own distillery, rushed the stage screaming, "Oh baby, where have you been all my life!"

She eluded the security patrol and tossed a paper, which must have had her telephone number written on it up to Harry. She then wobbled a bit, pulled her dress neckline down; exposed and flashed her bare chest, and then she reached up her dress, pulled off a garter belt, and tossed that up there too!

Harry deftly caught it! Then she reached inside of her dress, somehow as if she was a magician, removed her brassiere and tossed that up to Harry too. Harry eluded that garment, but he was now soaking it all up and his head was the size of Manhattan Island. He loved it all. The star of the show once more!

Then disaster struck!

While security closed in on her, the drunken gal shifted into super lust mode, and she attempted to climb up onto the stage. When she did, she pushed off on a table right next to the stage and the candelabra sitting on the table, which had multiple lit candles nestled in it, shook and tumbled over onto the tablecloth. The table went over, the people sitting at the table toppled over too, and the lit candles flew out of the candelabras and they landed on the edge of the cloth dressing on the stage. The flames from the candles and the spilled wax ignited the cloth, and it was suddenly on fire!

"FIRE! FIRE! FIRE!" Someone screamed, and people scrambled over one another.

The security patrol stood there frozen. They turned out to be a bunch of bums, so I quickly dismissed them as useless.

I looked around and then shouted, "Hey! Quick! Grab the fire extinguisher, over on the wall there!"

Since I had forgotten to open my mouth shutter, all that came out of my head was a very loud and inaudible, "HEYYY QUGRRBBBBBTHHHEFFFFIREEEXXXTING!"

No one reacted or understood what I was saying. Bedlam was breaking out in every direction, and the flames rose higher and higher along the edge of the stage! I reached up and tore the stupid bunny head off, chucked my head, sign, carrot, and basket, and dashed to the wall. I grabbed the portable fire extinguisher and ran towards the fire. Out of the corner of my eye, I spotted Harry leap off the stage and run over to the table. I ran up to the fire, pulled the pin, aimed, and blasted the fire with the extinguisher and put the fire out.

I turned and saw a young woman screaming, because she landed on the floor in the melee with the tablecloth now tangled at her feet, and the flames from some of the fallen candles rising all around her. She was panicking. The hot wax must have spilled on her, and she had a tablecloth tangled in her that had flames licking the edges of her legs.

"Twenty-seven! That chick is sitting in the fire!" Harry was busy picking up stunned persons who had tumbled over when the table tipped, and Harry pointed and yelled at me as he now ran in her direction. I grabbed her, pulled her by her arms, away from the table and the hot wax, while I yelled, "Stay calm, stay here!"

I pulled the edge of her dress out from under the lit tablecloth while Harry grabbed a vase of flowers, chucked the flowers out, and dumped the water on the cloth and the edge of her dress. Recalling the tag inside of my costume that told me that the Easter Bunny was now, "Flame Retardant and Fire Resistant," I knelt down and patted the edges of her dress and the tablecloth with my paws. Then I smothered the fire with my costume by plopping down on the entire smoking mess to make sure that I cut off the air supply to the fire. I stood back up and carefully checked to make sure that the fire was out. The flames were out and the young woman collapsed in my costumed arms.

I checked her legs for burns and miraculously, since her dress was long and flowing, the fire stayed far enough away from her skin so as not to cause any burns. Her legs were red, she had some scrapes and cuts and she was terribly frightened, but overall, she seemed to be in good condition.

"I think you are okay! Are you okay?" I asked.

The young lady looked down and checked her legs while she nodded her head to show that she was all right.

She turned to me, held me around the neck, and said, "Oh thank you, Easter Bunny guy! Thank you, part-time secret agent guy! You are my heroes!" She repeatedly kissed my cheek and then she gave me a big kiss on my lips. She held onto my costume with tears running down her cheeks. "I never knew the Easter Bunny was so good lookin'!" She was spouting off repeatedly.

People rushed in every direction and gathered around us. The fire was not that bad. In the big picture, it could have been much worse! Disco Dan bellowed out over the microphone that the fire was out and for everyone to remain calm. I could hear the fire horns sounding in the building and the strobes for the fire alarms were flashing. The grand ballroom suddenly filled with firefighters, fully equipped for fire duty and a team of medical personnel who were running in all directions to check on the situation.

"You okay, twenty-seven, or uh, uh, Easter Bunny guy?" Harry asked as he knelt down next to us and he patted my back. His sense of humor was intact.

"Yeah, yeah, yeah, I am fine, Ian Leadfoot. It was no big deal. It was just that no one was doing anything, thirty-five. They just all stood there like dopes!"

I stood up, held my paws out as Harry helped me in pulling the young woman to her feet. Teams of medical persons appeared, and they quickly led the young woman aside to check on her, as well as the other persons who had tumbled on the floor in the table-tipping incident.

I reached behind my head, tore out the hair tie, and shook my sweaty head. It felt so good to get out of that stupid inferno of a plastic head. Before I could even say anything, the newspaper reporter and his photographer rushed over, and snapped a picture of Harry and me standing there. Me in my remnants of an Easter Bunny suit, and Harry in his fancy Ian Leadfoot look-a-like suit.

"I have the headlines now! Hero Easter Bunny and part-time secret agent pal save the day!" He yelled out while feverishly fishing for a tape recorder in his bag. His photographer snapped one picture after another.

"What is your name there, pal? You are a hero!" He stuck a microphone in my face while two firefighters in full turnout gear arrived next to us.

This was my worst nightmare. My secret bunny identity was revealed to the entire world.

"No, no, I would rather not be in any newspapers. I am not a hero. Where is my bunny head?"

One of the firefighters came over and grabbed my paw.

"Are you the Easter Bunny and is this the part-time secret agent guy who put out the fire?"

This was incredible.

I looked around and since I did not see any other bunnies or any other persons dressed in a secret agent suit, I mumbled, "Yes, actually, I do not think there are any other Easter Bunnies. . .."

"Well, youse guys did a fantastic job. Quick work saved lives here today. Great work bunny! We are going to give youse guys a certificate and a badge for heroism and for honorary firefighting."

I shook my head while saying, "No, no, no. Thank you, you are very kind, but I would rather not have any badges or any certificates. This really was no big deal. I think everyone is being a tad bit, too dramatic here. You see, what really happened, was that the security. . .."

Flash bulbs went off right and left and the firefighters all stood next to me with big smiles on their faces as they shook my paws and posed with me. I officially gave up. I was too long-winded and besides, it was useless to try to stop this madness. I turned around to see Harry giving an interview to a team of reporters.

The big oaf was spewing drivel, and the reporters were busily jotting notes down on their pads, "Yeah, yeah, yeah, I play hockey and dabble part-time as a secret agent here and there. I also deliver sofas part time too. For obvious reasons, I cannot reveal the secret agencies, which I work for, but I will tell ya, my pal ovah there, ya know, the guy in the bunny suit, well he is one of the best. . ..."

Harry pointed towards me. Then he was posing for pictures, while he occasionally paused to sign some autographs.

Doom, doom, doom, and one more for good measure . . . doom.

Miss Rosenbloom and the Big Spike arrived on scene, congratulated, and thanked me, and then they thanked Harry for our quick action.

Miss Rosenbloom walked back over to me. She motioned for me to lean over and, to my sheer surprise, she grabbed my face and proceeded to plant a big, sloppy kiss on my lips!

"You are beyond awesome, hippie Henson."

I offered up some logistical advice, "I think you should have flame resistant and fire-retardant tablecloths next year, Miss Rosenbloom."

She screwed her mouth up at me as if she was not expecting technical advice, but she moved on rather quickly in conversation, "Yes, whatever. I will check into that bullshit. Anyway, the technical stuff is kinda sexy too. How I wish you were Jewish. I swear, I would find a rabbi and marry ya right now! Even with this interruption, sales are going through the roof! People loved the show and the fire only excited the drunken whackos even more. When the Easter Bunny and a part-time secret agent magically appeared in order to put the fire out, they went even crazier! They all think that youse guys are actors and that it was part of the entertainment. I think that for next year, we will have to work some type of other adventure into the program to get them all riled up like this."

Miss Rosenbloom turned around and waved to the crowd as she excitedly told us, "I must say that this has been the most exciting fashion show that I have ever conducted. Thank you, hippie Henson, for such bravery. I would dare say that you have made the real Easter Bunny proud!"

George walked over and patted me on the back, "Great work, twenty-seven."

"Stay right here, hippie Henson, now that the fire is out and the second part of the show is about to resume, and my duties are almost ovah, I am going to load up on martinis and chase your tail all the way back to the dressing room. Ya got me all kinda worked up now," Miss Rosenbloom told me, as she hustled off in the direction of one of the numerous bars. I watched as she disappeared into the crowd. She was a good kisser, very pretty, and she was very nice, however. . ..

I collapsed into a chair. What a disaster, yet despite the craziness of the entire incident, as I sat there, my long mop of sweat-soaked hair dangling down over my face and shoulders, I could not help but think, how in a strange way, this one was certainly going to be one for the books. I swear someday, I will write all of these Harry and Paul adventures down and very few people will ever believe what happened to us.

I might as well accept my fate. I did not think the Easter Bunny actually existed, but after today, who was I to doubt.

"Hi ya, Paulie. Wow, nice gig. You are a hero."

I looked up to see Glenda Flabbergaster looking at me and felt my heart sink deeply in my chest.

Glenda fluffed her long, red hair and smiled at me as she said, "Say, Paulie, I now realize that you really are quite the guy and despite Harry receiving all the attention from the ladies, well, I know who the best guy in this place really is! Paulie, I am very sorry and I want to explain about that night, when I acted so poorly. . .."

The show did go back on. Miss Rosenbloom, not wanting to risk another breakout of drunken, lust-driven women, asked Harry to refrain from another appearance. I dressed in my civilian clothes, and since the Easter Bunny was now anti-climactic, Mabel told me that I could hide in the back of the house, until the show finally ended and she would come looking for me. The Easter Bunny happily packed it in for today.

To say the least, it was quite the day.

Glenda apologized profusely to me for her previous behavior, and she even hinted around at a repeat date. When I resisted, she just outright asked me to take her out for a date. I told her that I would think about it, but I had no actual intention of calling her. To me, once Glenda showed me her true colors, then I felt it best if she saved her acting for the modeling gigs.

As the old man often told me, "All the actors ain't in Hollywood."

I preferred a real woman, and it was now very clear to me who that was. She was just as beautiful, did not put on fake and phony acts, and she had bought this spring dress with a very low-cut neckline.

Harry now required a file cabinet to keep in his basement for all the telephone numbers he had to index and categorize. I somehow escaped the end of the show with just a grab or two on my backside and another kiss or two from a tipsy and very tuned up Miss Mabel Rosenbloom. Most importantly, I earned the money that I required for the van repairs and new tires, and had a good bit of extra dough left over too. I put the extra dough in a savings account and I might just try to work out a deal with Vince for that jeep someday.

Despite the madness of the adventure, and a hit or two on my ego, it all turned out rather well.

However, I did have to admit that I came away from the entire incident with a very strong, lifelong dislike for the poor Easter Bunny.

5

Unwanted Fame and a Little Fortune

The next day, the headline emblazoned across the front page of the *Paterson Evening News* was certainly something I could have done without in my life.

"HERO EASTER BUNNY AND PART-TIME SECRET AGENT PAL SAVE THE DAY!"

The newspaper also had about ten pictures of Harry and me and various firefighters, police officers, and other people in the pictures. Despite my protests, Mum went down to the corner candy store and bought about ten copies of the newspaper for her scrapbook. The old man roared with laughter until he had tears streaming down his cheeks. My dear Mum kissed my cheek and told me how proud she was of me, and the telephone rang off the hook. Friends, relatives, people that I had not spoken to in years called. Maureen called and told me how proud she was of me and how she just knew that I would not flaunt myself in front of other women while becoming "involved" with her. She was very happy that all I did at the event was to hide inside the Easter Bunny costume until the time was right for me to make an "appearance."

I did not say a word, (other than twenty-two thousand and one, "Uh huhs") or even mention how the entire Easter Bunny thing came about.

It just was not worth it.

My hockey career suffered a few insults here and there. I could have done without my teammates on a team that I had joined up with for a short time, warming up in the pregame skate with bunny ears on. The bunny comments and jokes did wear a little thin, and it was hard to project a tough guy, goalie image, when you led a dual life and moonlighted as the Easter Bunny. The Nit-Nat kids dressed like little Easter Bunnies and part-time secret agents, and ran around the neighborhood while play-acting, making fun of us or honoring us. However, you wanted to look at it!

Harry was in his glory and relished every minute of it. He signed autographs in the neighborhood and called Miss Rosenbloom to ask her for a date and a full-time modeling job.

She turned him down on both of his offers.

Miss Rosenbloom did call me up and thank me once more while offering me a job next year to return as the Easter Bunny. She said that I was easily the best Easter Bunny ever, and she would find something else for Mr. Perkins to do.

I politely turned her down.

She then asked me out for a date "ovah" to her apartment for a candlelight dinner and as she said, "A little adventure later on."

Once more, I politely turned her down.

I thought the age difference between Maureen and me was a problem!

These women, these days, are so aggressive.

The old man bought the water pump and a few other parts for the van. We repaired the van, and it was back on the road with a new set of tires, purchased at a lower price than I expected with a very good deal from Vince Barroni. It was a big thrill when I walked away with the additional extra cash still stuck in my pocket. Let me tell you, the extra cash softened some of the blow of the trauma of the now famous "Easter Bunny" incident.

"Say Mum, do you think I should bring something to Easter dinner at the Zipperellis?" I asked my dear Mum one night during Holy Week as we were clearing the dinner table. Mum wiped her hands on her apron and looked at me. She seemed to be pondering the question a bit.

"Why, I would think bouquets of flowers would be nice to give to Maureen, her grandmother, and her mother. Yes, perhaps three bouquets, and maybe some type of dessert. I think a dessert and flowers would be nice. One of those Tiramisu cakes, yes, a chocolate one. I saw them in the dessert aisle at the Foodworld this week. They are in the exotic food section."

I smiled at Mum; she always gave me good advice.

"I will give you some flowers too, Mum."

Mum smiled back at me and insisted upon a hug or a kiss from her, as she still called me, "Her Easter Bunny hero son."

Right before we went to Tenebrae service on Good Friday, I picked up the bouquets of flowers and the cake, and while wandering around the aisles of the store, I had some inspiration of my own and picked up a pack of frozen meatballs. Once I checked the frozen food aisle to make sure that Maureen was not there, and the coast was clear, I picked out a large pack of meatballs. I figured that it was a good idea. The pack proudly proclaimed that they were Italian-style meatballs. Sure, why not? I liked them and after all, they all are Italian!

When I returned home, I gave Mum her flowers, suffered through another round of the hero stuff, and put the food in our refrigerator and freezer. Mum loaned me a foam cooler to use, and she explained that it was in order to transport them over to Maureen's house on Easter and keep everything fresh, cold and frozen. Mum looked at me a bit weird when I mentioned the frozen meatballs, but she did not comment. I tucked the cooler away in the corner of my bedroom until Easter. It was the same cooler we used once a year when we made a Henson family trip to Brady

Beach on the Jersey shoreline.

Easter Sunday finally arrived, and I proudly picked up Maureen Zipperelli at her house in my now-repaired van, and drove her to sunrise services on Garret Mountain. She looked captivating in her dress; let me tell you that it was hard to focus on such a holy day when you have such a gorgeous woman on your arm. I was the envy of all the men attending services. And finally, Maureen covered her amazing chest area with a sweater to take the pressure off! Sorry but, Miss Glenda Flabbergaster, eat your heart out!

Harry attended too, with the rest of the Redmond gang, and he had the gorgeous and lovely Joyce Dilber on his arm. Somehow, he always returned to Joyce Dilber these days.

That is, of course, a whole other story.

When the service was ending, just before he gave the final blessing, Father Mark mentioned all we had to be thankful for on such a holy day. He rambled on and on, while telling all of us, of the hope and promise of eternal life, the love of Jesus, and families gathered at Easter time, and heroes dressed as Easter Bunnies, and part-time secret agents, who rise out of crowds to save lives!

Oh, geez.

I could see Harry bowing to the attendees and signing more autographs on the back covers of the worship service programs.

Maureen reached over and squeezed my arm, and she kissed my cheek while telling me, "That she loved me to the moon and back."

After church, when we returned to the Zipperelli's house, I carefully carried my foam cooler with the flowers, the meatballs and the Tiramisu cake into the home. While Maureen ran ahead of me to greet what seemed as if it was a million family members, who all shouted loudly at one another in Italian and waved their hands and arms in the air, I looked around and set my stupid foam cooler down in the vestibule of the home.

As the family greetings went on and the loud and excited Italian language reverberated the walls of the home, I wandered into a living room, which had perfectly groomed green carpet vacuumed in a neat pattern, and had all the furniture covered in clear plastic. Matching green drapery, decorated with bright gold tassels and tiebacks, hung from a picture window in the center of the room. I noticed a ceramic statue of the Virgin Mary that stood on a fantastic, carved, and ornate table in the center of the room, in front of a large picture window. Numerous Rosary Beads and crucifixes on chains lay on the table, and the table had an expensive looking ivory crucifix on the opposite end of the table.

I took a few steps into the room when I heard Maureen shout to me, "NO PAULIE! Don't step on the carpet in the parlor. You will put tracks on the carpet!"

I nearly jumped out of my skin, slowly backed up, and when I realized that my footsteps had left imprints, I bent down and carefully ruffled the pile of the carpet with my hands to eliminate any evidence of my mistaken and errant encroachment.

Maureen grabbed me by the hand and she explained, "That room is only for funerals or when Father Mark comes over. Be careful. Stick by me. Now, come along. I want you to greet everyone and meet my extended family. Just smile, most of them do not speak any English. It is a good thing that you will not understand, my Aunt Sophia. I say that, because she already has had too much wine, she already spotted you, checked out your backside and commented on what she wanted to do with you."

Stunned at my terrible trampling of Italian traditions, I picked my stupid foam cooler up, while mumbling how sorry I was for stepping into the forbidden land of preserved furniture, religious icons and impeccably groomed carpet. I followed Maureen into the maze of garlic-exhaling relatives, as the hints of garlic and red wine wafted throughout the home. I carefully scanned the crowd for aunt whatever her name was, but it was hard to pick her out.

Maureen smiled widely while the family gathered around to meet me. Of course, I knew some of the family already, Mrs. Zipperelli, Mr. Zipperelli and some of Maureen's cousins and her brother, but the rest of the family seemed as if they just flew in from Rome. On a red eye flight.

There were hundreds and hundreds of them, short Italian guys, pretty gals, tall guys, older family members and young ones. All the men had large crucifixes around their necks and gold chains. Maureen had a very large family and, to be honest, they all looked about the same.

To make matters worse, they all gathered around me and stared at me.

A new boyfriend, a Lutheran of English and Welsh heritage . . . fish out of water Henson; you are a fish out of water. While they stared me down, the crowd parted wide open, and she appeared, sitting upon a golden throne at the head of a table that could seat twenty-seven thousand people.

They no longer mattered.

No one else on the entire face of the Earth mattered. We pronounced by a trumpet blowing proclamation that all other human beings now were useless and inconsequential. I swear there was a trumpet blowing loudly somewhere in the house. . ..

"Come along, Paulie. It is time for you to meet, Nonna. My beloved grandmother," Maureen said with a smile. "Don't be nervous. She will love you!"

Nonna! It was time for me to meet Nonna!

With a lump in my throat, and Maureen looping her arm through mine, we gathered ourselves to meet the most important person on the entire face of the Earth. I still carried my stupid foam cooler as an offering to Nonna, as we silently and reverently approached the shining throne.

"Nonna, this is my boyfriend, Paul John Henson. Paulie, this is my grandmother. Nonna," Maureen introduced me to the family matriarch. The grand Pooh-Bah herself, Nonna. Nonna was a short, very pretty, yet quite elderly woman, who was wearing the brightest and most loud, flower-printed dress that I had ever seen. She had a huge chest and a gold crucifix hanging on a gold chain hovered above her enormous bosom, with her hair neatly prepared in a fresh hairdo. I quickly determined from where Maureen inherited her chest genes. In observing Nonna, it could have been my imagination, but I couldn't help but notice that her white hair had many silver and blue highlights. Highlights, which reflected and captured the glow from the golden halo of light surrounding her.

Maureen leaned over and whispered to me, "Nonna does not speak English. Just smile, I can tell that she thinks you are sexy, have huge-sized male equipment, and have a nice ass."

That was indeed a comforting thought.

I set my foam cooler on the floor, smiled, reached out my hand and gently grasped hers while she smiled at me. I did not know if I should bow as if I was greeting the Queen of England, but I thought I was doing well, or at least, I thought I was doing well. I then remembered my stupid foam cooler. The entire family, led by Mrs. Zipperelli, Mr. Zipperelli, and the rest of the entire population of Rome and Vatican City, surrounded me to watch the introduction.

I excused myself, went over, and opened the lid. I reached in and pulled out the flowers, which I gave one bouquet to Maureen, another one to Mrs. Zipperelli and the remaining (and the largest) one to Nonna.

The flowers were a huge hit! Thanks, dear Mum!

Maureen squealed in delight, and she showered me with

kisses. Mrs. Zipperelli and Nonna smiled and blabbed loudly in Italian. Their hands waved in the air wildly and Nonna pointed at the lower extremities of my body, then at my hair and beard, and she winked at me! Then, Nonna, babbled in frenzied Italian. She winked at Maureen, who turned a little red and she answered her grandmother in frenzied Italian. I could only understand the body language, which had something to do with human reproduction. It was a bit embarrassing, but it seemed as if it was all evolving quite well.

I then reached in the stupid foam cooler, happily pulled out the Tiramisu cake and the meatballs, and while smiling broadly, I handed them to Maureen.

"Here you go, Maureen. I also brought this cake that I bought at the Foodworld and I bought this pack of frozen meatballs for dinner."

At the sight of the cake and frozen pack of meatballs, a quiet hush came over the formerly loud and cheerful crowd. Immediately, the frenzied Italian chatter died down, and you could hear a pin drop on a floor in Regina, Saskatchewan. My smile quickly faded as Maureen's eyeballs popped out and Nonna immediately grasped her chest, as if she was in severe duress and in pain.

"A STOREA BOUGHTA CAKEARINI! HORRIBLEIA FROZENINARINI ITALIANAO MEATABALLAS OHA NOA! OHA MYA HEARTA OHA MYA! Nonna shouted out, while Mrs. Zipperelli grabbed a dish towel and she fanned Nonna.

I needed to explain, "Yes, I mean, no! The meatballs are Italian style. We love them at our house. If you do not like the chocolate flavored cake, then I could bring it back and I would be happy to get a different. . .."

Nonna was spouting in agony, while gripping her chest as if she was still in pain, "Oha noa storea boughta stuffa! Storea boughta cakearini fora Pasqua! Frozeniarini meataballas! Wea haveata makea meataballas ourselvesa witha oura handas kneadiirini ina thea chopa meata! Oha noa! Oha noa!"

My goodness! I had given Nonna a heart attack! The rest of the family was yelling and hollering in frenzied Italian, waving their hands and arms in the air, pointing at me, while running around administering first aid to Nonna.

It was a bit of a bad scene!

Geez! I killed the family, Pooh-Bah!

All I did was to bring a cake, and some frozen meatballs for Easter dinner.

Maureen tore the cake and frozen package of meatballs out of my hands, threw them back in the stupid foam cooler, and she violently slammed the lid on the cooler. She then opened my arms and put the cooler into my hands, grabbed me by the arm and rather forcibly tugged at me and ran me to the front door of the home.

"Geez, Maureen. I guess I should have bought the vanilla cake and the regular meatballs."

Maureen was laughing now, and when we arrived in the foyer and we stood in front of the front door, she took the stupid foam cooler out of my hands and set it down on the floor. She then took my hands gently and leaned in for one of the most passionate kisses that I had ever shared with her. Oh, boy, garlic and red wine never felt, nor ever tasted, or smelled so good.

Maureen was so aggressive.

After the shock of the kiss subsided, and I propped my knees back up, she explained, "Paulie, it is not the flavors, it is the origin. Please remember, never, ever, bring store-bought food to a traditional Italian dinner. You are such a cutie and I love you dearly. Take your little, foam cooler and put it in your van. It will be okay. I will explain to Nonna that you did not understand, and that you meant well. She already knows that you are not Italian, but she doesn't care, because she loves you too. After all, the flower bouquets were wonderful and Nonna already told me that you and I are going to make handsome and beautiful babies someday. She added that we are going to have an amazing time making them too. Go now, I will wait for you here."

"Oh sorry, Maureen."

Oh well, at least dear Mum got the flowers right.

I put the stupid foam cooler in the van.

Back inside the house, Nonna, thankfully, had fully recovered. The cake and frozen meatballs were now lost in a haze of gallons upon gallons of wine and they were a forgotten memory.

Everything was now well in Italy or, ah, I mean, in the Zipperelli's house.

The Zipperelli family then proceeded to go wild. I must say, I never enjoyed food more than I did on that Easter Sunday. Mountains of meatballs (kneaded by hands and fingers in bowls) roasted lamb chops, piles of ziti, salads, Italian desserts (all homemade) on, and on it went.

All capped by Maureen in that dress.

Oh, boy! I thought the inside of that stupid Easter Bunny costume was hot.

We laughed, danced, drank wine and beer, and ate food all day long. I had a few sips of the Zipperelli's homemade wine here and there, along with, for me, way too much beer.

"Wea makea toasta toa younga Paulini! He buya wronga cakearini, anda bringa stupidirini frozena Italiano meatballas ina stupida littlea foama coolerini, buta hea savea mucha lifearinis and isa herorini!" Mr. Zipperelli lifted his glass of wine around the table and the family cheered loudly!

Nonna Zipperelli motioned to Maureen for her to bring me over to her. Nonna, of course, spoke little to no English and my Italian was very poor. I walked over and she motioned for me to lean over and to give her a kiss on the cheek.

I did, she smiled, and while gargantuan puffs of garlic and red wine floated in the air towards me, Nonna said in frenzied Italian, "Youa nota Italiano, anda boughta stupida storea cooka cakearini and frozenarini Italiano meataballas in a littlea, stupida, foama coolerini, but youa surea hunka mana anda nica yoosea guya! Youa gotta nicea buttarini anda Ia beta resta thata isa ahangina rounda insidea ofa youa pantas isa gooda tooa! Maureena picka outa gooda lookina, fako Eastah Bunnerino. I lovea alla thata hairorini."

I was not sure of all of what she said, but I took it all as a compliment.

Later on, when the wafts of garlic had vaporized the kitchen curtains, when most of the family had left, or they had passed out on the floor, and this wonderful day ended, Maureen and I sat on a bench in her backyard. I put a sweater around her and her plunging neckline. It was the least I could do; after all, she could have caught a chill down there! I put my arm around her and she leaned in for an incredible kiss. Red wine and a lot of garlic, but still full of magic!

"You know something, Paulie? I always knew you had what it took to be a hero. I do have to ask you, though—do you think that it was all worth it? Just how heavy was that sofa?"

"Oh, it was nothing. Not too bad actually," I instantly lied like the finest Persian carpet.

Even for a fleeting second, Maureen did not buy my statement, and she laughed aloud at my obvious fudging of the truth.

"Okay, well now. Harry told me that Joe Hinky and his son were taking bets from the entire neighborhood on you losing that glorious manhood of yours, so I am sure that you are not telling me the truth. So, instead, let's try this. How hot was it inside that Easter Bunny costume? I can make it a bit hotter right now for you, you know. In fact, I can make it really hot. I love it when you turn red, you are such a cutie."

She burst out laughing at me, tugged at her neckline under the sweater to emphasize her "abilities." While opening her sweater, she playfully maneuvered her dress and while slightly concealed by the cover of her sweater, she revealed a lot more than I should probably see at this point in the backyard where the entire population of Rome and Vatican City could see us.

She smiled an alluring smile at me.

Maureen was so aggressive.

After recovering my eyeballs, I laughed too.

"Maureen, oh my goodness, yes, indeed, it was worth it! I would do it a hundred times over to have this day back again! I am not ashamed to say that while looking at you in that dress and parts of you that suddenly . . . appeared . . . that it was all worth it."

Maureen smiled again and gave me another kiss. She lowered her voice, and her tone changed to a bit of a throaty growl.

She wiggled in closer to me as she said, "I told you that it would be, and the best is yet to come. All kinds of parts of me are going to appear. Everyone is almost passed out, or they have gone home and the night is still young, my dear Paulie. Very young. I plan to stress those same parts that the sofa tested and I am sure are intact, but I need to take them for a test drive. You are going to go home exhausted tonight, that is, if I even allow you to leave. . .."

Maureen was so aggressive.

However, deep inside of me somewhere, the logic remained, as well as the dreaded Old Lady Syndrome. Yet tonight, I was not going to allow it to derail me! I had just a bit of a sharp edge with me now.

"I promise that it takes quite a bit to tire me out, Maureen. I am a semi-pro athlete, you know."

"I am counting on that fact. We shall see, Paulie. We

shall see."

The conversation turned steamy, and while I knew and agreed that the night was still young, in hopes of living up to my promise, I decided to ease the conversation and situation back a bit.

Therefore, I added, "But you know, the whole fire and hero thingy . . . it was not a big deal. The fire was really nothing. I must confess though and tell you that once the fire was out, I had this terrible thought that it was too bad the bunny head did not catch a little lick of a flame or two!"

Maureen playfully hit me in the arm. "Shame on you, Paul John Henson! The poor children if the Easter Bunny had melted in a fire."

I sat back and pondered it for a moment. At first, I thought that I might reveal the Easter Bunny's well guarded and one of his innermost secrets—the fact that he was "Flame Retardant and Fire Resistant," but after giving it a few serious thoughts, I thought that it was best to keep that secret amongst us Easter Bunnies.

Fraudulent or otherwise.

After a few seconds, more of some deep pondering, I felt the familiar Old Lady Syndrome creeping into my soul. This time, I fought back. I tossed the touch of the Old Lady Syndrome aside. I pulled her in close to me, wrapped my arms inside of her sweater, and felt the paradise contained therein.

While slowly closing in on her lips, I began a sultry kiss, while mumbling, "Yeah, yeah, yeah, it would have been such a shame. I would feel terrible. . .."

I returned to reality and realized that I was now sitting on the steps of the small porch in front of my apartment. The sun was setting a bit in the west and it lit up the sky with some early spring colors of red, yellow, and a little blue haze. I laughed a little more at the memory of it all. Dusting off my backside, I picked myself off the porch steps, walked back inside the apartment, and closed the door behind me. I picked up the newspaper that I had tossed aside and reread the advertisement about the upcoming fashion show.

My memories spun out of control. There was no way that I could keep up with them all. Even though at times I felt so very lonely, I had this barrel full of endless memories. I could dip into them at any time, and enrich my life with the things I had done, the people whom I met, and the adventures that I shared with the greatest friend that anyone could ever have.

Most of all, I could always recall the memories, faces, and voices of the persons whom I love. These wonderful memories made me a very wealthy young man, and they swept over me in giant waves of the past.

One thought stuck out in my mind. I could not help but imagine how any moving men, years later, could have possibly managed to remove that sofa out of Cricket's apartment. Even if they knew about the tricky bolts.

Easter was just around the corner now, and it brought with it the hope of eternal life, the rebirth of the Earth in springtime, the love of Jesus, the fun and joy of families gathering.

Oh yes, and please do not forget, young men with love-struck stars in their eyes, carrying store-bought Tiramisu cakes and frozen Italian meatballs packed in stupid foam coolers, gorgeous women decked out in fantastically tight dresses with flower prints, fraudulent Easter Bunnies, and guys dressed as part-time secret agents too.

THE END

Frankie the Garden Gnome

"Look, dear Mother. This cute stone guy would look so happy sitting in our garden. He has such a cute face and a cool, red hat. Can we buy him, dear Mother? Can we?"

I looked up and saw a cute, little red-haired girl, staring at me and waving frantically for her mother to come over and look at me.

Hey, cute, little red-haired girl, I am a garden gnome, not a stone guy!

Much to my chagrin, she did not hear me.

No one ever does.

A beautiful, tall, blonde-haired woman came over; she smiled, bent down, and looked at me. Wow! What fantastic blue eyes she has, and what a figure, too! She is gorgeous. Yeah man, I only look like Frankie the garden gnome, but cement gnomes have feelings and eyes too. You may find that a bit difficult to believe, but it is true. The beautiful woman looked at me; she tugged at the price tag around my neck. Hey! Easy there, honey, that hurts! I don't go around a-tuggin at your stuff. Looking at ya though, that might not be a bad idea.

"I agree, he is soooo cute."

Darn right, I am cute there, pretty lady. Ya ain't too bad yaself. Maybe we can go for a drink latah.

"I think he is perfect, Heather Sarah, and he is on sale. He is very cheap!"

Wait, a doggone minute there, pretty lady, I ain't cheap. I might be on sale, yes, but cheap, well, no! I much prefer the word inexpensive. Cheap has a deeper meaning.

"I think he will look good, right at the base of the hollies near where your father likes to plant those sweet peas. Let's buy him!"

Oh no! Those bloody sweet peas give me a headache. They are so strong and fragrant. Hey, easy there, baby. Oh geez, she is picking me up, oooohh la, la, right next to her soft and ample chest there. Wow! She smells so good. Oops, inside a shopping cart I go. Off on a little ride now, through the garden center. Yippeee! Yippeee! I am going to have a home. This is great. I am very excited; after all, that shelf was terribly hot during the day, but kinda cold at night. Hey, wait! I will miss all my friends here at the garden center. Slow down, honey, because I want to say goodbye to my friends.

Much to my chagrin, she did not hear me.

No one ever does.

So long birdbath, I hope no one sees the crack in the corner of your basin, and you finally sell someday soon. Goodbye to my old friend, the stone toad. See ya down the line there, Mr. Pink Flamingo. I am sorry that you are still stuck here. Maybe they will put ya on sale too. Goodbye to all my friends! I will miss ya guys. I will not miss that lazy punk kid they hired this spring who would shoot cold water from the hose when he watered that cherry tree in a pot next to me. If only I had hands that moved, in order to blast your ass back with cold water, like ya did to me.

"Hello, I see you picked out Frankie today, ma'am. Frankie is what my wife named him. He was our little garden gnome. Good selection. He is on sale too."

I looked up and saw the owner of the garden center, Mr. Ashley, smiling as the pretty lady agreed, and the little, cute red-haired gal laughed. I will miss ya, Mr. Ashley. So long, buddy. Ya were a kind and a good guy. I gotta say that ya just shoulda fired that punk kid. Ya know, he hides in the woods on the side and smokes some funny lookin' cigarettes, when ya think he is watering the shrubs. Anyway, that's right, my name is Frankie the garden gnome and don't forget it, pal!

"Thank you, Mr. Ashley. Yes, he is a wonderful bargain. Come along, Heather Sarah. Let's bring Frankie home now."

Hmm, okay, I get it now. The little cute, red-haired gal's name is Heather Sarah. She has a very pretty name. I wonder what her mother's name could be? Heather Sarah is as beautiful as her mother is. Okay, here we go, across the parking lot, out of the cart, up against that fantastic chest again and into the back of some old jeep. Geez! I hope this old wreck makes it to their garden. Hey! Slow down there, baby doll. I ain't got no movin' hands to hold on to anything. Wondah, where we are going? Oops, there I go, first to one side, then to another . . . weeee . . . I am slidin' around here, folks. Wooops. I am rolling over here, can't stop! Ouch, that side of the jeep there hurt. Sorry, I weigh a little bit here. In case that you did not notice, I am made of cement.

"Let me pull over here, Heather Sarah. I need to stop Frankie from rolling around back there. I did not realize that he shifted so much while we drove. I do not want him to break or get a scratch on him."

Well, good idea there, pretty lady. Thank you, after all, I am a big shot here, ya know. Ah yes, that is better. I can rest against this bag of other stuff ya bought. Yawn. The motion is making me a little sleepy. . ..

Wait. Hello? Where am I? I am sitting next to some holly shrubs and I see, well, a nice yard, small but nice, and there is a quaint little house in front of me. Oh, wow. I wonder how long I was asleep? This must be my new home. Well, this is not too bad. Fantastic oak trees, some pine trees, and over there is a little children's play-set, a sandbox, a swing, a little patio with a grill sitting out there and a vegetable garden over to my right side. Hmm, okay, I think that I am going to like this new joint. Very quiet and very idyllic. From this location, I can see everything. Oh, look. A pretty bird, maybe a Blue Jay, sitting on the tree branch above me. Yewwwww! Yuck! Hey, Mr. Blue Jay! Come back here and wipe that off my back! Whom do ya think ya are? Doing that all over me? I swear, if I only could move my arms or if someone could hear me. Come on back ya bum!

Much to my chagrin, Mr. Blue Jay did not hear me.

No one ever does.

"I bought him today at the garden center, twenty-seven. He looks good there. Do you not think he is cute?"

"Sure, Binky, sure, he is nice. I think I will plant my sweet peas over there this year. They can climb up the trellis there. I like him very much. Heather Sarah and you did a great job. Plus, you got him on sale. Is dinner ready, honey? I am starving!"

Binky. That is the gorgeous chick's name, huh? Weird name, but such a beautiful woman, and that must be her husband. Twenty-seven? Must be some type of nickname. Look, he is giving her a smooch. The gorgeous chicks are always married. It looks as if he is a pastor. The guy is wearing a black suit with a pastor's collar and he has long hair and a beard, too. If I did not know better, he is justa hippie, not a minister!

It sure is hot sitting out here, and now, this little long-haired boy comes along and shoots hockey pucks off me. I wish he could know how much it hurts. He must be Binky and the minister's son and the little, cute, red-haired gal's brother. Oh yes, what was that? A name. I heard his name called out there. Hey, his name is Paul William and his sister is Heather Sarah. They actually are nice kids. I like watching them from here. I love when the cute, little red-haired girl, uh, huh, I mean, Heather Sarah, comes and talks to me. She is so cute! Could do without her dressing me up with flowers and puttin' girly hats on me. After all, I am a tough guy, ya know. A garden gnome. Yeah, yeah,

yeah, Frankie is my name. She is a cutie. What's that ya said there, Binky? Oh, oh, oh, I get it now, the long-haired guy, he *is* a minister. Pastor Paul, huh? That is what ya guys call him. He seems like a nice guy. I like it when Pastor Paul and Binky sit by me in their chairs and talk, or they pull the weeds growing in front of me, or when I watch Pastor Paul cut the grass. Hey, could I have a sip of that ice-cold beer, Pastor Paul? Ya are a nice guy, and I sure am thirsty. Hope it is a Big Boulder beer, and not one of those horrible Dingleberries. Well, I hear from all of your friends that they are way too sweet!

Could do without those smelly sweet peas. Maybe next year ya can plant them farther away from me.

Hey, it is cold out here. I am underneath all of this snow. Can you hear me?

Much to my chagrin, no one can hear me.

No one ever does.

More of the snows came, and then another spring, and another summer, and still, I am out here. Next to these smelly sweet peas. I have watched from here while this family played in the yard. They laughed, and they cried. I watched the children play games and run around in front of me, and watched Binky get mad at Pastor Paul, and then they kissed and made up. Ooh, la, la, and how did they make up! I had to look the other way that night when they snuck out here in the corner of the yard in the darkness and, well, I ain't supposed to tell. I watched parties full of people when they danced until dark and laughed and played games. They decorated for holidays, carved pumpkins for Halloween, they played games in the yard in front of me, and they had family parties and cookouts in the summer. Pastor Paul's friend Harry is a kick. So is Pastor Paul's old man and Binky's dad, well, he is nice but he is a whacko. From here, I watched when they launched some fireworks for Fourth of July. I sit here and watch it all. Hey, shoot another bottle rocket off, would ya, Pastor

Paul. I like them. I have been out here in heat, cold, snow, and rain and I enjoyed it all. I really did . . . being a part of your lives. Now, listen to me, be careful around the lawn mower, and watch out for that ground hornet's nest over in the corner by the oak tree, Pastor Paul. OUCH! Don't say that I did not warn ya!

Much to my chagrin, Pastor Paul does not hear me.

No one ever does.

The children have grown so much as of late; I swear they grew up so soon. Actually, maybe it is not so soon after all. Sometimes, I wonder just how long I have sat here, watching everything.

Being a part of their lives.

The snows came, and then another spring, and another summer, and still, I am out here.

Now, there is a young man hanging around my beautiful little red-haired girl. Well, she is not really a little girl anymore; actually, she is all grown up. When you are a garden gnome, time is hard to tell. It is not as if I have a watch, or anything like that ya can use to tell time with, ya know. Hey, don't kiss her. I want to kiss her. I miss when Heather Sarah used to come by, talk to me, and tell me stories. No one ever comes along much anymore. Just Pastor Paul. He comes by and cleans up around me. Hey there, Pastor Paul. Can ya hear me? Now look, Paul William has a young woman following him around now too. They are laughing and chasing one another. She really looks a lot like that little girl who used to come with that crazy Harry guy. Maybe, or maybe not. It is hard to tell. Then they stop and kiss in front of me, too. Oops, wish I could move my hands to cover my eyes, or that I could close my eyes. They are holdin' on to each other in some pretty risqué locations. Hope Pastor Paul doesn't catch 'em. There they go . . . runnin' off somewhere. Don't stay out too late, youse guys. Please be careful and safe and come home soon.

Much to my chagrin, no one can hear me.

No one ever does.

The snows came, and then another spring, and another summer, and still, I am out here, watching everything go by.

Being a part of your lives.

I have to say; it is harder to see. My eyes are not quite what they used to be, ya know. I hate to admit it, but I am gettin' old. Pastor Paul is too. I noticed he has a little stiff back these days. When he works in the yard, he is slower to move around and he lets out with a bit of a grunt and groan too. His long hair has just a touch of grey along the edges, and in the tips of his beard too. But, Binky, wow! She is still such a hot little numbah. Binky wears eyeglasses now. Wonder if that would help me to see? I never see the kids much these days. I wonder where they went off to now? Never see the old man anymore either, or Mr. Hobnobber. Only see that crazy Harry guy and his wife. I am sorry to say that I can't remember her name anymore.

"Oh my, twenty-seven! Look at poor Frankie, his hat is faded so much now, and all the red color from it is almost gone. My dear husband, look at the paint in his eyes. The colors are so faded that you cannot see them much anymore."

Oh, huh? Hey, I was sleeping here. Who? Oh, hi there, Pastor Paul. Hi Binky. What is that ya were sayin'? I think ya said something about my eyes.

"I think he is old now, Binky. How long has he been out here? It has to be at least twenty years or maybe even more. I can bring him inside and put him on the workbench. Clean him up a bit and repaint him. What do you think?"

"Why, that would be wonderful, Paul. After all, Frankie is part of our lives too!"

Hey, easy there, big guy. Oohhhhhh . . . hey! Hold on there, Pastor Paul. What are ya doin'? I have not moved in a very long time. A little stiff here. He is pickin' me up and

I am goin' in the house. I never get to go in the house. My job is to watch the house. Be a part of your lives.

Ya know, guard ya guys. Who is goin' to watch?

Much to my chagrin, no one can hear me.

No one ever does.

Hey! Wow! I can see really clearly. The world looks so bright again. All clear, all shiny and alive. Thanks, Pastor Paul. Ya sure are a nice guy. A great guy. It is nice to be back in my spot. I missed it. After all, I guard ya guys, ya know, watch everything. That is my job, just being a part of your lives. I sure wish that I could have a match and light this stupid pipe in my mouth. Held this damn pipe for all of these years and never took a puff yet. Sorry for the bad word, Pastor Paul, but it is a little frustrating. Hey, look it is, Heather Sarah! She looks so beautiful; all dressed in that white gown, or is it some kinda fancy dress? What do I know? I am just a garden gnome. I think she is gettin' married! Hey, don't cry Binky. Ya goin' to make me cry too. Sometimes, I wish that I could cry, but I can't. I am just a cement garden gnome. What's this now? Now, Paul William is all dressed up with his buddies, and they are takin' pictures of them all in the yard here in front of me. Oh look! It is Harry and his wife, the old man, and there is, dear Mum. She was always so sweet and nice. Mrs. Hobnobber is here. Wow, she is still so beautiful. Mr. Hobnobber too. He is all bent over, barely movin.' He is still yellin' at Pastor Paul, though. They all look so different. So old now. Hi guys. It is I. Frankie the garden gnome. Remember me?

Much to my chagrin, no one can hear me.

No one ever does.

The snows came, and then another spring, and another summer, and still, I am out here watching everything go by.

Being a part of your lives.

"Oh, dear Mother. I love him! Please, please, please,

could we take Frankie for our yard? Grandpa does not have a large yard in his new house, and he would look so nice next to our rose bushes."

Hi, Heather Sarah. Hi, pretty little girl. I do not know your name, but you sure are pretty, too. I wondah who you are? Maybe you are Heather Sarah's daughter. If you are, then let me tell you that you are gorgeous, just like your mother is. I wondah where Binky is? I have not seen Binky in a long time. I love her and I miss her, too. What's this about takin' me somewhere? I do not think so. My job is to be here. Ya know, guard the house. Watch and be a part of ya lives. . ..

"I think we will. Grandpa will be pleased that Frankie has a nice backyard to live in. We will take him to our house and sit him next to the garden. That would be so nice. Frankie would look good there. It is early spring, so I will plant some sweet peas nearby him, just like Grandpa used to do. Let's pick him up and bring him over to our house."

Oh no! More of those smelly sweet peas! Oooooohhh . . . Here we go again. Easy now, been sittin' a long time. Oh my, ya smell so good, Heather Sarah. Wow, nice and soft here next to ya chest. Hey! Slow down, baby doll. I ain't got no movin' hands to hold on to anything. Ooops, there I go, first to one side, then to another . . . weeee . . . slidin' around here, folks. Wooops . . . I am rolling over here, can't stop. Ouch, that side of the jeep there hurt. Sorry, I weigh a little bit here. In case you did not notice, I am made of cement.

"Let me pull over here, Sarah. I need to stop Frankie from rolling around back there. I did not realize that he shifted so much while we drove. I do not want him to break or get a scratch on him."

Well, good idea, there pretty lady! Thank you, after all, I am a big shot here, ya know. Ah yes, that is better. I can rest against this bag of other stuff back here. Yawn . . . the motion is making me a little sleepy. . ..

Wait! Hello? Where am I? I am sitting next to some holly shrubs and I see, well, a nice yard, small, but nice, and there is a quaint little house in front of me. Oh, wow. I wonder how long I was asleep? This must be my new home. Well, this is not too bad. Fantastic maple trees, some pine trees, and over there, is a little children's play-set, a sandbox, a swing, a little patio with a grill sitting out there and a vegetable garden over to my right side. Hmm, okay, I think that I am going to like this. Very quiet and very idyllic. From this location, I can see everything. Oh look! A pretty bird, maybe a Blue Jay, sitting on the tree branch above me. Yewwwww! Yuck! Hey, Mr. Blue Jay! Come back here and wipe that off my back. Who do ya think ya are doing that all over me? I swear, if I only could move my arms or if someone could hear me. Come on back ya bum!

Much to my chagrin, Mr. Blue Jay did not hear me.

No one ever does.

Hey, look. It is that pretty, little girl again, she kinda, sorta, looks like Heather Sarah does. She is coming my way with Heather Sarah. She has blonde hair though. . ..

"My dear daughter, I think Frankie the Garden Gnome looks wonderful here in this spot. He has been part of our family for a very, very long time. Your Grandpa cleaned him up, he painted him a few years ago, and he looks so good now. Do you like him here?"

"Oh yes, dear Mother! He is so cute! I love his little face, and his red hat!"

That's right cute, little girl! I get it now. Ya must be Heather Sarah's daughter. I came to live with youse guys now. I hope I get to see Pastor Paul once in a while. And Binky too. Been a long time since I have seen Binky. I miss them. I love them. I love 'em all. Thanks for lettin' old Frankie be a part of your lives. But, hey, that's my job. To sit, guard ya and watch the world go by. I am Frankie, the garden gnome.

Much to my chagrin, they did not hear me.

No one ever does.

It does not matter because I just enjoyed being a part of your lives. I hope that you enjoyed it too.

I wonder if someone would come along and wipe these tears away from my eyes. I can't move my arms, but I sure can shed a tear or two. Better yet, if anyone around here has a match, then someday, I swear that I will take a puff on this pipe. . ..

THE END

For You

If you need me, I will always be there.
When you need to laugh, then I will laugh with you.
If you need me to dry your tears, I will kiss them away.
If you need someone to hold you, then I will hold you forever.

For You, I will always be there.
For You, I can only give myself.
That and my love are all I have.
For You.

Whenever you want me to listen,
then, I will lend an ear.
If you want me to help you to dream, then
I am here to dream endlessly of endless dreams with you.
We can dream together.
Of our children's laughter, or dancing on moonbeams, or holding the sun in our hands.

For You, I will always be there.
For You, I can only give myself.
That and my love are all I have.
For You.

If you need someone to smile,
then, I will smile at you.
If you need someone to be angry with,
then be angry with me.
Hand me all your burdens.
Give me your sorrow, your joy, and your heart.
And I will give you mine.

For You, I will always be there.
For You, I can only give myself.
That and my love are all I have.
For You.

Forever, until the stars dim and the sun fades away.
I will still be here to love you.
To care when you need me to care.
To hold your hands gently,
after a long night together.
To feel the pounding of our hearts while I hold you and we honor our love forever.
Until the early morning light steals away our nights.

For You, I will always be there.
For You, I can only give myself.
That and my love are all I have.
Until the end of all time.
For You.

The Rock

I sat on the front steps of the parsonage of Reunion Lutheran Church, staring out into an early spring sunset. For me, there is not too much in the world that can exceed the majesty of a glorious sunset, while it is announcing the pending darkness of a spring evening.

Oftentimes, it is indescribable.

To a great extent, sunsets are almost incomprehensible. The colors, reds, oranges, yellows, shifting clouds and the reflections of light.

With a sunset, we exemplify God's great creation and broadcast peacefulness that this day has ended, and darkness will fall, but tomorrow we can start anew. It is the end of the day and somehow, a promise too. A promise of hope for a new start tomorrow. In my opinion, there is nothing quite as magnificent as the beauty of the glory seen in a soft, golden sunset. I have always enjoyed sitting and watching the sunsets. Not only to admire, and to enjoy the beauty of them, but to capture my thoughts at the end of the day. There is something very calming to my soul about watching sunsets, and in fact, it has been a fascination of mine since I was just a small lad. If I live to one hundred years old, and I watch a sunset every single day of that long life, then it still will not be long enough to comprehend it all.

Here at Reunion Lutheran Church, we were all very lucky. The church sat nestled in an enclave of natural beauty. It was an unusual property, a magical setting, a setting carved out of the woods in northwestern New Jersey. The trees, peace and serenity, were magnificent. The setting often made me think that the leaders of this church had to be steered by the hand of God, in order for them to have been so fortunate to find a property of such beauty and peacefulness, to build their church upon this very special location.

My mind traveled back to the first moment that I arrived here, with my wonderful wife by my side, holding her hand tightly as we began a journey into the next phase of our young lives together. A journey filled with hope, love, God's plan, and our own dreams and desires. It had been worth it all to be the pastor of this wonderful church, which despite the challenges, truly lived up to the name on the charter, the name Reunion Lutheran Church. In many ways, the church reunited not only many people's lives that grew up here with this church, but it also reunited my family, friends, complete strangers, and my own soul. In fact, this church accepted me while I was still a young man, when I was struggling with my past life and with my doubts, and the church gave me back my purpose and then laid perfection upon my soul.

It had to be part of the plan because in my mind, no other explanation could be true.

I sat here on the front steps, enjoying the glory of the sunset in front of me and enjoying the sunset, yet reflecting rather pensively on where I was right now in my life, marriage and career. Reflecting on how far I had come, how much we had left to do and what brought me to where I was right now.

My wife had set out earlier with our two children on some shopping excursions and it would be a bit more time before they returned. Therefore, here I sat and relaxed, thinking deeply, taking a few moments out of my harried life to enjoy God's creation and to reflect and ponder while I waited for them to return.

I leaned back and felt it in the front pocket of my vest, while I stretched my long frame backwards on the cold concrete of the parsonage steps.

There it was in the pocket of the vest, just as it has been for a very long time.

I felt the rock.

I reached into the pocket, grabbed the rock, and pulled it out. I studied it, felt it in my hands, rolled it around, and then smiled. It was just a rock, a small, round rock. Nothing special, no brilliant colors, no vibrant lines, cold, dark and dull, but it was not the appearance of the rock, which made it special.

It was what it symbolized to me.

After all of these years, the rock was still the same, and the memories it brought to me were not only joy-filled, but in many ways painful too. While I sat there holding the smooth, little, rock in my hand, I returned once again to another front stoop and another set of front steps, a place of my boyhood, a place where I often, just as I did tonight, sat, watched sunsets and passed my time.

A special place, called 182 Belmont Avenue.

"What are you up to there, Paulie boy? Sitting out here again, eh? Watching our world go by, eh?"

I was somewhat startled by the voice, as well as the disturbance, to the haphazard peacefulness from the foreground of the city noises on the busy street in front of me. The traffic whizzing by on Belmont Avenue in front of me had some type of mesmerizing influence upon me. It was a bit hard to explain or describe. One would not think that a busy city street full of trucks, buses, traffic and blaring horns could lull anyone into complacency, but I imagine the many years of watching and listening to the same scenes and noises had somewhat dulled my senses.

I looked up to see my grandfather standing on the sidewalk in front of me. I had no idea of how long he had been actually standing there watching me.

I smiled and answered him, "Hello, Gramps. Yes, sort of, well, somewhat daydreaming, I guess. You know, thinking about things at the end of the day. I am not sure what I am thinking about but, I am thinking."

He smiled back at me, waved his hand a bit, tugged at his trousers, and took a sip from the bottle of Big Boulder beer that he held in his hand. He was dressed in his usual wool sweater, with a crisp white tee shirt underneath it. His trousers were just a bit too big for him, but he pulled them up when he moved a bit in my direction. Despite the somewhat cool weather creeping in as the sun started to set, my grandfather only wore his favorite English wool sweater. I only wore my favorite light vest, which covered a tee shirt emblazoned with the logo and name of my favorite rock-and-roll band. A grandfather and grandson, cut from the same mold. We were both impervious to the cold or a chill of the late afternoon and early spring evening.

"Do you mind if I join you there on the front steps, Paulie boy? I would like to share a bit with you in your meandering thoughts and pensive ways tonight. You do not mind now, eh?"

I nodded and smiled while motioning for him to come ahead and sit next to me. I admired his English accent gently framing his words with a golden lace. The echo of his voice; I can still hear in my mind many years later, in fact, all of my waking days.

His many years of living here in the United States had done very little to fade his accent, which he acquired from his native land. I was indeed quite happy that he retained it, since it was a part of my own heritage.

In actuality, as my grandfather settled in next to me, this was a scene that we had replayed countless times over in our lives. We had viewed many a sunset and passed many early evenings sitting together upon these same front steps. In fact, ever since I was old enough to remember, he and I sat here together while we were both thinking and watching.

Gramps settled in next to me. He wiggled a bit, looked over and smiled at me, while taking another sip of the beer he had in his hand.

After a period of a long silence, he asked me, "So have you read a bit more from the book I gave you? What story are you up to there, Paulie boy? What is our favorite detective up to these days?"

I smiled, reached down next to me and pulled up the leather-bound book, a book containing the adventures of a certain detective, who lived at a famous address of Baker Street in London, England.

"I forget the name of the story, Gramps, but it is the one where the snake comes down the bed pull and he gives it a bash with his walking stick. Love it. What a great story!"

Gramps laughed at my enthusiasm, and he patted me on the back. He joyfully told me, "Ah, yes. The speckled band story. Indeed, it is a good one. I knew you would like them. However, I have to say, they are all great stories. One after another, from a great mind, a storyteller. . .."

Gramps looked at me and he seemed to be admiring how I held the leather-bound book tightly in my hands while I studied it.

He continued to speak, "Are you writing anymore, Paulie boy? I rather enjoyed the story about the time bomb of troubles and mayhem that Ronzo created. I know that I told you how much Chadwick down at the bookshop enjoyed the draft that I allowed him to read. Chadwick knows books and authors better than any person whom I know of. You have a talent. I dare say that, I hate to see you stop writing. You are a captivating storyteller too. You watch everything, and you capture it in your mind. I find it quite remarkable. I marvel at how you will use it later on, not only for you to entertain us, but to allow it to escape in your mind and touch others with what you have experienced. Not too many people can do that, Paulie boy. I must say that it is a gift. A very special gift that you have. You do know that. Do you not?"

I shrugged my shoulders and did not answer him. I was actually writing many stories but keeping them all in my mind. My mind never stopped; I just did not think they were good enough to put down on paper. I smiled at my grandfather, put my head down and then glanced over at him while he studied me with his eyes over the rim of the beer bottle he was sipping.

I finally answered him with an honest reply, "I write a little here and there, Gramps, but mostly, I just enjoy sitting here thinking. You are correct, in that I am capturing the entire world, and keeping it close to me, in order to write about later on. Right for now, work, reading, and hockey are what I mostly do. When I am not playing hockey, I am thinking about it. Watching the shooter's eyes, playing my angles, keeping my body square or in the right position. I play it all over in my mind. When I am not doing that, then I think about what I will write, and I watch the world go by here on Belmont Avenue. Besides, the stories I have in my mind, I am not sure that anyone would be interested in them. I rather sit here, when I am not hanging with Harry or Jeff, or playing goal, and watch things go by. It gives me ideas. I think someday, maybe, way down the road, the stories will come out of me. Until then, I gather what I need. Does that make any sense, Gramps? Or am I a little strange?"

Gramps put his beer down and he laughed a bit at me. He shook his head. He shifted off to speaking in his second language of Welsh, as he described me a little in the Welsh language, "Paulie boy, you are a rhyfedd (weird or strange is what he categorized me as) one! All goalkeepers are, in football or in hockey. You goalkeepers are all the same. You are complex and a very deep thinker, but I do understand. The best writers are the people who gather what they need. Use it all later on in your life. Sir Arthur did that very same thing, too. He was a medical doctor before he became a writer. The medical practice served him well to conjure up adventures."

I nodded in agreement, but did not comment. We sat in silence for quite a long time, neither of us saying much.

We watched two cars stop for the red traffic light at the corner. The driver's doors flung wide open, the two drivers of the cars both jumped out. They met in the roadway and argued and screamed at each other in Spanish, and shook their fists in each other's faces. Obviously, they knew each other and the argument must have boiled over from a previous adventure, and it now was going to culminate on the street corner in front of our house. Gramps and I carefully watched the wild scene unfold.

"Bloody well, those two chaps might create a bit of a tussle for each other, Paulie boy. Perhaps, a spot of too much cheap wine, eh?"

"I suppose so, Gramps. Let's see how it goes."

Was this just another scene to provide more wild adventures for inspiration later on down the road? Who knows?

Car horns blared, obscenities screamed out of many car windows, traffic snarled, and life went on around the two irate combatants. Even though neither Gramps nor I understood Spanish, we managed to follow the general gist of the conversation. The two men settled their differences with a few shoves here and there, yelled a few more words at each other, and happily, they resolved this one without a gunfight, fist fight, a knife fight, or other potential assorted methods that were all too common in our old city neighborhood.

Northern New Jersey, home to the most amazing

varieties of life in which you could ever imagine! Mobsters, street life, tortured souls, happy people, sad people, natural beauty and urban decay, all within a step or two of the front door of our home. It is one of the unique places on the face of this Earth, yet I would not trade growing up here for a million dollars.

As we watched the scene dissipate, I turned to Gramps and said, "That is why I sit here, Gramps. So many scenes unfold before my eyes. Some are happy, some sad, some terrible and some enlightening. I have seen it all pass by the front steps of our house here. It is better than any movie or television show in which you could ever imagine."

"Only because you absorb it, and put a positive approach on it, Paulie boy. You have a huge heart and are a magnet for people and happenings. Your mind needs to absorb it all and capture it forever. You are very much the same as I am. In England, as a young boy, I would wander the meadows outside of Sherwood Forest, listening to the whispers of the wind in the meadows, retaining the stories that the wind told to me, whilst it whistled through the dry grass that leads up to the edge of the forest. There, the wind gave up on the meadow grasses and focused on moving the mighty limbs of the forest. The whispers became a howl, and I understood that the wind was, as our lives are. Sometimes, we need to whisper, and sometimes, we need to howl. Something as simple as the wind, invoked my imagination. Retain it all, Paulie boy. It will serve you, and others well, someday down the road."

Gramps had been studying my eyes as he spoke to me, as I was studying his. He now moved his focus away and leaned back more into the stairs.

He shifted his position on the stairs, and I imagined that some beer was now influencing his speech, as he became a bit deeper in his thoughts.

Gramps then tapped his chest with his right hand as he spoke again, "All that you need to do, is keep your heart open, stay strong and tough as you are, and imagine that everything is speaking to you. Understand your potential to imagine, retain and share it with others. You will be a great storyteller someday, maybe, not a great author, but a great storyteller. There is a difference. I for one prefer to read great stories rather than eloquent and glorious, flowing prose. After all, in the end, a grand story is what the reader desires most. Your ability to imagine and create, well, it is limitless, Paulie boy. It will touch people's lives."

I smiled at his profound words and captured them in my memory banks forever.

My grandfather watched me out of the corner of his eyes and I watched as he chugged the last of his beer. He placed the empty bottle next to us on the steps; he then slowly stood up and walked over to the small section of grass between our sidewalk and our home. Gramps seemed to be studying the mixture of grass and dirt, and his actions were a bit puzzling to me. I did not say a word, but I studied him while he poked at the ground with his feet. He then seemed to spot what it was that he was searching for, reached down and picked up a small stone that his foot had uncovered on the ground. He picked it up, turned and walked back to where I was sitting, all the time holding the rock in his hands. His amazingly clear, blue eyes sparkled as he walked over to me and he held the rock in his hand. Most people would call it a stone because it was too small to be a rock. Yet, held tightly in my grandfather's powerful hands, I would never say that he picked up a meager stone.

Therefore, it was a rock.

Forever more, it would be a rock. In Welsh, we would say, "Am byth." Forever.

"Here, Paulie boy. What is it that you see?"

I studied the rock for a few moments. It had some dirt along the edges. It was small, but solid, not colorful, rather dull, and it was nothing very special. I reached out, took the rock from him, and held it in my hands. I turned it over repeatedly in my hands and then I smiled at my grandfather.

Finally, I spoke, "I see the spot on the ground, in which you and my grandmother first stepped on, when you first came to America from England. Perhaps, this rock was part of the actual ground where your feet first landed. It was underfoot as you stepped off together, arm-in-arm, hand-in-hand, together into a journey of the unknown. The rock did not break or give way and it helped to lead you. It became a little smoother, but the rock remained solid and powerful. It was here before you came and will be here long after we are gone. It is part of a new life, a symbol of hope, a part of the pathway to where we all are right now."

I looked up and Gramps put his hand on my shoulder, and he squeezed it tightly. I could feel the power in his hands. He was a powerfully strong man, both in emotion and in physical prowess. A man of unparalleled strength. His grip was strong and deep.

This was, however, not a grip of control; this was a grip of encouragement, a sign of his love.

Gramps smiled widely as he told me, "Bloody amazing! You see how well, in which you can imagine, Paulie boy. Wonderful! Study for now. Then you can write when you decide the time is right. However, please, someday write. Most of what I have learned in life, I learned by reading. It is a gift that we all can take advantage of and share."

"I will, Gramps. I promise, someday."

Gramps looked at me, smiled a bit and said, "I do, however, think that is a stone you are holding there, Paulie boy, because rocks are larger."

I shook my head and replied, "Sorry, but with respect, you are wrong, Gramps. It symbolizes you. You are too powerful to be just a stone. I have to say that what I hold right here in my hand is a bloody rock!"

Gramps laughed aloud, loosened his grip upon my shoulder, and waved his hand in the air at me.

"Oh, bloody well! Please, do not let your mum hear you say that bloomin' word. She will blame me for teaching you! Then a rock it 'tis. Good night, Paulie boy. And, my dear Paulie boy, please remember that sometimes, you will need to whisper and sometimes, you will need to howl. The rock will remind you of that, and you are smart enough to know when you need to choose between the two. Cheerio for now."

"Cheerio, Gramps. Thanks for the rock and the chat."

I brushed off the dirt from the edges of the rock, spun it and placed it in the front pocket of my vest. It fit perfectly in there, smooth, solid, it felt good. It reminded me of my grandfather and I thought about how I would keep it.

The spring gave way to a hot summer, then the seasons passed quickly and soon I found myself still sitting on the front steps of our home on another spring night.

Watching and waiting, gathering information as the world flashed before my eyes.

I was now about nineteen years of age, or thereabouts, tall, strong, lean, and powerful. Long hair, down past my shoulders, a solid growth of a blonde and red beard growing upon my chin and face, and I was now on the cusp of manhood. Yet, I remained blind to so many things, all the information gathering was far from complete.

Other than my best friends, Harry M. Redmond Junior, and Jeff Porter, my hockey teammates and a few on and off again girlfriends, I was a loner. I enjoyed being alone; I found nothing wrong with it. I was able to pass the time on my own. I read books on the front steps and in my bedroom at night. In and amongst the pages were where I escaped to far-off lands. Enjoyed wild adventures, fought wars, confronted pirates, sailed the high seas, solved crimes, sought pretty women, and I captured their hearts too. It was easy to imagine that I was driving down lonely country roads in fancy convertibles with the top down, all while never leaving the front stoop and the front steps of my own home.

It was magical.

I read, The Bible too. In fact, I read anything that I could. Gramps was correct. All we need to learn in life comes from genuine experiences and from reading. It all unfolds for us; we just need to absorb and keep all of it.

Gramps often joined me on the front steps, and sometimes, I remained alone. I often took the rock out of my vest pocket and rolled it around in my hands, while I watched and thought, or read.

I spoke to neighbors who passed by, chatted with strangers, petted dogs on their head, spoke to our resident stray and often pet cat, Pussface, when he decided to stop by and hang out with me. Sometimes, my faithful pet fox terrier, Skippy, would sit with me and he, too, watched the world go by our front door. I knew when to run back into the house when I heard some random gunfire or other trouble emitting from the darkness of the neighborhood. I refused to partake in the illegal drug deals occurring in front of my eyes; the lure of their promise to escape to far-away places had no appeal to me. I had my dreams of a hockey career, my words, and books for that!

It was amazing what scenes unfolded here on these gritty streets, right before my eyes.

Then in the late spring, when the summer was closing in, and the heat seemed to be creeping in closer and closer, my world changed a bit. The trees had now all bloomed out, and the leaves were proud and fresh upon their branches. The large maple tree in front of 182 Belmont Avenue now had left a deposit of dried, brown spinners chasing all around in front of me as a reminder of the lateness of the spring. The usual vest that I wore to fend off just a touch of the spring evening chill, was almost ready to return to the confines of my closet, because I found sitting there on the front steps that the nights were not quite as cool as they had previously been. Yes indeed, my world changed a bit, because it was on one of these late spring evenings that she came by.

I noticed her one night, looked up from my book and watched her pass by me. She looked at me and smiled, and I smiled back. I did not say anything to her, but I caught her eyes, and then admired her from a distance, when it was safe to steal a glance, without the embarrassment of her catching me.

You know, I was checking her out.

My goodness, she was gorgeous!

She walked by me, and I could not help but to notice how well she was dressed. As she wiggled by the front steps, wearing a pretty blouse with a light sweater over it, along with tight bellbottom pants, I could see streaks of red wisps in her blonde hair and most of all; I caught a whiff of some intoxicating type of perfume that was floating around her.

Oh, how in such a short period of time, the scenery had dramatically changed.

The usual roar of trucks, city buses, guys yelling at each other, car horns blaring, and the occasional gunfire in the distance all no longer mattered.

She had smiled at me and I had smiled at her. I found myself captivated, and as a result, I purposely arranged my daily timetable to ensure that I was sitting out on the front steps at that same time each night, which I had seen her first pass by me.

One night passed, and she did not walk by, then two nights, then three. Perhaps she was just passing through; maybe, she did not live close by. After all, I had lived here for a very long time and I had never seen her before. On the other hand, perhaps, she was new to the neighborhood.

A million different scenarios ran around in my mind. All I knew, and all that I could recall, was her smile. Her smile had lingered upon my mind's eye, and the image of it was a bit difficult to overcome. With one simple walk by me, on a late springtime evening, she had cast a spell upon my heart.

One night, about a week or so after I had first seen her, I looked up from the book that I was reading, and there she was, strolling down the sidewalk in front of me. I felt my heart jump in my chest and my throat close up. Playing it cool, I leaned back and casually flipped the pages of the book. There you go, Paul, make as if you do not even see her.

Yet, it was impossible. Our eyes locked and I could not prevent the wide smile that came upon my face.

It just came over me.

She passed by and she smiled widely at me, melted my heart with one smile, and mouthed a gentle, "Hello" to me. I was too love struck to answer, too much in awe of her beauty even to murmur a single word. She wiggled by and continued on her way.

In a flash, she was gone. I had blown it!

Geez. I could not even begin to imagine what a bum I was.

Now, it was not that I was uncomfortable around young women. I had a few gals chasings me here and there, and even at my young age, I had chased a few back. A friend of my sister, Maureen Zipperelli, had taken a bit of a fancy to me since we were very young, and even though she was older than I was, we had shared many special moments together. It was not as if Maureen and I were dating one another exclusively, but time would tell. Maureen was great fun to be with, she had an amazing personality, and one more thing stuck in my mind whenever I thought about Maureen Zipperelli, and that fact was that she was knockout gorgeous too.

I also had a long-time and long-distance romance and pen pal relationship with a gal named Debbie Boatwright, but that is a story for another time and place. Debbie sure was a pretty gal, too. When you are young, well, you know how it is. . ..

"Beautiful lassie, eh?"

My grandfather's voice echoing from behind me had made me jump off the steps, and in shock; I almost dropped the book that I had been reading.

Gramps had caught me gawking at the young woman!

"Yeah, yeah, yeah, she is Gramps," I humbly admitted. There was no sense in denying that I had admired her.

Especially from the rearview. . ..

Gramps laughed at my embarrassment. He turned the corner from behind me, patted me on the back, and he said, "Don't blame you! She is quite the lovely young woman. Do you know what I think, based upon that brief encounter? Next time she will stop, Paulie boy. I will bet upon it. You are a handsome lad. I agree with my sister Alma that you look very much like our Cousin Percival. Percy does not have all that longhair and a wispy beard upon his chin, but you look like him. He is a handsome man and has had all the women in town chase him around for years. He never settles down with any of them. Instead, he allows them to continue to chase him. Nothing wrong with that. You share his position in sports too. He was a football goalkeeper. Unlike your skills, Percival was a poor one at that!"

Gramps stood in front of me, while I sat on the front steps, he stomped the ground a bit, waved his hands in the air as if he was duplicating a soccer goalkeeper waving at a shot towards him, while allowing the shot to go by him into the goal net. I laughed at his demonstration. As a goalie myself, I felt the pain of allowing a goal.

Gramps continued to speak, "I hear you are quite a bit better at the position than your relative is, even if it is in a different sport. More and more, as time goes on and you grow older and more powerful, I see touches of your father in you too, and that is an exceptional thing, Paulie boy. Your father is still a very handsome man, and he might be stubborn as an ass, but he is a good man. A harder working chap does not exist on this good earth. My Joanie, she picked a good one in that father of yours. I am quite proud of him and love him as a son."

I nodded in acknowledgement of the description of my father. Gramps leaned back, pulled at the sleeves of his sweater, and he smiled at me. Gramps seemed to be transporting to another place within his mind.

He smiled, sighed a bit, then said, "Young lassies. Eh? Pretty, cute, yes. Enjoy and be smart about it! Please, be smart, Paulie boy, a young woman as beautiful as she is, or that, other woman . . . what is her name, eh? It escapes me a bit now and then. The gorgeous, Italian lassie?"

"Maureen Zipperelli is her name, Gramps." I helped Gramps with the memory of the name of the captivating and quite alluring, Maureen Zipperelli.

"Yes, indeed, Maureen. She is a beauty. What a beauty she is, Paulie boy. You do attract them. It is best not to let her catch you with another lassie, because that might ignite a bit of fireworks. She has been after you for years upon years, Paulie boy. I suppose that she can be a bit emotional and difficult to control. The gorgeous ones always are."

Gramps laughed and tugged at his waistline again to pull his pants back up a bit.

"Young lassies can also bring you a bit of trouble, too. They can peddle their wares, flitter about, captivate you with their beauty, and lure you into a spot where it might be a bit difficult to control. You are very smart. You will remember my words and when the time comes, you will make the correct decision."

He winked at me, and I understood very clearly where his advice was coming from.

"What is it that your father always says? He does have quite a few of those, New Jersey street-wise statements that he blurts out here and there. Statements that are actually quite profound and are meant to teach, meant to coach, and often are, spot on in their meaning." Gramps looked at me as if he wanted to see if I could recall the words and lessons that my father gave to me about relationships with young women.

I did, and smiled as I relayed it as proof that I paid attention, "Five minutes of pleasure has to be measured against a potential lifetime of pain."

Gramps laughed and nodded, but after our laughter faded, his face changed to a more serious look as he said, "On the same subject, you are only young once, and as long as you keep your wits about you, and remain smart, then enjoy it all. This young lassie will not stop for most young men. When you are that beautiful, then you can select whom it is that you want to stop for in life. Yet, she will stop for you. I can tell. She might be a bit older than you are, Paulie boy. Time will tell, be careful, and keep your wits, eh? Say, I am going to the corner for a six-pack of Big Boulder beer. Would you enjoy a cold soda?"

I smiled. Gramps was so cool.

"Sure, thanks."

A few days later, my grandfather's prediction came true.

While I was sitting at my usual front step post, she passed by me and, after an alluring smile and a nod of her head, she turned around quickly and she stopped.

I had just set upon clandestinely admiring the rear view of her, and I did not expect her to stop and whirl around so quickly. I was quite sure that she caught me gawking at her backside!

My heartbeat increased, my face turned red, and I watched while she slowly walked over to the sidewalk in front of me and asked, "Is that all you do with your life? Do you always read and only smile at the gals as they walk by? Or can you actually speak?"

"I speak and I read and I do other things and, well, I watch too." At this point, since I figured that she had caught me gawking at her beauty, that a dose of honesty could not hurt me.

She tilted her head a bit; her body swayed and leaned in closer to me.

Her mouth turned into a bit of a seductive smile, and her voice lowered as she asked, "Oh, yeah, huh? What is it that you watch? Never mind answering, because, I think I have an idea of some of the things that you might check out here and there."

She stood up straighter, smiled, and posed a little by tilting at the waist a bit and placing her right hand upon her hip.

Well now, I was not quite ready for this type of dialogue, and I found my tongue tied up in knots. I made a mental note to read a bit more of the romantic stuff, because I needed to steal some sappy material for use in real life. There was no doubt now that she obviously had caught me in my rather poor efforts to conceal my admiration of her beauty while she passed by.

"Do you have a name?" She asked.

After a few stops and halting starts, the words finally came out with a forced and rather dumb sounding laugh, "Sure, sure, sure. Paul. Paul John Henson. How about you? I am quite sure that you have a name too."

"I like your humor and style. Very subtle. Yes, I do . . . Kyra. Hello, Paul John Henson. Nice to meet you. My full name is Kyra Lovell. I see you read an awful lot when you are not watching certain things, or actually or more specifically, watching and admiring female body parts. So, what do you read?"

Oh well, I was now proud that I had not fudged the truth at all and confessed up to my gawking.

I held the book cover up for Kyra to see it. The book cover had the name of the great detective emblazoned upon it in large block letters. Certainly, it was not hip or cool, and not the type of book that one would expect a long-haired, hippie young man to read, but I did not care. I marched to my own drumbeat, and I never really cared to lockstep with what other people did.

"Oh, I see. Very impressive . . . Sherlock Holmes. So, the classics are what you usually read."

"I do read the classics quite often, but I read all kinds of books. My grandfather gave me this one. It is a leather-bound edition. He brought it with him from England. He was born there."

Kyra walked closer to the front steps. Now that I was interacting with her and studying her closely, I surmised that she was around twenty-two or twenty-three years old, and in my heart and in my mind, I hoped that I could appear to be a few years older than what I actually was. While she stared at me, I noticed that her eyes were green. Deep green, sparkly, yet very warm. Her eyes were wide, and she laced the lashes of her eyes with some type of eyeliner to enhance them, her hair was blonde, it hung down in gentle curls to her shoulders and in the setting glimmers of the waning sunlight, I could detect some red highlights. She was tall for a woman, and I could see that she wore low-heeled shoes with soft bottoms. They were the perfect pair of shoes for walking, and perfect shoes for a tall woman to wear. Kyra Lovell had a long neck, a thin face, with perfect features. Kyra wore tight, black, bell bottom hip huggers, which clung to her amazing figure. She wore a white blouse, and on top of the blouse, she wore a black knit sweater. She left the sweater open and unbuttoned, and with her blouse being a rather tight fit on her, it was impossible not to admire her petite, yet shapely and perfectly formed breasts. Around her neck, she wore a thin gold chain that only enhanced her long neck.

She was gorgeous.

"Oh, I see. England . . . that is very cool. What is your favorite story of the great detective's adventures? Mine is the one where the criminals put an ad in the newspaper for red-haired men, in order to lure the banker out of his office, so they can dig the tunnel under his office into the bank vault."

I now, officially, became a mess. Suddenly, waves of emotions captured me, and I encountered all types of difficulty in forming even simple words, huge troubles with speaking, and in formulating simple sentences. In fact, I became speechless!

A love struck, babbling fool.

A gorgeous gal and she read and knew the stories of the great detective!

A rare and precious find. She was a gem.

I finally managed to find some words deep within my mind, take my focus off her smile, her hair, her eyes, and her other attributes and say, "I forget the name of the story, Kyra. It is the one where the snake comes down from the bed pull and he gives it a bash with his walking stick. Love it. Great story!"

Kyra smiled, but she did not answer me. I had a feeling that she actually knew the name of the story, but did not want to reveal it to me.

I recovered enough to gain a bit of ground and asked her, "So, I have lived here forever, and I have never seen you around here before. Did you just move into the neighborhood? Are you living close by?"

Kyra walked even closer to me and she leaned up against the wall next to the front steps of our house. Her green eyes now reflected a bit of the spring sunset lowering rapidly in the sky. I could tell that she was very keen on my interest in her.

"I am staying close by here, over on North Tenth Street, at my grandmother's house. She has not been feeling well. My home life over in Great Falls is complex right now, and in a little turmoil, so I came to stay with my grandmother for a few weeks. I start a new gig in college in a few weeks, my final year. I transferred in from a college in New York and I plan to finish here in a college down in south Jersey.

Near Philadelphia. I am a literature major. Things were not the greatest in New York, and being a Jersey girl, I decided to return home."

"I see. That explains it. Well, I hope it works out for you. Literature, eh? And that also explains the interest in books and Mr. Holmes, eh?"

I felt a bit deflated; she was quite a few years older than I was, and she was heading off for a new life. A life where I knew that I did not exactly fit in. Kyra stopped leaning on the wall. She pulled her sweater around her, as it was obvious the night air was growing colder. She smiled at me.

"Thank you, for the well wishes. Yes, it does explain some of it, not all, but some. I love to read, and my plans are to teach and write someday."

Kyra studied me carefully; she was deeply looking at me, almost as if she sensed my deflation at her plans.

She took a few steps and waved in the air to me while saying, "Well, I guess that I will continue my evening walk. It has been nice meeting and speaking with you, and while I do not want to pull you away from such an engrossing evening of your own, the neighborhood is a bit rough around here. Would you care to join me? You know . . . would you like to walk with me?"

I closed the book and smiled. An invitation, an opening and now, do not blow it, Henson! You usually mess up these types of situations. Think hard and do your best not to blow it. I stood up from the steps, bent over and placed the book on the step next to me, and noticed how intently Kyra studied me.

"Oh my, I did not realize how tall and athletically built that you are. You did not look so tall and muscular sitting there on the steps. I think that you will be quite a protector of me!"

"Kyra, I can assure you that no one, actually messes with us around here. My family has been here so long, we, along with my buddy Harry and his family over on John Street, we are the anchors of the neighborhood to some extent. Newcomers might test the waters, but all the older residents, they know better than to test us in foolish ways. I will be glad to walk with you, and I can assure you that, you will be fine."

"I imagine so. You are quite imposing. I never thought you were as big, as tall, and as strong as you look right now while standing there. When you sit, you must slouch."

I think I surprised Kyra by my height and size. Or she was turning on the flirting big time. Perhaps it was a bit of both.

I reached down, grabbed my book, and picked up the rock, which I usually kept in my vest pocket. I had set it aside while I was reading, and must have forgotten about it, until I stood up and noticed it. I saw Kyra's eyes study me while I grabbed it and placed it back in my vest pocket. I was now officially doomed, since she now knew that I was a whacko.

"Why do you have a stone that you keep in your vest pocket, Paul?" Kyra asked the question which I knew would be coming.

"It is not a stone. It is a rock. It helps me to think, to imagine, and to create. I am a bit on the rhyfedd side. That is the Welsh word for strange."

Yes, I was a doofus and blowing this big time. Geez, a stupid rock.

What a dorky and goofy thing to have.

After spilling the explanation for having such a silly item to carry around with me, I immediately looked up at her and brushed the long hair from in front of my face. I was studying her face for a reaction. I was sure that she would laugh at me and recognize that I was just some weird young guy, sitting on the front steps of his house while dreaming endlessly. Kyra did not answer me right away, but she watched me as she started out first to walk up the sidewalk and head north on Belmont Avenue. To my surprise, instead of dismissing me, she smiled at me.

"You speak, Welsh?"

"Very little . . . some, well, I dunno. I guess a little more than just some. Just what I picked up from an aunt of mine and from my grandfather . . . a few words here and there."

"I see. And what do you create, Paul?" Kyra asked as she walked ahead of me with a few steps. I was still fumbling with my book and placing the bookmark in the pages.

"Oh, not much right now. I wrote a draft of a book consisting of three short stories a bit ago. Now, I just study things, compile adventures and scenes, until the bug bites me to write again."

Kyra stopped dead in her tracks; she turned and smiled as she studied me. Her hair, her eyes, her beauty was riveting.

It sent a shudder down my spine.

"Really? I would love to write well. My writing sucks. It is a weak point for me in my studies. Of course, being a lit major, I read and write, and I try so hard to write well, but I cannot ever come up with storylines to write something decent. Characters are easier. I just do not know where to place them in the stories, nor do I compose any meaningful dialogue. My goodness, what a surprise it is to me that you write. You are full of surprises, Paul John Henson. I would love to read what you have written and I hope that perhaps, someday, you would share it with me."

I did not answer her, I guess the writing did take her by surprise, but right now, the last thing that I would want to do is to show her some draft of my short stories. She knows great literature, not my hokey writing. I did not want her to read my silly short stories about life in this old neighborhood. It would be very embarrassing.

Kyra still stood and smiled at me, and when I had no reply or reaction, she pointed towards my vest pocket and pronounced, "And by the way, that is a stone, not a rock there, Paul."

She waited for me to catch up to her. When I did reach her side, she reached out towards me, and to my profound and complete surprise, she took my hand and pulled me along as we continued to walk. It was without the slightest hesitation that I took her hand, and she gripped my hand rather tightly. I was now close enough to catch another whiff or two of her perfume, some type of magical scent in which lured me to a place that I had never been before, and now embedded into my senses forever.

In the spring evening we walked, we talked, and we shared conversation. It was a conversation of a deep level. We spoke of writing, and of literature, of how to create a dialogue between characters and how to create story settings. Her intelligence was amazing, her thoughts were captivating for me, and the discussion took me to a new level.

Somehow, it seemed as if I had known Kyra Lovell for my entire young lifetime.

What a profound connection.

Suddenly, this early spring evening had turned into quite an exhilarating situation. I only just met this woman.

Geez, even though we were only casually dating, and we had no formal agreement or commitment, Gramps was correct. In the fact that Maureen Zipperelli would be a bit ruffled if she saw me right now with Kyra Lovell. What a tangled web we weave sometimes!

"So, other than reading, writing or pardon my correction, but studying for future writing, and observing the asses of women who pass by your front steps . . . what else is it that you do, Paul John Henson?"

I laughed. Kyra Lovell was indeed honest and I could tell she was a reader and literature major. Her vocabulary was quite extensive, and to be honest, very appealing.

"I play hockey. Kinda started out on the street, then

roller hockey leagues and now I am playing on the ice rinks. I am a goaltender. Currently, I am in a part-time goalie clinic over at Ice Land in Great Falls. I want to play professionally someday."

Kyra stopped walking; she dropped my hand and put her hands on her hips.

"Ice hockey? Ice skating? Very cool. You write books, read all the time, sit on the front steps, I must say that you are indeed, whatever that word in Welsh for strange was that you said, Paul! However, that makes sense now, and it does explain your athletic build and body. You have a remarkable physique."

"Thanks, at least, I think. I do dabble in quite a bit of different things."

"I'll say, and you are what, eighteen or maybe nineteen? I am twenty-three by the way, in a month and just a few days, I will be twenty-four."

Kyra looked at me for an answer. I would not lie to try to close the gap between us.

"Nineteen. 'Be twenty in November. I graduated from a vocational school. I am a journeyman electrician and electronics technician. The service shop should promote me to master someday soon. Just need more field time now, already passed all my exams with close to one hundred percent scores on 'em all. I hope that they promote me soon."

Kyra waved to me to take her hand, and I did so, while once again, we resumed walking.

"They will. It does not surprise me that you passed all the exams with such a high score. Very nice. A tradesman. Very sexy, a man with a tool belt. By the time that you are twenty-five, you will be quite the amazing man, and I must say, quite a catch for some young woman too. I think that you are already quite the catch."

We stopped walking for a moment and while still holding hands, she studied me. I stood taller. Her eyes looked me up and down, and I knew what was going through her mind. Part of playing the position that I played in hockey, was to remain confident, and I knew what you projected forward, came back to you. A weak posture, sitting back on your skates, a lack of challenge, all of them combined to allow a shooter to think right away that you would allow a goal. I learned to project confidence by standing in the net playing goal, walking through tough neighborhoods and by passing through life, and it was a powerful lesson. A lesson that Gramps and my old man both taught me, and we all used well.

Kyra finally spoke, and I relaxed.

"You are a fantastic looking guy, amazing looking, in fact. That hair, wow! My goodness, you must have all the women fainting. Paul, I want to say. . .."

I abruptly cut her off. Embarrassed a bit, or perhaps actually playing it cool, would be a more accurate description.

"I think that we should keep walking," was all that I said, and this time, I took the lead and gently held her hand. We walked together, hand-in-hand and as we did, I decided to project some of that confidence. I held her hand tightly, and we continued to walk all the way to North Tenth Street.

Just to ice the scene, and not be a complete idiot, I added, "You are gorgeous, Kyra. Stunning and pretty amazing looking. Yes, indeed. You are totally gorgeous."

She only gripped my hand tighter and did not say a word.

We spoke about seemingly hundreds of subjects in five city blocks, and by the time we made it to her grandmother's house, the sun was set, and darkness, framed upon a backdrop of smutty city streetlights, was all around.

"This is my grandmother's house. Right here, Paul," Kyra said as she let go of my hand, turned, and faced me.

We had stopped in front of a narrow, small home, tucked back from the street a bit. I had passed this house a million times or more, during my times wandering all over the old neighborhood. Previously, I had never given it a second thought. Now, it would embed in my mind forever. It had a small fence lining the front yard, which was a strip of land about six feet wide, leading to a small wooden porch. It was a typical Paterson, New Jersey home. It was neat, clean, and well maintained. I looked at the home, spotted a light glowing in the front window, and then I looked back at Kyra. I was making my first move to reach out, shake her hand, and say goodbye. When she gently reached out, she took my face in her hands, stood on her toes, and kissed me.

She tasted better than candy, her lips were very sweet, and her kiss was soft and passionate. The smell of her perfume made me weak in the knees. I was too stunned to say a word; I leaned in and, well, enjoyed it.

I had swapped many spits with Maureen Zipperelli, and; I am not ashamed to say, shared a bit more than just a few kisses with Maureen, too. I had enjoyed a few kisses and such with other young women in my short nineteen years, but I never shared a kiss quite like that kiss was.

Kyra let go of me, stood back, smiled and without speaking a single word, she opened the gate, went up the stairs, turned the knob to the front door and she disappeared into the house. I stood there in front of her grandmother's house for a long time, while recovering my sense of awareness and collecting my thoughts.

Geez! What the hell just happened to me? That was the only thought that came into my mind. I had stolen a kiss with some gorgeous, older woman on a fine spring evening and I had not a single regret.

It was exhilarating!

I reached into my vest pocket, grabbed the rock, and held it in my hand. I tossed it up and down and caught it in my hand while I began to think.

This was going to make one helluva story someday!

Most every night, I sat on the steps watching and waiting for Kyra to come by, and most every night she did. We walked, we went to the local park and sat on the benches and talked for hours. We spoke about books, stories, and people, and joked about the simple things we saw and observed. She laughed easily and often, and her mind was keen, her words were poignant and carefully selected. I took her to the Paterson Diner where we had dinner, chased down with coffee, tea and snacks, and we sat and talked for hours about nothing that was very special. Or so it seemed to be nothing special.

I never did, despite her gentle prodding, share the draft of the book in which I wrote. For some reason, I was too embarrassed to do it. Her magical use of the English vocabulary floored me, and I felt my writing was too simple, too quaint and uneducated, in order to compete with her ability to link glorious words into sentences.

We laughed, we joked, and we kissed, and we shared some magical times together.

I knew that our time grew short, however; I just did not realize that it would come so quickly. The springtime was waning now and the end of the month of May loomed closer; the days grew longer and the evenings grew much warmer. Spring was now becoming a memory.

One rainy Saturday evening, I was sprawled across my bed, reading a hockey magazine. I was being lazy. Harry and Jeff were both busy and not around, so I was goofing off and killing time reading an article, in which I had already read a few hundred times before.

I had an intense hockey practice and hard skate earlier in the afternoon and I was a bit sore. It was time to relax and recover.

I heard the front doorbell ring, but I knew the old man was in the living room watching television and he would answer it. Usually, a ring at the front door at this time of night meant it was just a neighborhood bum seeking a few coins or a handout. Even Skippy, my faithful fox terrier, did not get up from the foot of the bed to check out who was at the door.

It was that kind of evening.

I was a bit stunned when the old man appeared in the doorway of my bedroom and he smiled at me.

He looked at me for a second or two and finally said, "Better get off ya lazy ass and get your act together there, twenty-seven. Some really gorgeous twigeon is at the door, bundled up in a raincoat and hat, and she is asking if you are home."

I looked up, tossed the magazine aside, and sat up.

"Really? Do you know who it is?"

"Nah. Geez, man, what the hell do I look like, a detective? How many ya got chasin' ya now? Damn. I think she is that cutie ya been walking with from the other block. Better, not let Maureen spot ya with her. The fireworks from that explosion would be a son-of-a-bitch. But, if I were you, I would not keep her waiting too long. Maureen is a hot little numbah, but this gal, whoo wee. She is amazing."

"Yeah, okay, I got it, Dad. Thanks!"

I nodded, jumped up, ran in the bathroom, washed my face, brushed my teeth, took the hair tie out of my hair, combed my long mop of hair, smoothed my clothes out, and ran to the front closet. I pulled an old ball cap off the top shelf and my trusty vest and almost ran to the front door. As usual, I was dressed in my rock-and-roll tee shirt and canvas sneakers. My attire seldom changed, but later on in my life, it would suit me well.

"Hey there, Kyra. Geez, I did not think you would be around tonight. You know, with the rain and all."

She winked at me and waved as she quickly descended the front steps, where she stopped at the base of the stairs to make sure that I was following her. If it were even possible, Kyra Lovell looked even more captivating than she usually did, wearing her raincoat and a hat, her smile shining through the raindrops.

"Does the big, strong, tall and handsome, hippie goalie melt in the rain?"

I smiled at her description and question.

"No, not at all."

"Then, let's go! A walk in the rain is the ultimate pinnacle of romance!"

Kyra was correct. We walked in the rain for hours and hours. Around and around the city blocks we went until we were both close to being soaked to the skin. While we walked, we talked, and we shared in one another's magic. When we once again finally reached the front of her grandmother's house, instead of remaining on the front sidewalk, Kyra dragged me by the hand to the front porch.

"Here, let's get out of the rain now," Kyra explained as we walked up the three short steps leading to the porch and stood in the darkness together under the cover of the porch. I knew the same scene that we had replayed repeatedly during the past three weeks or so would be different this go around. I could tell by the look in her eyes and the huskiness in her voice that something was different.

Very different.

I was young, only nineteen, but I already had a strong sense of when the look in a young woman's eyes had become different towards me. This was not a casual look in her eyes; instead, this was a very intense stare.

Kyra unzipped and removed her raincoat, pulled her hat off and she placed them on the seat of a rocking chair sitting on the porch. Underneath, she had on her usual blouse and sweater, and of course, she wore those glorious, tight-fitting dungarees.

"There, time to get out of those wet things," she said as she walked over to me and slowly and seductively unzipped the zipper to my vest, removed my hat and placed it over the top rail of the rocking chair. She then reached up, moved wayward wet strands of my long hair out of my face and then despite her height, she did as she always did, and stood up on her tippy toes, took my face in her hands and kissed me. This was a longer, deeper, and more intense kiss than we had ever shared. After our kiss, she rested her head against my chest and relaxed, while I wrapped my arms around her and she wrapped her arms around me, too. Even in the dim light of the front porch, I could see her close her eyes, and heard her exhale a gentle sigh, while she nestled into the folds of my chest. As she rested upon me, we remained enfolded in each other's arms, while we gently rocked back and forth, not speaking a single word but simply enjoying each other's warmth and closeness.

Kyra's hands wandered from my back to my chest, where she lingered with her hands, for some time, while exploring my chest with her gentle touch. Her breathing changed to deeper breaths, almost gasps, long and deep breathing, all the while growing increasingly deeper.

We shared an intense stare, and I marveled at how, even in the dim light of the porch, her green eyes sparkled and glowed.

Kyra softly spoke, "Oh, Paul, you are a remarkable man. Tell me, how a woman does not fall in love with you? I guess that question is too late because I have fallen in love with you."

I did not answer her because the truth is that I would not know how to answer her. Now, it was my time to breathe deeper and while she explored my body with her hands; I studied the look in her eyes. As they grew even more intense, her breathing remained deep and hard, even with a shudder or two between breaths. Her hands worked some magic in various locations on my body, and I am not ashamed to say that parts of me reacted. Kyra then her hands slowly glided around me and she placed her hands upon my backside. There, she slid her hands inside the rear pockets of my dungarees, and once again, she rested her head upon my chest.

Kyra then whispered to me, "Paul, I leave tomorrow. Tonight, is my last night here in Paterson. My grandmother is not home. She will not be home until late tomorrow. I would like very much for you to come in and we can say goodbye together. We could share one, last very special evening together, in each other's arms."

Waves of emotion and pangs of seduction came over me, shaking my body, rippling through my soul. I knew what she meant; I just did not know exactly how to react.

While pushing the long hair out of my face, I bent down; we kissed again, deeply and powerfully. We held each other, and I, too, allowed my hands to wander. My hands first gently wandered from her face, to her neck, to gently caressing her lovely breasts and then I began rolling my fingers and hands over the hardness of her nipples. After releasing her breasts and while kissing her, I held each side of her glorious backside and I firmly pulled her body into mine. When I pulled her into me, even while kissing, I could hear her throat throttle with a slight gasp at the power of my grasp. In a somewhat out of character and bold move for me, I now held her glorious body next to mine with a seductive yet a powerful clasp.

There was no doubt that I held her so tightly that our souls welded together. We were so close, and so tight, that I could feel the hardness of the nipples of her breasts tucked against my chest. I could feel every inch of her body next to mine, and I was certain that she could feel every inch of mine too. It felt glorious, and the smell of her perfume, combined with the feel of her body next to mine, was magically intoxicating, and it was difficult not to wither in the grips of her beauty. When I felt my soul and willpower collapsing, I then remembered the words of my grandfather.

They echoed in my head and resonated into my inner being.

"Young lassies, can also bring you a bit of trouble too. They can peddle their wares, flitter about, captivate you with their beauty, and lure you into a spot where it might be a bit difficult to control. You are very smart. You will remember my words and when the time comes, you will make the correct decision."

I knew what to do. It was not going to be easy, but I knew what to do.

While still holding her closely, I looked into her eyes, smiled, and told her, "Kyra, I would love to, but I can't. Believe me, when I tell you that you are gorgeous and captivating. Our exploring hands only make this decision even more difficult. You are a woman beyond description. However, I am not about that. Commitment is a word that I know all too well. I write books, ya know, and study the use of words. That is just not, where I am at right now in my life. Someday, it might be my style, but not right now."

As soon as those words left my mouth, I wanted to retract them. While shaking my head to display my disagreement, I corrected my words, "On second thought, it might never be my style."

I took both of my hands, gently held each side of Kyra's face while looking in her eyes, and I told her, "You are a one-of-a-kind beauty, with a diamond for a personality and gold for your heart. Yet, try as I might, I can't light a flame like that, then walk away, and try to forget you for the rest of my life. You are unforgettable, and after sharing a special night, then I might never let go of you. Instead, I would rather remember these special three weeks for what they have been, not what they might have been. I want to keep them as a special dream in a nineteen-year-old, young man's heart."

I let go of her face and once again hugged her tightly.

She wrapped me in her arms and rested her face against my chest while she listened to me.

"Kyra, dreams do not cost anything and they allow me to whisper my greatest secrets and wishes to the sunsets every night. Dreams just might be God's greatest gift to us. If I pretend, and put this moment into retrospect, then it is easy to say that despite the fact that you are older than I am that we are both way too young. It is a fabulous excuse for my actions and my decision. Maybe it is correct and maybe it is not. Yet, I rather keep the dream close and then someday, when I choose to write this story, then I might be able to finish this story. Finish it, in the manner that I wanted it to end . . . not how it actually ended."

Kyra smiled a wide and glorious smile. A smile of understanding, a smile of love.

She kissed me long, deeply and profoundly, one last time and she whispered gently in my ear, "That is not what I wanted you to say, but rather it is what I expected you to say. Mature beyond your years, you are. Amazing. Only a powerful and special young man would turn down an invitation such as this, in a manner such as what you just did. You will someday, Paul, fill some very lucky woman's heart with joy and with love. I too will dream. I will dream of you. You are going to write a great story about this someday, Paul. Promise me that someday, you will write this story."

She looked at me for confirmation and I nodded to indicate that I would, and then I mouthed, "I will."

For a brief second, Kyra looked away, and then returned her eyes to mine.

She continued speaking with tears in her eyes and just a hint of a smile on her face, "I will read that story, with tears in my eyes, and joy in my heart. I too, will never forget the last three weeks, or ever forget you. You are so correct, when you said that we are both going to always remember this time for what it has been, and not for what it might have been. You are too special to describe or to forget. There are no words. Other than, perhaps, one word . . . love. I love you. No question that I do. I will never forget you. Ever."

She started to let go of me to turn and to walk away, but she stopped, leaned back into my arms, and spoke in a low voice, almost a whisper, "By the way, you were right and I was wrong. Very, very wrong. That is not a stone, which you carry around with you in your vest pocket. It *is* a rock."

With a lingering handhold that slowly and somewhat painfully faded away, Kyra let go of me. I watched as she turned, picked her rain garments off the rocking chair, walked away, put the key in the lock, opened the door and disappeared forever.

She never looked back.

I grabbed my hat off the chair rail, reached into my vest pocket, grabbed the rock and held it in my hand while putting the hat on my head. I tossed the rock up and down and caught it in my hand while I began to think. I zipped up my vest, adjusted the hat on my head, and walked back out into the rain and into the night.

Yes, indeed, this was going to make one helluva story someday.

Spring gave way to summer, and the night air was warmer now.

June weather was quite unpredictable.

The seasons changed, but I did not. As usual, at the end of the day, I sat on the steps of 182 Belmont Avenue, reading, watching the world go by. Watching another incredible sunset in front of me.

This was going to be a special one. I could tell by the colors. Red, gold, a touch of yellow, but it was the whispers of red, which made it special.

Hockey season ended a week or so earlier, and now, if I was not out with Harry or Jeff conquering the world, I was here on the front steps gathering all that I required for use later on in life.

On the other hand, was I?

All of it was passing by in front of me, the cars, buses, trucks, taxicabs with horns blaring, all of it. I loved every minute of it.

Yet, somehow, I secretly hoped that she would magically appear in front of me, smiling, with her green eyes glowing in the early evening, the whiff of that perfume and all the rest of her magic.

"Eh, so whatcha up to there, Paulie boy?"

The voice of my grandfather echoing from behind me made me jump once again. I turned and looked at him, placed the book that I was reading down on my lap, and smiled at him. He stood in front of me now, his blue eyes wide open, his white hair crisply tucked on his head, not a hair out of place. Even at his advanced age, my grandfather was a powerful man and his large barrel chest, with his ample muscles, displayed sturdily underneath his sweater.

He wore a smile a mile wide.

"Reading, Gramps. As usual, I am reading and watching our world go by us."

"I see. Visiting Baker Street again, eh?"

"Nah, not tonight. Tonight, I am in a garden and reading some Kipling."

"Oh my, a good one. The gardener story. Mind if I join you?"

I patted the stairs next to me. I watched as Gramps settled in next to me with a bit of a groan and a creak of his legs. He carried a Big Boulder beer with him, and once he sat down, he took a long swig of it.

We sat in silence for a long time.

Finally, he spoke to me, "You have been quiet as of late, Paulie boy. The pretty lassie is gone now I guess, eh? Off to university."

I did not answer him. Instead, I only nodded.

"You fell a bit hard, eh? It will not be the first time, Paulie boy. I hate to tell you that it will never be easy. I think, by looking at your face, that you had to make a difficult choice. A very tough choice, eh? Maybe, what I had warned you about, Paulie boy. Have you reached a point that you are now wondering if it is a deep regret or not? If I had to bet, you spoke in a whisper and not a howl, eh?"

"Definitely, a whisper. As far as the regret part of this goes, I am not too sure, Gramps. I kinda think that she was special. Maybe, one of a kind. And yes, it hurts like bloody hell. She was more than just beautiful, it was her laugh, her conversation. Damn, just the words she could put together, geez, she made me jealous. I could never construct sentences like that. She will be a great writer someday."

Gramps looked over at me and he spoke a bit softer. I could tell that he felt my conflict and pain. I had a feeling he had been here too, at some time in his life.

"Oh, I see. And, you will write many great stories too. Don't sell your talents too short, Paulie boy. The young lassie might have the benefit of the university education, but you have this front stoop and these amazing front steps with the window to our world all in front of you. I have to admit, I have no glorious words to make you feel better. Nevertheless, I do hope that you recall what your father and I taught you so long ago, when you were just a young lad, shining shoes and earning a few coins. I hope that you do recall that afternoon in the Widow's Pub when that crazy, drunk bloke went a bit on the wild side and then he regretted his actions. Do you recall that lesson, Paulie boy?"

I leaned back and smiled while I closed the book and set it aside. The lesson was very clear and bold in my mind. It would be there forever, just as so many lessons that Gramps and my parents taught me would be.

I answered him boldly, "Sure do, Gramps. I will never

forget it. Not that one. Regrets are for fools. Regrets are only foolish doubts of decisions that we made. They serve no purpose. They only cause us angst and worry. Make a choice, be a man, then move on. Never doubt."

Later on, in my life, I would use that lesson a few times more.

Gramps smiled at me. He took another swig of beer and patted me gently on the knee.

"Good show. I am very proud of you. You should be proud of yourself too. It takes quite a bit to admit what you passed up and to stand up proudly for your actions."

"I guess, but still . . . it hurts."

"It does, I am sure of that. Yet, you are very young, strong and remarkably handsome and you have my word that there will be many other young lassies that will come along, my dear Paulie boy. You will fall in love and out of love. You will find some special lassies, and eventually, you will make the correct choices. You are too smart not to make them."

I reached into my vest pocket and pulled the rock out. I tossed it up and down while Gramps watched me.

We did not say a word for a very long time. Instead, we studied the sunset.

Gramps finally handed me the beer bottle, and he said in a low whisper, "Here, Paulie boy, take a long sip and do not tell your mum, eh."

I set the rock aside, took the bottle, tilted it back, and took a sip. It tasted cold and good. I handed it back to Gramps, took the rock once again in my hands, and held it tightly.

"Ya know something, Gramps? Someday, I have to think that all of this will make one helluva story."

He smiled at me, reached out, took my hand, and squeezed it tightly.

I felt his power, his encouragement and his love, as he told me, "Well then, Paulie boy, my suggestion is that someday, you write it, eh?"

I saw the headlights of our jeep pulling into the church parking lot and I knew that it was my wife and children returning from their day of shopping. I returned to where I was, back to reality, back on the front steps of the parsonage, and I left 182 Belmont Avenue behind once more.

Or did I?

I never did write that story in the manner in which I hoped that it would have ended, but I did keep my promise to Gramps and to Kyra, and I wrote it. The storyline and plot were a bit different. The characters changed to the point where only Kyra and I would know of whom I based them upon, but I wrote it.

Wrote that story and a whole helluva a lot more of them too.

I never searched for Kyra Lovell to see if she became a writer, or a teacher, or if she fulfilled her dreams. I often wondered if she ever sought me out and if she ever read any of my material. Who knows? Yet, I know that I have no regrets about anything I wrote or anything that I ever did. Regrets are only foolish doubts of decisions that we made. They serve no purpose. They only cause us angst and worry. Make a choice, be a man, then move on. Never doubt.

I held the rock tightly in my hand and thought deeply about the decisions that I had made in my life.

I lost my beloved grandfather when I was about twenty-five years old. Gramps was well into his nineties and he was still strong and powerful. His death was not a sign of his weakness; instead, it was the pinnacle of his strength. He died, as he lived, strong, proud and brave. I was lucky enough to be with him and hold his hand during his last moments in this world.

I felt his strength.

I felt his power and his love. He was a really cool guy, and I loved him with all of my heart.

Not a day ever goes by that I do not think of him, or wish that he were right here with me. To sit with me on the front steps on a warm spring evening, to feel his power, tap his wisdom and capture his advice. He taught me more than I ever could imagine. He encouraged me to write stories, of which I never dreamed that I could ever create. He taught me the power of words and the joy of books.

If I could be half of the man that he was, then I would be proud.

I squeezed my hand tightly around the rock in my hand. I opened my hand and studied it. Dull, colorless, yet full of power, solid, strong, and forever.

Am byth.

Yes indeed, no way was this just a stone.

It is, was, and always will be, the rock.

THE END

The Look in Your Eyes

Cold reality that I cannot escape.
Joy filled and heartfelt, but somewhat sad.
You follow me everywhere, everyplace that I go.
There is nowhere to hide, no place I have found yet to forget.
The look in your eyes.

In the hills or in the trees, in the warm winds of spring.
In the snow of winter, or riding on a road to nowhere.
Cold reality, I cannot escape.
You follow me everywhere, every place I go.
There is nowhere to hide, no place I have found yet to forget.
The look in your eyes.

I know every inch of your body.
The look on your face in the morning.
The sound of your voice in the evening.
The smell of your perfume and the softness of your hair.
I can feel the gentle touch of your hand upon my chest while we lie together.
Yet, there is nothing to compare to in my life when I remember.
The look in your eyes.

The Lord knows that I have tried.
I prayed, begged, and pleaded.
I wished and dreamt upon endless stars for you to be with me, here and now.
Or for me to try to forget.
The look in your eyes.

There is no place for me to hide.
I have tried.
In the mountains, or in the hills.
In the thrashing of storms, or in the wilds of the wind.
In the blizzard of memories.
I guess I need to leave it all for dead.
The hope of ever forgetting.
The look in your eyes.

The memory of your touch upon my hand.
The image of your smile.
The beauty of your soul.
The sound of your voice.
Everything about you is beyond compare.
Yet nothing can replace in my heart,
the look in your eyes.

You laugh at something I say.
You tell me how much you love me; how much you care.
You tell me how silly I am being, and I pull you in close.
I hold you tightly while the light trickles in and your soul
appears to me.
Bare, naked, exposed, full of love, full of our joy.
It illuminates our love and only enhances,
the look in your eyes.

Sometimes, I do not know what love has to do with joy.
If it has anything to do with it at all.
All I know is that I love you.
I miss you, the smell of your skin.
The softness of your body when you hold it against mine.
But most of all, I miss,
the look in your eyes.

Maybe someday soon I will see it again.
Maybe in a quiet whisper of the wind.
Or, perhaps, in the ripples of a pond.
Until then, I know I am hopelessly lost.
There is nowhere to hide.
I can never forget.
The look in your eyes.
The look in your eyes.

Epilogue

Yes, indeed! Spring has sprung! Tomatoes and peppers sit in the peat pot trays, under the grow lights, safe and warm inside while waiting their turn in the garden.

Oh, boy, those tulips just poking out of the ground there might suffer a nip or two, because tonight, it is still a bit cold. The peas in the garden will love this weather, the radishes are happy and the lettuce that the insects are not ravaging is crisp and green. Let us not forget those glorious sweet peas that I planted in front of the barn.

Soon, their sweet scents will float all the way into our kitchen window, carried along by warm spring breezes, which pop up this time of year when the sun dips over the top of the trees.

Yes, indeed! Spring has sprung! Glorious, breathtaking, and full of wonderment.

A few runny eyes, some sneezing--my goodness, those Easter Lilies closed up poor Grandma's throat!

The women sporting their pretty, new dresses in the center of town always look so gorgeous in the springtime. The men all eye them as they flitter about the town. Oh, my, yes indeed, spring brings a rebirth, in more ways than one.

Everything is wonderful; however, all too soon, it passes.

Spring hands off the cool mornings and warm afternoons to the heat and humidity of summer. Another season passes and a few more trips occur around the circle of life.

I sit, as I often do, on those proverbial front steps, sipping a cup of hot tea while pondering it all, and I cannot help but to smile. This is so enjoyable, so relaxing, a light vest in the morning, short sleeves in the afternoon.

Now, I for one, wish that spring would hang around a bit longer, you know, hold off on the summer. However, when you look at the grand scheme of things that would grow a bit wearisome. God's great creation works so well, the ebb and flow, the changes of the seasons, the changes in our spirit. Yes, I smile a bit, take a sip of hot tea, and think how in a few short hours, I will trade this tea in for a cold beer. Memories of the past, people, adventures, all come rushing back to me.

Where were all of these thoughts when I was writing this particular collection? Suddenly, my mind is flooded with potential stories. Stories of springtime. Stories which eluded me until now.

I have to remember to write the story of how the drunken bum, who was standing in front of us in the communion line in church on Easter morning, downed the entire communion chalice of wine. That should be a good one!

Yes, indeed! Spring has sprung! Glorious, breathtaking, and full of wonderment.

My teacup is now empty. I set it down on the steps and gently sigh. Looking at my watch, then at the empty teacup, ah what the hell, it is a Saturday and if I try really hard, then I can convince myself that it is not too early for a nice cold beer. Yes, indeed, Gramps was right on. . ..

"Sometimes, we need to whisper, and sometimes, we need to howl."

I think it is time to howl. Down a beer or two and go find that pretty woman of mine. I need to see the look in her eyes, and perhaps just a tad more too.

Yes, indeed! Spring has sprung! Glorious, breathtaking, and full of wonderment.

ABOUT THE AUTHOR

If you ask Paul John Hausleben, he will tell you that he is not an author, he is just a storyteller. His mission is to continue to write and tell stories to warm your heart, make you laugh, and sometimes make you cry, just a little. Most of all, he deals in memories, and helps you to remember the good times of your own life, and the special people who touched you along the way. Paul was born and raised in Paterson, and then nearby Haledon, New Jersey, and began writing at an early age. He revisited a writing career later in his life, and he now is the author of a number of novels, compilations, short stories and audio and video works. Most of his work touches upon nostalgic remembrances of simpler times, and tells the stories of heartfelt, humorous, and special human relationships. Other than writing, among many careers both paid and unpaid, he is a former semi-professional hockey goaltender, a music fan and music reviewer, an avid sports fan, photographer and amateur radio operator. He now resides in Somewhere, U.S.A., but his heart always remains along Belmont Avenue in good old Paterson, and Haledon, New Jersey.

You may write to the author at ctte27@gmail.com

Other seasonal collections by Mr. Hausleben that you also will enjoy:

The Autumn Collection

The Christmas Tree and Other Christmas Stories.
Tales for a Christmas Evening

The Summer Collection

Reflections. The Christmas Collection

Where We Used to Live
The Home for Christmas Collection

Christmas Cocktails

Published by God Bless the Keg Publishing
Somewhere, U.S.A.

You may write to the publisher at
Godblessthekegpublishing@gmail.com

"Life's simple pleasures are so often the best ones!"

www.ingramcontent.com/pod-product-compliance
Lightning Source LLC
LaVergne TN
LVHW020708110826
845149LV00012B/2157

* 9 7 8 0 9 9 0 6 9 7 9 4 7 *